Scream If You Want To Go Faster

Russ Litten was born at the end of the 60s, grew up in the 70s and left school in the 80s. He spent the subsequent decade in a bewildering variety of jobs before becoming a freelance writer at the turn of the century. He has written drama for television, radio and film. *Scream If You Want to Go Faster* is his first novel. He lives with his family in Kingston-upon-Hull

Praise for *Scream If You Want to Go Faster*

'A powerful debut: ambitious and mesmerising. Paints a kaleidoscopic – and heartbreakingly funny – portrait of where we are today.'

John Niven

'*Scream if You Want to Go Faster* is a gem. Terse, truthful, and teeming with good old Yorkshire lyricism – Russ Litten effortlessly spins together the disparate lives of his characters, like the sharpest, bittersweet candy floss.'

Richard Milward, author of *Apples*

'This is a rollercoaster ride of a novel . . . Rough and rousing, Litten's novel vividly evokes Hull's rich past and its diversely uncertain present.'

Guardian

Scream If You Want To Go Faster

RUSS LITTEN

WINDMILL BOOKS

Published by Windmill Books 2012

2 4 6 8 10 9 7 5 3 1

First published in Great Britain in 2011 by William Heinemann

Windmill Books
The Random House Group Limited
20 Vauxhall Bridge Road, London SW1V 2SA

Addresses for companies within The Random House Group Limited can
be found at: www.randomhouse.co.uk/offices.htm

The Random House Group Limited Reg. No. 954009

www.randomhouse.co.uk

A CIP catalogue record for this book
is available from the British Library

ISBN 9780099537977

The Random House Group Limited supports The Forest Stewardship
Council (FSC®), the leadng international forest certification organisation.
Our books carrying the FSC label are printed on FSC® certified paper. FSC
is the only forest certification scheme endorsed by the leading environ-
mental organisations, including Greenpeace. Our paper procurementpolicy
can be found at: www.randomhouse.co.uk/environment

Typeset by Palimpsest Book Production Limited,
Falkirk, Stirlingshire
Printed and bound by CPI Group (UK) Ltd, Croydon, CR0 4YY

Hull Fair!

Hull Fair!

Everyone's going to Hull Fair!

There are sideshows to tease you

Oh please take me with you

To join in the fun

At Hull's Famous Fair!

(Traditional)

KINGSTON-UPON-HULL
Friday 19 October 2007

Hedon Road: 10.04am

Marshall said the drop was due in at ten o'clock, but there's no sign of any lorry out here. All Dave can see is a load of empty pallets and a big empty yard. He's got two jackets on, but that wind is whipping off the docks and it goes right through the pair of them. No point being out here when the only warm part is his arse on this seat. He starts the forklift back up, spins it round and zips back into the warehouse.

Butch is leaning on his brush, yapping to that young Kosovan lad. What an introduction to English culture – an audience with Butch. The lad is smiling politely and nodding away, but it's obvious he hasn't got a clue what Butch is on about. He's not alone in that respect though. Dave doesn't think Butch even knows what he's on about half the time. Butch is not the sharpest tool in the box. The more ungenerous of his colleagues have even been known to use the term thick as pig shit.

– Teatime, ladies, shouts Dave as he whips past. Butch's brush clatters to the floor and the pair of them follow Dave into the Bun House. Kenny Rose and Little Stu have already got the kettle on and the cards out. Dave lines another three mugs up and drops a tea bag into each one. The sugar situation is looking a bit desperate;

they're down to the last scrapings in the bag. Kenny has two sugars, Little Stu has none and Butch, the big fat bastard, he has three. Four if it's a big mug.

Dave holds the bag up to the Kosovan lad.

– How many mate?

The lad just smiles and gives Dave the thumbs up.

– No, how many? Dave holds up one finger, two fingers and both of his eyebrows. The lad smiles and nods.

– I'll take that as two, then.

Dave gets the brews on and Kenny deals him in, but no sooner have they got sat down and settled than Marshall's in the doorway, tapping on his watch.

– Dave, what about this lorry?

– What lorry?

– Them panels from Shrewsbury. Ten o'clock drop.

– Not here.

– Well it will be in a minute, so go and get that bay cleared.

Dave tells him he's just got sat down. Marshall moves to the worktop and touches the kettle with the back of his hand. He tries to do it dead casual so the lads don't see what he's doing, but he's about as subtle as a clown at a cremation.

– We need to get that Wilkins order boxed off today, ASAP, he says.

He picks up one of the papers off the side, the one with all the tits. He flicks the pages over, pauses and gives a low whistle through his teeth.

– Would not say no to that.

– What is it, says Kenny, – a picture of a cream cake?

Marshall folds the paper up and slings it back on the side.

– Don't be sat here all fuckin' morning!

A stern nod, a swift about-turn and he's out the door.

– Cream cake. Cream fuckin' puff more like, says Little Stu, and Kenny laughs.

Butch looks up from his cards, puzzled.

– Cream puff?

– Arse bandit int he, says Little Stu.

– Who, Marshall? Joking aren't yer?

– Nope, bent as a nine-bob note. Complete fuckin' deviant.

Little Stu looks up at Dave and winks. – No offence, like, Dave.

– None taken.

Dave studies his cards. Two queens. Not bad.

They play a few hands and Kenny tells them about the rugby club do he's going to tonight. Some charity thing for a bain with leukaemia. They want to raise enough money to send her to Disneyland. He's getting a Rovers shirt signed by all the players for a raffle. Kenny has that peculiarly sentimental streak commonly found in headcases. Butch tells them about some new fish he's got for his tank. Some little blue 'uns, apparently. Little Stu rolls a tab, sticks it behind his ear, rolls another one and tells them a joke about a nigger who goes for a job as a gynaecologist. Butch asks him what one of them is. What, a nigger? says Stu. A nigger is one of them blokes your mam shags, he says. No, says Butch, that other word you said. The Kosovan lad sits by the sink and reads the papers. Well, he looks at the pictures, anyroad. The radio plays the golden hits of the eighties and the wind rattles the plastic sheeting in the Bun House window.

3

Dave plays his cards and says nowt. He's thinking about the weekend and Denise and he's counting down the minutes till he can get out of this filthy place.

There's the rumble of an engine from the yard and then the hiss of brakes. Dave slings his hand in, stands up and gulps down his brew.

– Right, he says, and he puts his two jackets back on.

– Careful you don't break a fingernail, says Little Stu.

There's a hand shovel leant against the wall next to the sink. Dave picks it up. Stu's eyes go all wide and he takes the tab out of his gob.

Dave lays the shovel down on the table in front of his colleague.

– There you go Stu.

– What's that for?

– That's for them long dark days down the diamond mine.

Then Dave flings his shoulders back and sings out at the top of his lungs:

– HEIGH *HO*!

The Kosovan lad looks up startled from the football and tits. Dave gives him a big grin and a double thumbs up.

Then he goes out and gets that fuckin' lorry unloaded.

Boothferry Estate: 12.23pm

No skeletons, that's what she tells them. They both have to agree on that point. Rose doesn't like people playing silly buggers and she's too old for surprises. It's not like she's asking for much anyway; all she wants is a bit of civil company, someone to pass the

4

time of day with. Enjoy a nice afternoon out maybe, a bit of a meal of an evening, summat like that. Nothing complicated. Companionship, that's what she's talking about. Donna said it would be good for her to meet new people, and she said that this would be an easy and safe way to get started. It's the modern way, Mam, she'd said. Everyone's doing it. There's no shame.

Course, Rose is not daft. She knows what men are like. Pack of hounds at the best of times; dirty bloody dogs they are, sniffing around with only one thing on their mind. But she makes it quite clear to each and every one of them from the off – no funny malarkey. That usually sorts the wheat from the chaff. Don't get her wrong; she's no prude in that department. Rose and her Malcolm enjoyed a normal healthy marriage in that respect, thank you very much. One beautiful daughter and one fine son, both of them doing very well for themselves. Course, they don't call as often as they should, but that's another story. They're both healthy and that's the main. But Malcolm was the only man Rose ever took into her bed, and she intends to respect his memory.

And that's the end of that.

This latest one, though, he seems like a decent enough chap. Rose turns the laptop on in the back bedroom and gets on the internet. It's running a lot smoother since she took it into the shop. They did a very good job, it has to be said. Damn thing had been giving her all sorts of bother, running slowly, taking for ever to get onto sites – sometimes even freezing up altogether. Crashing, they called it in the shop. Rose was a bit chewed up about it, cos she had everything on there, her addresses, her emails, her diary, everything. Anyway, the chap sent it to their repairs department and they sorted it all out. Said she had Trojan Horses, whatever they are. Rose doesn't pretend to understand computers. Anyroad, she left it with them and they got it all going again. They even organised all her photos, put them into separate little files for her. There's one that comes up on the screen now when she's not using the computer, a photo of her and Malcolm, took on the cruise ship off the coast of Majorca. Rose loves that photo. Happier times.

She logs onto the Local Link Up site and goes into 'Flirty Fifties'. Yes, there he is: LEO123. She invites him to a private chat and he accepts straight away.

Yorkshire_Rose: Hello again.

LEO123: hello rose, how r u?

Yorkshire_Rose: Good thank you, what have you been up to?

LEO123: usual really ... work, etc ... been painting the back room ... how about u?

Yorkshire_Rose: Just pottering round the house. Nothing too exciting!

LEO123: doing anything over the weekend?

Yorkshire_Rose: Seeing my Grand daughter this afternoon. Taking her round Fair with her Mam.

LEO123: i've not bothered this year ... seems to get dearer every year!

Yorkshire_Rose: I agree, it's all commercialised now isn't it.

LEO123: well if u r not doing anything this weekend maybe we could meet up?

Yorkshire_Rose: I don't know what I'm doing yet. I might be seeing my friend on Sunday, I haven't seen them for ages, we are due a catch up.

LEO123: which friend is that rose?

Yorkshire_Rose: Just an old friend, anyway don't be nosey!

LEO123: LOL, sorry rose, just don't want to be getting my hopes up if u r already spoken for!

Yorkshire_Rose: Well if you must know it's a lady friend. Not that it's any business of yours!

LEO123: LOL I know I am sorry, but just checking! Forgive me?

Yorkshire_Rose: You daft haporth!

LEO123: not cross with Leo?

Yorkshire_Rose: Don't be daft! Course I'm not!

LEO123: gd gd ... hey rose I had a look at that site you mentioned, that hessle road one ... by, there's some memories on there eh?

Yorkshire_Rose: Oh yes, some wonderful old photos.

LEO123: u must know half the people on there eh?

Yorkshire_Rose: Oh yes, a lot of them have passed on now of course, but some of them I still see from time to time

LEO123: hard to imagine st andrews dock like that now eh?

Yorkshire_Rose: Aye, it's a shame, but there you go. Like I always used to say to my husband, the only thing that stays the same is change!

LEO123: ooh very profund rose! you should get a job writing christmas cards!

Yorkshire_Rose: Cheeky monkey!

LEO123: LOL jst jkn . . . so, are you going to be going on any rides at Fair then?

Yorkshire_Rose: I might do! Think I'm past it do you?

LEO123: LOL, no I don't think that at all love . . . just u b careful though!

Yorkshire_Rose: I always am Leo! So . . . what are you up to tonight?

LEO123: nothing 2nite, staying in reading I'm going 2 church with my mother 2morrow nite

Yorkshire_Rose: It's Saturday tomorrow isn't it?

LEO123: yes, mother hasn't been for a bit and I said I'd take her . . .

Yorkshire_Rose: Well have a nice time, I'm going to get off now and get meself ready for this afternoon.

LEO123: ok . . . r u taking bella for a walk

Yorkshire_Rose: Yes, I will do at some point. She wears me out she does!

LEO123: well, good to stay active especially at our age!

Yorkshire_Rose: You'll get a clip in a minute! Our age! Speak for yourself!

LEO123: LOL promises promises!

Yorkshire_Rose: What's that supposed to mean?

LEO123: nothing . . . see u on here later?

Yorkshire_Rose: Maybe. If you're lucky. And you stop being cheeky.

LEO123: I was born lucky rose

Yorkshire_Rose: Well it's alright for some isn't it!

LEO123: LOL . . . ok, speak later?

Yorkshire_Rose: We'll see. Maybe tomorrow night.

LEO123: at church, remember?

Yorkshire_Rose: Oh, OK. Well whenever then.

LEO123: we finish at 9. I'll b on here after that

Yorkshire_Rose: OK

LEO123: see u then?

Yorkshire_Rose: OK

LEO123: it's a date?

Yorkshire_Rose: I told you, I don't do dates.

LEO123: LOL, you're a tough nut to crack rose!

Yorkshire_Rose: It's you who's the nut!

LEO123: LOL, ok have a lovely time at fair, take care

Yorkshire_Rose: And you Leo.

LEO123: speak soon xxx

Yorkshire_Rose: OK

She logs off the site, shuts the computer off, goes down to the kitchen and makes something to eat. Tomato soup and a ham sandwich with a spot of mustard. Bella gets up and starts trotting round after her.

– You've had your dinner, Rose tells her. She's after a treat, but she's got no chance. She gets spoilt enough as it is, that one.

– Down, she tells her, – down Bella!

Bella stands there gazing up at Rose with them big brown eyes. Thinks Rose is a bloody soft touch she does. Thinks Rose's here just to fill her belly.

– Lie down Bella, there's a good girl.

Bella realises there's nothing doing and she curls back up in her basket.

Rose puts the radio on while she potters about. She likes listening to them phone-ins on Humberside;

Soapbox, with that Blair Jacobs. You get some good debates going on there. Some proper ding-dongs sometimes. Some of them get right on their high horse. There's some chap going on about Hull Fair today, how it takes all the money out the city and should be banned. Miserable old bugger! Why's he getting so worked up about it? It's not even aimed at people his age, it's for bains! Rose is off round Fair this afternoon with Donna and their little Jessica. She's been twice already, has Jessica. She absolutely loves it to bits she does. She gets that excited and her little face lights up like a Christmas tree. Why deny a bain a nice time? It's not like it's every week of the year is it? Grumpy old so and so!

Mind you, at least they've stopped going on about the floods and the council. That's all they had for weeks on end, council this and council that. Rose knows it was a terrible thing for all those people who had to move out of their homes, but there's no point trying to blame the council is there? What could the council have done? They can't control the weather can they? Malcolm knew that better than anyone, all them years he went to sea. You can't account for acts of God, he used to say.

This chap on the radio, he won't let Blair get a word in edgeways. He sounds a bit like that Alex fellow off the site, the last one she met up with. Not his voice as such, more his manner. Oh, totally in love with himself that one was. If he was a bar of chocolate he'd have ate himself, as Malcolm used to say. Rose should have known as soon as she clamped eyes on him, with his tinted glasses and his daft yellow cravat. What sort of man wears a yellow cravat? Sat with him nearly two hours in Norland one Sunday dinner time before she gave it up as a bad job. Two hours of him and his wonderful career as a travelling sales rep for Smith & Nephew. Oh, all over the shop he'd been. Not a town or city in the country that he hadn't visited. Abroad as well; Germany, Denmark, all over Europe. India even. The people he'd met and the places he'd seen. All me, me, me, he was. Not in the slightest bit interested in anything Rose had to say.

Mind you, he wasn't as bad as the second one. He proper put the heebie-jeebies up her did that bugger. Dickie he was called. Dickie Dirt she ended up calling him. He seemed alright at first. They had a couple of nice afternoons out, went up to Beverley, did some shopping, had a nice walk on the Westwood. Then he started on about all the other women he'd met up with. Some of the tricks they used to get up to. Rose told him, she said she wasn't interested in that type of relationship and she'd thank him to keep them kind of details to himself, thank you very much. But he didn't seem to take any notice. Only seemed to encourage him, in fact. They met up a few more times, but Rose was always a bit wary. Somehow he'd always manage to turn the conversation a bit . . . well, smutty. That's the only word for it. The final straw was when he pulled a bundle of photographs out of his jacket one teatime in Medici's. Rose had never seen anything like them in all her life and she never wants to again. Disgusting they were. And not just women her age, some of them were young lasses as well. But he seemed to think it was the most natural thing in the world.

Said he'd met them all on the internet and it was all between consenting adults. Well, that sealed the deal; Rose told him exactly what she thought of him and she walked straight out, just left him in there she did, with his half-eaten dessert and the bill still to come. Rose said if her husband had have been there he'd have took his bloody jacket off to him. He rang her up a few more times but Rose threatened him with the police and then she never heard from him again.

It was a while before she got the nerve up to even go back on the site, let alone meet up with anyone else. But you can't let these type of people win can you, these Percy Filth types with their one-track minds and their grubby little habits. Why should she miss out on meeting new people just because of one bad apple?

So Rose is hoping it's third time lucky with this Leo chap. He seems normal enough. She's been chatting to him for a couple of weeks, off and on. He seems keen on a meet up, keen as mustard. But she'll see. No rush, is there?

This chap on the wireless is still banging on. Poor old Blair still can't get a word in:

– *NOW HOLD ON A MINUTE PETER, IF I CAN JUST STOP YOU THERE FOR ONE SECOND . . . HULL FAIR HAS BEEN AN INSTITUTION IN THIS CITY FOR OVER SEVEN HUNDRED YEARS AND . . .*

– *YES, BLAIR, I APPRECIATE THAT, AND I AM A RESPECTER OF TRADITION, OH HELL AYE, YES, PLEASE DON'T MISUNDERSTAND ME ON THAT SCORE, BUT WHAT I AM SAYING TO YOU IS THIS – IT HAS GOT OUT OF HAND.*

ARE YOU WITH ME? IT'S BECOME AN ABSOLUTE MONSTER. DO YOU UNDER-STAND WHAT I'M SAYING BLAIR?

– WELL WHAT YOU SEEM TO BE SAYING IS . . .

– NO NO NO NO NO, WHAT I'M SAYING IS THIS

Rose switches off the voices and takes her soup to the table. That's enough of that. She'll read a magazine instead. Can't stand to listen to any more of him, mouth all bloody mighty. Become a monster indeed! Some people, she thinks. They haven't got the sense they were bloody born with!

Lime Tree Lodge, Cottingham Road: 12.34pm

First thing Kerry noticed about this place was the smoke. Out of the twenty or so residents about ninety per cent of them smoke like chimneys; chaining them an'all, some of them, lighting one straight off the other. Kerry spends half her time wandering round emptying ashtrays. That telly room is the worst, the designated smoking room; you go in there sometimes and it's like someone's lit a bonfire. Can hardly see the screen some nights for all the smoke. Stinks an'all, clings to every-thing; the furniture, the wallpaper, even the carpet, no matter how many times you spray the room or sling the Shake n' Vac about. They've got these automatic air fresheners on the walls that give out the occasional blast, but they're no match for the twenty-four-hour smoke-a-thon that goes on in here. And anyway, half of them don't work now, since Pete Craven marched down the hallway the other night, smashing them all to bits with a sweeping brush. He said they'd been put there by the government to poison him in his sleep. Maggie's son Gary who works here, and him who does the drawings, that Barry, they both had to get him down on the deck and sit on him while the doctor came with the injection.

They're certainly not supposed to smoke in here when they're having their dinner, but you're fighting a losing battle with most of them. Like Frank, for instance. Frank's the eldest one in here, well into his seventies Kerry reckons. Skinny little feller, a crumpled-up bag of bones in shirt-sleeves an' braces. Always got a rollie dangling off his bottom lip. She clocks his bacca pouch; he's rolling one up now under the table with trembling brown-tipped fingers. He's not even touched his sausages and mashed tatie, and that's his favourite an'all.

– Come on Frank, Kerry tells him – you know you can't smoke in here. Have a tab after you've had yer dinner.

– Oh aye, he says, – I know, just doing it for after. He slips the roll-up into his shirt breast pocket and picks up his knife and fork, starts smearing the grub round his plate.

Frank's not really mental, he's just an arsonist. Been in prison half his life for setting fire to things, including himself on a few occasions. He ended up in here after he set the curtains alight in his last old people's home. But he's not really properly crackers, not like Christopher or Alec Nelson or Marjorie upstairs, who never comes out of her room, not even for mealtimes. Frank's just one of them who has had a bit of a hard

14

life, like most of the others in here. Alkies, druggies, victims of abuse, nervous wrecks, self-harmers. Manic depressives, or bi-polar or whatever they call it nowadays. Some of them are just people who have lost their way for whatever reason. They never had anyone to look after them and they just ended up slipping through the net. Most of them have had summat horrible done to them. Or they've done it to themselves. Like Maurice, muttering away in the corner there, dinner untouched. He was a skipper on trawlers; wife, four kids, two new cars, big house up in Swanland, the full lot. Drove home pissed up one teatime and mounted the kerb near a school crossing, killed two mams an' a bain in a pushchair. Tried to do himself in about four times while he was in prison and now he can't live on his own. Needs constant supervision. Shame, really. He's quite a nice bloke once you start talking to him.

Half of them aren't even looking at their food and the other half are just plastering it all over the table or dropping it on the floor. Kerry can see she's going to have to get the Hoover out again, for the fourth time today. Keeping this place clean is like shovelling snow in a blizzard. Kerry must go through about ten gallons of Flash a week. When everyone's finished and left the dining room Sandra helps her clear all the plates up and stack them in the washer. Then Kerry gives all the tables a good going over while Sandra gets the brews on. When she goes back through to the kitchen Christopher's hanging around in the doorway.

– What do you want Chris love?

– Can I help yer?

– No, you're alright petal, we've nearly finished.

– I'll do the drying up for yer.

He goes to go inside the kitchen, but Kerry puts her arm across the doorway. He's just trying it on. He knows he's not allowed in there because of the knives and that.

– There's no drying up to be done love, we've got a machine. Now go in the telly room and I'll bring you a cup of tea. A biscuit an'all if you're lucky. Go on, skedaddle.

He peers over her arm into the kitchen.

– Who's in there?

– Sandra. Come on, Christopher, be a good lad.

– Have you got a cig, please?

– I'll bring you one wi' yer brew. Now off you pop.

He turns and strides off down the hallway, disappears into the telly room. Kerry was a bit wary of Christopher at first, but if you let him know who's boss he soon falls into line. The main thing with him, with all the schizophrenics really, is to keep it all on a certain level. Stick to basic instructions. Don't get too deep. They can sometimes take things the wrong way, and the slightest remark can set them off. When Kerry first started here she made the mistake of getting into this big debate with Alec Nelson about summat on the news, and he went totally off on one, put his fist through the glass in the front door and had to go to Infirmary. Fourteen stitches up his arm and a visit from the social. Maggie went absolutely ballistic at her. Kerry thought she was going to give her the bullet, but she stood her ground, told Maggie she was new to all this mental illness lark and didn't know the proper way to carry on with people like Alec. After a bit Maggie calmed down and said Kerry could stay, but she was still on trial. Ever since then Kerry keeps it short and sweet, especially with them like Alec and Christopher and that other lass, that Joanne. Usually if you give them a cig it keeps them off your back for a bit. But you have to watch it with the cigs an'all. Make a rod for your own back if you're not careful. Kerry was going through about thirty a day at one point, and only smoking half of them herself. It's a balancing act, when to dish them out and when to say no. But you soon learn. Sandra, she won't give any of them a cig. Says she doesn't earn enough to hand her wages back to the residents every week. Sandra's firm but fair, and none of them ever play her up. Kerry's glad she's on with her tonight. The nights are long in here.

Kerry doesn't particularly like doing nights, but it's a case of needs must. She's been out of work too long and she doesn't want to mess this job up. Doesn't want to start shouting the odds about what hours she can and can't do. Maggie can soon find herself another care assistant, no problem. And anyway, not sleeping doesn't bother Kerry, she can always read a magazine or talk to one of them in here. There's usually at least three or four of them traipsing about well into the small hours. Kerry thinks the medication stops them sleeping. Either that or the voices. Good job she's got her helpful head on today. The hours soon disappear if you keep yourself busy. And there's always plenty to have a go at round here, night and day.

When they've finished clearing up Kerry and Sandra bring two trays of tea and the biscuit barrel into the telly room.

Twenty minutes later Kerry's getting the Hoover out again.

Itlings Lane: 1.17pm

Michelle's popped round to her mam's, but she's starting to wish she hadn't have bothered. She's been buzzing her tits off all day – all week in fact – but ten minutes with her mam is enough to piss on the brightest of bonfires. Plan was to show her face, stop for a quick cuppa, get back to their Chrissie's, get changed, then meet Darren at the top of Walton Street for three. All Michelle wanted was a quick in and out with no head stress. Instead, she walks slap-bang into the middle of yet another domestic drama, number four hundred and twenty-six in an ongoing series.

One of the builders has sawn through some pipe under the sink and now there's water pissing all over the kitchen floor. Marvellous. Michelle's dad's going berserk. She's sat in the caravan with her mam and she can hear him shouting and bawling from inside the house.

It's dead cramped in this bloody thing. There's the portable telly from the kitchen jammed up on the side and a few of her mam's ornaments dotted about, but it's not exactly home from home. Michelle doesn't know how her mam and dad haven't murdered each other, the pair of them in here. It's only a matter of time though, surely. She'll come round one afternoon and one of them'll be dumped in that skip, along with all the old kitchen units and bits of sodden lino.

The little electric kettle clicks off and her mam pours the brews.

– It's just one thing after a bastard 'nother, she says.

She's always been a gloomy get has Michelle's mam, but since the floods she's been unbearable. Michelle knows it can't be much fun stopping in a caravan on the front drive, but it's not like her mam's the only one who's been inconvenienced. Both Michelle and Nathan have moved out, him to his mates in Anlaby and Michelle to her Auntie Chrissie's, just off the square. Chrissie's place isn't exactly a five-star luxury hotel, but you don't hear Michelle moaning and groaning. They just have to get on with it, all of them. Michelle's mam though, she's never happy unless she's totally miserable.

She treats Michelle to the full run-down on all the things that have gone wrong this week and all the bastards who are to blame – the council ('them bastards'), the loss adjusters ('them clueless bastards'), the insurance company ('them thieving bastards'), the builders ('them lazy bastards') and last but not least Michelle's dad ('that useless bastard'). Michelle will say one thing for her mam, she's very fair minded. She doesn't leave anybody out.

Michelle sits and listens to her go on and on. It's vaguely amusing at first, but after about ten minutes of useless bastard this and clueless fuckin' twats that, Michelle's good vibe is in very real danger of being totally wrecked.

She sups her tea and tells her mam she has to get off.

– What, already? You've only just got here.

– I know but I've gotta go and get changed.

– Why, where yer going?

– Round Fair, then off on Prinny Ave.

– Oh aye, is this with your new bloke then?

Wonderful. How does she know about that? Best thing to have happened to Michelle all year and now her mam's going to rag him to bits before she's even met him.

– What new bloke?

– Don't give me that, says her mam. – Angie said you were seeing some new lad. Danny innit? Danny off North Bransholme?

Their Angie. Michelle might have known. Can't hold her own piss, that one. It's a wonder that bain's stayed in her belly these last nine months.

– I've only been seeing him two weeks, Michelle tells her. – I wouldn't go buying a new hat just yet mother.

– Who is he anyway, this Danny? What does he do?

Michelle's mam lights a tab up and opens the caravan door.

– His name's Darren, says Michelle. And he's a builder.

Her mam takes a long hard drag on her cig and exhales a plume of blue smoke. She's always moaning about being skint but she must get through about forty tabs a day, at least.

– Oh well, she says, – at least he won't be short of work.

She leans out of the caravan and flicks ash.

– Can't he come and sort that bastard lot out, she says.

– I don't think he does houses, I think he just does shopfitting and that.

– Shoplifting more like, if your track record with blokes is owt to go by.

Before Michelle can answer her back, this builder comes stomping out the front door of the house, closely followed by Michelle's dad. Neither of them look best pleased. The builder goes off down the driveway, jabbing a number into his phone. Her dad kicks his boots off and stands them outside the caravan. The entire thing shudders with his weight as he steps inside. He has to constantly stoop down to move about.

– You have to stand over these bastards twenty-four-fuckin-seven, he says.

He clocks Michelle sat up at the other end.

– Alright Shell? No college today?

– Hiya Dad. No, no classes on a Friday.

Her dad picks a mug out of the sink and swills it under the tap. He looks completely knackered, like he hasn't slept for about a week.

– What's happening Joe? asks Michelle's mam. – Have they sorted that mess out?

Michelle's dad shakes his head.

– He's turned the water off and patched the pipe up, but they're gonna have to rive it all out again an' have a proper look. I'm not happy with him leaving it like that.

Michelle twists herself round and pulls back the net curtain. This builder is stood out in the street next to the skip, his mobile clamped to his ear. He looks seriously pissed off. Her dad's head bobs down next to hers.

– I know what it is, he says, – they're cracking up to get back to Middlesbrough so they can go out on the piss. If he puts them tools anywhere near that van I'll wrap them round his bastard neck.

– Middlesbrough, says Michelle, – why are they going to Middlesbrough?

– That's where they're from.

– Why do we have to have people from Middlesbrough to put a kitchen back in? Why can't a Hull firm do it?

– Cos these are the insurance company's preferred builders.

– Why?

– I don't know, do I? Probably give them the cheapest quote. There int a fuckin' plumber among them though, I know that.

– Me mate Sarah, her uncle's doing their house up. She reckons they'll be back in for Christmas.

Her dad ignores this comment. Probably not what he wanted to hear. Instead, he asks Michelle if she's been round to see her grandad.

– I went round last week with Chrissie, she tells him.

– You do know he's going into hospital on Monday don't yer?

Shit, Michelle had forgot all about that. She knew he was going back in at some point, she didn't realise it was so soon. He's only been out a month or so. The cancer's all in his liver now. Michelle had heard Chrissie on the phone to her dad the other night. It's not looking good, she'd said.

– I'll go and see him, she says.

– Yeah, you do that.

These three other builders come traipsing out the house laden down with spades and pickaxes and heavy bags of tools. Two young lads and an older feller. One of the lads is a bit of alright, thinks Michelle, quite fit in fact. Not as fit as Darren though. They go up the driveway and start chucking all their gear into the back of a van that's parked up at the side of the road.

– BASTARDS!

Her dad goes flying out the caravan, nearly tipping the frigging thing over, ornaments bouncing about on the shelves. Her mam pelts her cig and she's right behind him. Michelle hopes for the builders' sake that her dad gets to them before her mam does.

Michelle rinses her mug out in the little sink while they all argue the toss in the street. She glances outside. The first builder's still got his phone to his ear, one hand held up to Michelle's mam, like he's trying to ward off a vampire with a crucifix. The other three are stood leaning against the van, rolling tabs and grinning at each other behind their gaffer's back.

Oh dear, thinks Michelle, not a good move.

– WHAT THE FUCK ARE YOU LAUGHING AT, EH?

Michelle's mam's livid. The older bloke looks like he's trying to calm her down. Michelle can't hear what he's saying, but whatever it is, it's pointless. Like trying to put a blazing fire out with a can of petrol.

– YEAH, IT'S ALRIGHT FOR YOU INNIT! YOU'VE TURNED THE FUCKIN' WATER OFF! I CAN'T EVEN GO FOR A BASTARD SHIT!

All that money on that Swiss finishing school, thinks

Michelle. Wasted on me mother. And her mam wonders why Michelle doesn't bring any of her blokes back to meet her.

She taxes two Mayfair out of her mam's packet, gets her coat and bag and gets out of Dodge City, smartish. Michelle hasn't got time to hang about and watch the show. Places to go, people to meet.

Well, person.

She says her ta-ras as she hurries past them. One of the lads grins and nods, gives her the once-over. Michelle can feel his eyes boring into her as she goes down the street, so she puts a bit of a wiggle on, just for his benefit. Put that in your wank bank and take it back to Middlesbrough mate!

She texts Darren:

RUNNIN L8. W8 4 ME!

Thirty seconds later her phone beeps:

NO PRBLM BABE.

And there isn't.
Not as far as she's concerned, anyhow.
Not one.

Lime Tree Lodge, Cottingham Road: 2.14pm

There's nowt on the telly. Kerry goes through to the other front room and Barry's got his sketch pad and pencils out. He's quite a good artist is Barry. Went to art school in London, or so he reckons. Says he used to be a roadie an'all, working for loads of big rock bands in the eighties and nineties. He looks the part, like one of them old biker types, the long hair and the denim jacket and that. He comes out with some right tales does Barry, although he's actually one of the more normal ones in here. Kerry doesn't think he's a schizo or a manic depressive or owt like that. She think he's just had a bit of a bad time with the old Class As. His arms have got all faded trackmarks and scars and cig burns dotted up them, so Kerry thinks he used to do a bit of the old dirty digging. Best not to ask, though, really. Take people as you find them and all that.

She looks over his shoulder at what he's drawing.

– That's good Barry. What is it?

He holds it up. It looks like a load of horses stampeding through a whirlwind.

– What d'yer think it is?

– Dunno.

– Can't yer tell?

– Looks like a load of horses stampeding through a whirlwind.

– It's a merry-go-round.

– Ah right, yeah, I can see it now.

And she can, now that he's said. It looks ace an'all, the horses with their flared nostrils and raised hooves, charging after each other across the page in a mad circle. The way he's done the lines and that, you can almost see it spinning round.

– That's brilliant that Barry. You gunna colour it in?

– Dunno. I was gunna keep it like this. Why, do yer reckon it needs colour?

He holds it out at arm's length and tilts his head this way and that, like he's checking out one of them big old paintings in Ferens Art Gallery. Kerry can't draw to save her life so she doesn't feel qualified to give out advice. But Barry obviously wants her opinion, and besides, it's good to encourage 'em when they do summat constructive.

– I'd mebbe put a bit of yellow in it. Shining down. For the lights and that.

– Yeah, I think you're right.

He picks a dark yellow pencil out of his box and starts adding long swooping lines alongside the black. It really brings it to life, even more than before. He's definitely a talented bloke. Zoe was artistic an'all. She once did this brilliant drawing of Jennifer Lopez that she copied out of *heat*. Kerry's still got it somewhere, along with a few other ones she did. Kerry always wanted Zoe to do her one of Jay-Z, but she never got round to it.

– Me and Gail are off round Fair in a bit, says Barry.
– Fancy coming?

– Can't can I. Supposed to be on duty.

Barry smiles to himself as he scribbles away. Kerry can tell he doesn't like to think of a young lass like her being in charge of him, but he never acts all clever about it. Some of 'em, like that Alec Nelson or Pete Craven, they're always testing the boundaries, seeing how far they can push her. Like bains really. You can understand it to a certain extent, and Kerry does make allowances; especially as how she's only just getting to know 'em all. But there comes a point where a line has to be drawn. At the end of the day she's responsible for their well-being, and if owt happens it's down to her, and that's that. Barry's alright though, he never gives her any grief.

– It'll be alright, he says. – You'll still be supervising, won't yer?

– Yeah, but I told Sandra I'd give her hand with all that ironing. Can't leave her to do all that on her own, it's not fair.

Barry glances up at the clock.

– Gary'll be here in a bit. He can move an iron about can't he?

– Suppose so.

– Well there you go then. You ant stopped since this morning. Sandra won't mind you popping out for an hour or so.

Kerry's not been to Fair this year. Not really fancied it to be truthful. Her and Zoe used to go at least twice every year. Zoe loved it, always did, right from being a bain. Good memories. Kerry's mam always says to her, if you're going to dwell on anything, dwell on the good times.

– An' we're not prisoners are we, says Barry. – Not under lock an' key. Free to come an' go as we like, aren't we?

He's got a point.

– Yeah, alright fair enough, Kerry says – I'll see if some of the others want to go. Be a nice afternoon out for 'em, eh?

– Do some of 'em a bit of good to get up from in front of that bloody telly.

It will an'all. Spend too much time brooding, most of them lot. A walk round Fair . . . yeah that'll be spot on. Before it gets too busy. Bit of fresh air in their lungs. Do 'em a world of good.

– Right that's nailed on then, she tells him. – Long as we're back for tea, though, yeah?

– Absolutely.

He rolls up his merry-go-round and starts slotting his pens back into his box.

– Right, he says, – I'll go and get Gail and you see who you can round up. Back here in ten?

– Back here in ten, she says.

Lambert Street Nursery, Newland Avenue: 3.10pm

There's loads of 'em round here now, thinks Carl, these Poles or Ukrainians or whatever the fuck they are. Eastern Europeans. This one here, she's jabbering away to her bain, giving him a bollocking as he's twisting round in his seat, pulling on the wall display behind him. She swats his hand away and he slumps back down, sulking, his little feet swinging a good six inches off the floor. Little pair of Adidas Superstars. Carl thought they were meant to be skint, these refugees or asylum seekers or whatever the fuck they are. She doesn't look too impoverished though. Nice leather jacket, if a bit eighties, like. And that gold rope round her neck, that must have cost a few bob.

She glances up at Carl, catches him staring. He slides his eyes slowly to the pictures behind her: WE WENT TO THE PARK! Stick people on slides and swings. Fixed smiles on enormous balloon heads. He wonders which one's meant to be Ella. Must be the one with the mad candyfloss curls and the red trousers. Dead proud of her hair, Ella is. She'll hate it when she's older,

Angie reckons. Hair straighteners for her fifteenth birthday, she says, you watch. She's already started raiding her mam's make-up bag. Four years old and blathered in lippie. Fuckin' wrong, really, thinks Carl, but what can you do.

The little lad starts singing a song under his breath, in time to his swinging feet as he bangs his heels on the underneath of the chair. He gets another dig off Mamski, another hissed rebuke. The little lad crosses his arms and scowls.

She looks across at Carl, rolls her eyes. He takes the opportunity to weigh her up. Nice eyes. Dark brown. Bit too much eyeliner though. Blue an'all. Bleached blonde hair with black roots. Straight out of a Hot Gossip video, this lass. A lot of these Polish birds seem to be caught in the same 1980s time warp. The blokes are all sunken-eyed shaven-headed army cadet types and the lasses are all out of *The Hitman and Her*. Trust Hull to get the lookers. Carl thought they were all meant to be professional people, dentists and doctors and that?

The little lad's legs start swinging again. She must have another one, if she's here at this time. Wonder why this little feller's not in the nursery? He must be about the same age as Ella. Maybe there's a limit on overseas visitors, thinks Carl. Like they have with the football teams.

A few more parents start to arrive, some with kids, most of them on their own. Gets a bit crowded in this reception bit if you turn up too early. Big fat Lilly from down the street wheezes in. She's weighed down with carrier bags from Iceland and so, like the perfect gentleman he is, Carl stands up and vacates his seat. Right on cue, the buzzer goes and the young lass comes and unlocks the door and they all go through to the main playroom.

Ella clocks him straight away, flies over and flings herself round him.

– DADDY! she yells.

Her hands are all covered in some blue gunky shit. Fuckin' marvellous. All over his best Fred Perry. Clean on an'all. Come on, he says, and they wash her hands at the basins and join the throng in the narrow little corridor for coats and shoes and bags. Ella's chattering away ten to the dozen about Mrs Wilkins and Carrie and Archie Brown and some game they were playing where Archie Brown was being a wolf but he's not a wolf really he's a badger and is her new sister or brother here yet and can they go and get a comic on the way home cos he promised her this morning, can we Daddy, can we, can we, can we?

– Come on, he says, and they get her stuff together and get outside.

They pass Russian Mam on the way out. She's got her other little lad with her, a dark-haired little carbon copy of his brother. They're having a mini-battle at the door, pulling each other about, yelling and arguing in whatever language it is. She looks pretty pissed off and Carl opens the door for the lot of 'em. She bundles her kids through with barely a glance.

Charming, thinks Carl.

– We say thank you in this country, he remarks loudly to the back of her peroxide head. But she's off through the outer railing gate and down the road, part of the tide of big and little people all making their way home to tea and CBeebies and a last half-hour larking out, riding bikes and kicking balls about till it gets proper dark and it's time for bed.

His mobile bleeps a text message from Ange:

GET MILK, PAPER, DIET COKES, HEAT, GRAZIA

– Who wants to go to goodie shop? says Carl.
– Me! says Ella.
– C'mon then, says her dad.

Hull Fair: 3.15pm

So there's Kerry, Barry, Gail, Christopher, Gordon Green and Pete Craven all walking down Chants Ave towards Spring Bank, towards Walton Street, towards Hull Fair. Gordon's come out without his coat, he's just got a City top on and a thin pair of trackie bottoms. The sky's getting darker by the minute and it looks like it might pelt down. Kerry tells Gordon he'll catch King Cough coming out like that, but he just grins and nods. Gail keeps trying to link her arm through Barry's, but he's not having any of it, keeps pushing her away. Gail thinks she's Barry's girlfriend. Sometimes Barry agrees with her and sometimes he doesn't, depending on what mood he's in. Christopher's dawdling along at the back, stopping every two minutes to pick tab ends up off the pavement. Kerry has to keep making everyone stop and wait for him.

– Come on Chris! Fair'll be shut by the time we get there!

But eventually they all get down Chants and onto

Walton Street. Kerry tells everyone to stay together and not get split up cos even though it's not that busy now you can easy get lost round Fair. Gail takes this as her cue to grab tight hold of Barry's arm and this time he lets her keep hold of him. It's nice to see an'all, thinks Kerry.

Kerry tells Peter and Gordon and Christopher to hand over their money and she'll look after it for 'em, but nobody's got any money apart from Gordon and he's only got about seventy-odd pence in change. He hands it over, good as gold. Pete Craven though, he's not happy about this at all. He starts muttering away to himself under his breath, and Kerry can tell it's aimed at her by the looks he's giving.

– What's up Pete? she asks him.

– Why should you look after Gordon's money?

– Cos I'm responsible, she tells him.

– Who says?

– Maggie says.

– Well I never heard Maggie put you in charge.

– Well she did. An' if owt happens, I'm to blame.

– No you're not, he says.

Kerry just ignores him. If you get into owt like this with Pete it can only end in a row. He's like a dog with a bone. Kerry asks Gail if she likes Hull Fair and Gail says she hasn't been for a while but she loves it, yeah. She wants Barry to win her a teddy and she wants to take some brandy snap back for Sandra, but she won't be having any herself cos it's too sweet for her. She's not a lover of sweet things, she says. Kerry asks her what about Barry then and Gail giggles like a little lass and Barry says give over the pair of yer.

– Give Gordon his money back, says Pete.

– No, he'll only lose it, says Kerry. – Now give it a rest please Peter.

– Fuckin' give him it back, now.

– I said no dint I? An' don't use language like that please.

They go on and on like this but Pete keeps raising his voice and then Gordon starts getting all agitated and bursts into tears, starts wailing, big style. People are looking. Barry hears all the row, stops and turns round, asks what's up.

– It's her, says Pete, – she won't give Gordon his money back.

– I'm looking after it for him, Kerry says.

Barry looks at Pete and then Gordon.

– Gordon, did you ask Kerry to look after yer money for yer?

Gordon nods, his face all shiny with snot and tears.

– No you fuckin' dint Gordon, says Pete, and Gordon clamps his hands over his ears, starts shaking his head and running on the spot, really shrieking and bawling now. Gail's straight over to him and giving him a love, and he wraps his arms round her, clamping his face into her neck, his skinny little shoulders shuddering up and down. Barry glares at Pete.

– Why do you have to cause trouble Pete? We've all come out for a nice time, why d'yer have to spoil it for everyone?

– I aren't spoiling fuck all, it's her, says Pete.

– Look, Kerry says to Pete, – I'll give Gordon his money back, alright? But if he loses it, it's your fault. Alright?

Barry asks Gordon if he's happy with that and he says summat that Kerry think sounds like yeah I'm real happy Barry, but he's in that much of a state Kerry doesn't think he really knows what's going on. Barry takes the money off Kerry and holds it out in his hand for Gordon to see.

— Ere y'are Gord, I'll look after it for yer, alright? That alright, yeah?

Gordon says yeah, his head still buried in Gail's neck.

Barry turns to Pete, who looks highly delighted with himself and all the bother he's caused.

— An' what about you? You happy now, yeah? All sorted?

Pete shrugs.

— Just as long as she's not in charge.

This is the main problem with being new, thinks Kerry. She's only been at Lime Tree Lodge for three weeks. It takes a while for some of them to accept you as a figure of authority. Kerry thinks they see that many people coming and going, they like to know that you're stopping before they drop their guard. That's what Sandra told her anyway, and she's been working there for God knows how long. So she'll let it go this time, but if Pete gives her any more grief she'll have to report him to Maggie and then he'll end up in Morton House again. He's just trying it on, testing the boundaries. Seeing what he can get away with.

They all set off down Walton Street again, Barry and Gail and Gordon all propping each other up and Kerry and Pete trailing behind them.

Kerry looks round for Christopher.

Where's Christopher?

She's gripped by a proper belly-fluttering panic for about three seconds, but then Kerry spots him stood at this stall a short way behind them. She trots back to get him. He's stood staring at these little glittery plastic windmills, a big rack full of 'em, their sails spinning hard, round and round in the wind. The bloke on the stall looks at Christopher and then at Kerry. Kerry can tell he's a bit wary. Christopher can properly freak you out if yer not used to him, the way he just stands and stares with those dark ringed eyes.

– Two pounds fifty they are love, says this bloke.

Christopher points at the lit cig between the bloke's fingers.

– Can I have a drag, please? he says.

The bloke looks at Kerry.

– It's alright mate, I've got him, she says, taking hold of Christopher by the arm and pulling him back up the street after the others.

This bloody job, thinks Kerry. You can't turn your back for two seconds.

Hedon Road: 3.31pm

Dave's helping Butch clear up in Bay One when their Janice calls him on his mobile. She wants to know if he fancies going round for his tea after work. He tells her he'll pop in for a cuppa, but that he'd promised Lindsey he'd go and see her at Fair, so he can't stop long. He tells her he'll bring them some chips or summat. She asks if Denise is coming, what with it being Friday and that, but Dave tells her no, not tonight. Not to Hull Fair. Not with all them people there.

Then they yap about this and that, her job, the bains,

their mother's recent move into the hospice. Graham and his ongoing mid-life crisis.

Butch is trying to tune in. He's got his back to Dave, sweeping up, but Dave can tell he's ear-wigging by the way he's got his head cocked to one side.

– Anyhow Jan, I'll be finished here in about an hour. I'll go home and get changed into me ceremonial robes and I'll be round at yours for about six-ish, half six, yeah? You light the black candles and get the virgin tied up, I'll sharpen the sacrificial dagger . . . yeah, alright love. Ta-ra.

Dave puts his mobile away and claps Butch hard on the back.

– Did you get all that Butch?

The nosey fat four-sugared bastard nearly jumps clean out of his skin.

Hull Fair: 3.34pm

Michelle said she'd have nowt to do with lads after she finished with Scott. Not for a good bit, anyhow. Too much head stress. This one, though, this Darren, there's summat different about him. He's not all full of himself like most lads. Doesn't walk around giving it the big I am. He's real quiet and dreamy, like he's miles away, sometimes. But Michelle likes that. And she liked him the minute she first met him. He was sat with his mates in White Hart, in the beer garden. They were all dead loud and carrying on, but he seemed separate from them somehow; not acting like he was above them or anything like that, just sort of cool and detached. Self-contained. She found herself sat next to him and they just talked and talked. They talked about all sorts. Well, Michelle did, mouth almighty. He just listened, mainly. Smiled and listened. He didn't try it on or owt like that, didn't even ask for her number. But Michelle made sure she got his. And two nights later she rang him up.

Four times now they've been out. Every time Michelle sees him she prepares herself for the catch: mental ex-bird, abandoned bain, hard drug habit, jealous streak, possessive streak, mad paranoid bastard behaviour. But there's been none of that. So far he seems like that most rare of creatures, the Decent Bloke. And, as an added Brucie Bonus, he's a brilliant shag; although she had to take the lead in that department as well. Had to invite herself back to his gaff on the third night, after it became obvious he wasn't going to invite her back himself. Even then he was all coy, even when they got back to his place on North Bransholme. For a minute Michelle had thought he might be gay; but no, she took the matter in hand, so to speak, and he fair stood to attention alright. After that it was all systems go, proper full on. Michelle had forgotten what it was like to be properly fucked – Scott was either too pissed or too stoned. Usually both. Like Michelle said to her mate Jennifer, more interested in his Xbox than her box. After six months of crap sex and non-existent conversation she kicked Scott firmly into touch. Mind you, he probably didn't even notice. Probably still sat there in his grotty little flat full of empty pizza boxes and overflowing ashtrays, hypnotised in front of Grand Theft Auto, wondering why she hasn't rung him up for the last two months.

But this Darren, though. He's different. Michelle keeps telling herself it's early days yet, but she can't help feeling there's something special happening here. Something proper.

Oh God, she hopes so.

She gets off the bus just before the flyover and walks back to Walton Street. For a second she can't see him and her heart's in her mouth but no, there he is, stood outside Parkers, looking the other way up Anlaby Road. She sneaks up behind him and puts her hands over his eyes and he nearly jumps out of his skin. He spins round and grabs hold of her by the shoulders.

– Jesus Christ, Michelle! he goes. – Don't ever do that again!

Michelle laughs and gives him a big kiss, gets hold of his hand and they set off down Walton Street. She likes Fair at this time, when it's not too busy. She can't be doing with it late on a night when it gets packed, struggling through gangs of hood-rats and mobs of pissed-up idiots. They'll have a nice leisurely stroll round Fair and then get to pub before the crowds start. Michelle fancies a good drink tonight. A good drink and a good laugh. The Fair feels like it did when she was little, her breath hanging in the cold air, the smell of hot dogs and ketchup and fried onions, bright lights, dark nights and raw excitement. Halloween, bonfire night and Christmas all on the way. Good times to come and someone there to share them with.

She pulls her new bloke close up against her as they wander off into the noise.

Hull Fair: 4.32pm

Jessica, bless her, she's that excited. Fair's not too busy yet, but Rose still makes her hang on tight to her hand as they go down Walton Street. She's got a fiver to spend, but Rose tells her to keep that in her pocket for now and Nana will pay for the first few rides. Donna makes a bit of a face but if Rose can't spoil her own grandbain who can she spoil? Besides, she doesn't see her as often as she'd like, so she's entitled to make a bit of a fuss of her.

Course she wants everything in sight, the sun, the stars and the moon on a stick! Rose tells her to wait till they've been round the rides and when they come back down Walton Street she can choose one toy to take home with her. So they watch her go round on the teacups and the mushrooms and Donna films her on her mobile phone. Every time Jessica goes round she waves like mad and her nana is telling her to keep tight hold of the handlebars. Rose has visions of her flying off and splitting her head wide open. Donna tells her not to be so daft, that it's not going nowhere near fast enough, but Rose tells her she's been coming to this Fair for nigh on sixty years and she knows full well that you don't have to be going fast to hurt yourself. She remembers when Dorrie Taylor's little lad stood up on top of that horse, pretending to be Roy bloody Rogers. Showing off to some lasses he was and went flying off, smacked face first onto the ground. Bit his tongue clean in two, straight to Hull Royal Infirmary. So don't tell Rose about Hull Fair.

They go round a few more stalls and have a few more rides. Rose helps Jessica hold the pole for the Hook-a-Duck and they manage to lift one out. They're a twist, though, thinks Rose, half of these bloody stalls.

You don't win owt except a load of tat. You used to get a goldfish years ago, but they stopped all that. All this political correctness. Barmy. Now it's just bits of plastic rubbish that fall apart before you get them halfway home. They don't even have the sideshows they used to have, the World's Strongest Man and the Bearded Lady and all them. There used to be a boxing show as well with a big coloured chap. American, Rose thinks he was. Course, all the fisher kids used to queue up and try and knock his block off, but they were usually half cut and most of 'em ended up stretched out on the deck. And he was a big chap, this darkie, remembers Rose. Strong bugger. She used to kid Malcolm up, tell him she was going to run off with him, take off to America and become a showgirl.

Donna's saying it's getting on now and they've got to get off, so they have one more go on the round-about with the little motorbikes and cars and then they set off back down Walton Street towards Anlaby Road to catch the bus to Boothferry.

It's getting busy down Walton Street now. There's a Gypsy woman leaning out of her caravan door, smoking a cigarette and watching the people wander past. Her face has got more creases than an old accordion, but Rose bets she's not that much older than her. That's what a life outdoors does for you. Weather-beaten, that's how she looks. They used to scare Rose when she was little, the Gypsies. Her dad always said they'd steal her away if she didn't behave herself. Rose seems to remember them looking a lot more like Gypsies back then though. She's sure they used to dress up a bit more, in their headscarves and big earrings and what have you. Like you imagine a Gypsy in a story book to look like. Probably just did it for effect, she supposes. This one though, she looks just like any normal middle-aged woman you might see shopping down Hessle Road: quilted coat, dyed-blonde hair with an inch of grey showing at the roots, sucking away on her ciggie. She catches Rose's eye as they draw level and Rose looks away quick, but the Gypsy's holding her hand out, beckoning her.

– Lady! Yes, come in lady! Best reading for you!

Jessica stops dead and so Rose has to stop an'all. Her grandbain points up at the photos dotted all over the side of the caravan, all pictures of this Gypsy woman with famous people off the telly, *Coronation Street* and *Emmerdale* and what have you. There's one with that ventriloquist chap that always used to be on, him who had that big green duck.

– Look Nana! Look at that!

This Gypsy, she swings open the bottom half of her door.

– Come in lady, come in.

– I'm alright thank you very much, Rose tells her.

– Oh go on mother, says Donna, – it's only a bit of fun.

– Best reading for you, says the Gypsy.

And she stands back, holding the door open for Rose.

– Go on, says Donna, – I'll go on them machines over there with Jessica and then we'll get her a toy or summat and get off home.

Well, it's just a bit of fun isn't it? Can't do any harm now, can it?

Rose asks this Gypsy how much it is and she tells her it's ten pounds. A tenner! No wonder people say they're all a bunch of bloody robbers!

– Oh, go on, get in, don't be daft, says their Donna. – Might bring you a bit of good luck.

Three steps up and Rose is in this cramped little caravan. It's immaculately clean, but absolutely jam-packed full of tat. Like Aladdin's cave it is, little ornaments and trinkets going all the way round the walls and along the windows. Little gold and silver figures, painted dolls, framed photos. There's stuff dangling down from the roof an'all, wind charms or bains' mobiles they look like. Some lanterns an'all. All manner of gaudy little knick-knacks twirling and glinting and twinkling away. Spotless though, Rose'll give her that. She must spend all her days dusting and polishing. The kitchen quarters are at the far end, a small gas cooker and a sink. The Gypsy puts her cig out under the tap and rinses it down the plughole, wipes her hands on a tea towel.

– Sit down lady, she says.

There's a little table near the window with a chair on either side. Rose can't see any crystal ball or packs of cards though. There's a teapot and a couple of little china cups on saucers but they're clean, no tea leaves in 'em or owt like that. It's a bit disappointing, actually. Rose thinks they should make a bit more of an effort. Dress it all up a bit, give it some of the old hocus-pocus.

Anyroad, she sits down. The Gypsy parks herself opposite her and reaches across the table, takes a hold of Rose's hand in both of hers. Rose tries to pull it away, natural instinct like, but this woman's got tight hold. Her fingers find Rose's wedding ring and start turning it round and round.

– It won't come off, that, y'know, Rose tells her. She says it like she's making a joke, but she's not. That ring went on her finger on the twelfth of October 1965, and she'll be wearing it in her wooden overcoat, you mark her words.

– OK lady, says the Gypsy, – OK, and she starts mumbling to herself under her breath. She has these bright little brown eyes, like the squirrels you see darting around in park. They don't leave Rose's eyes for a moment as she twists on her wedding ring and mutters away. God knows what language she's talking, it's not English. Doesn't sound like English to Rose, anyroad. Sounds like a load of jibber-jabber to her.

Then she falls silent and they're just sat there, both of them staring at each other like a pair of bloody lemons. Oh, this is just ridiculous, thinks Rose! She has to bite down on her bottom lip to stop herself getting the giggles.

Then the Gypsy says: – There is a man.

– Oh aye, says Rose, – am I going to meet a tall dark stranger?

– No, no . . . The Gypsy shakes her head. – Many men . . . but only one for you.

– Well yes, I should think so. I think one's more than enough, don't you? And Rose laughs. But the Gypsy's not laughing, her fingers twisting and rubbing on Rose's wedding ring.

– He has a gift, says the Gypsy.

– Oh does he now. What is it? Summat nice I hope.

– It is . . . not . . . no . . . the one man. He knows you. The only man for you.

Them little brown eyes fixed on Rose.

It's too hot in this caravan. Too hot and too cramped. Too many bright lights, they're making Rose feel a bit giddy. She's sweating an'all. She's not taken her coat off. She won't feel the benefit when she goes outside.

She mumbles some more nonsense, this Gypsy, but Rose is not listening. She feels a bit nauseous, if truth be known, what with this heat and all of them lights twinkling away. She wants to be out of here now, but the Gypsy's still got tight hold of her hand.

– I'll have to get off, Rose says. – Me daughter's waiting for me outside.

A tenner out of Rose's purse, and then she finally lets go.

Rose is out the door and down the three steps back into the crowds of Walton Street. More people now, seems to be twice as many as before. Rose can't see Donna or Jessica and for one horrible second she thinks they've gone off without her. But no, there they are, shoving coins into a machine in the arcade over the road.

– Any good? asks Donna.

– Load of bloody rubbish, Rose tells her.

Hull Fair: 4.45pm

They don't go on owt, cos no one's got any money. They just wander round, looking at all the stalls and rides and that. But that's alright. Everyone seems happy enough. Gordon's got a smile on his face again, and even Pete seems to have calmed down. They go once right round the Fair and then stop to watch the Dive Bombers on the way back to Walton Street. Barry's telling them all how he used to come and pick all the money off the floor that had fell out of people's pockets. He's pointing up at how high they are but Kerry doesn't like to watch them, all them people being slung about, all clinging on and screaming. Makes her feel proper sick. The Fair's starting to get a bit busier now, a few more families and big groups of young kids roaming about. It's getting dark an'all. The lights on all the rides have come on. Or maybe they were on before and they never noticed 'em. Anyway, thinks Kerry, we'll have to be getting back in a minute.

There's a shrieking noise coming from behind them, like a whistle or a siren and then a long low cackling laugh. Kerry looks round and they're stood right in front of the Ghost Train. The big double doors fly open and the train scoots out and jolts to a stop. People get off, some of 'em laughing, some looking a bit less happy. One poor little bain is sobbing his heart out. Then the ride fills up with people again, and goes lurching through the entrance, gets swallowed up by pitch black, the double doors banging shut behind the last carriage. Laughter cackling from the speakers again as the screams disappear inside. Kerry clocks that Chris is staring up at the roof of the ride, at all the skeletons and the monsters and that. There's a zombie with blood dripping from its mouth and next to that a big white skull with a top hat on, a cigar clamped in its teeth, billowing smoke up into the sky.

Kerry catches Barry's eye and nods at Christopher.

Christopher can go off at stuff like this, he's got a bit of a thing about it. He can't watch owt even a bit scary on the telly, definitely no horror films or owt like that. Sometimes even the news sets him off, if there's summat dodgy on, like a war or a murder. Gets him all agitated. Works himself up into some right states. You sometimes hear him in his room, shouting about ghosts and evil demons and what have yer.

Barry says they'd best be getting back, and Kerry agrees, but Pete Craven's noticed Christopher staring up at the Ghost Train.

– Fancy a ride Chris? Pete asks him.

Horrible trouble-causing get, thinks Kerry. She's about to say summat when she catches sight of this couple at a burger van across the way. Summat about 'em makes her look, and then look again.

This lass, she's laughing and pushing this lad away, he's trying to grab a chip out of her tray, just messing about, but then they both turn round and walk off and oh my God, thinks Kerry, it's our Zoe, but it can't be their Zoe, no, no, no, but she's just like her, the absolute image, her face, that smile, them big dark laughing eyes and she's the same height, same length and colour hair, good God, the same laugh even, it's like someone's sent a ghost back to haunt her oh my God oh my God oh my . . .

And him.

That lad she's with.

Kerry feels like someone's punched her right in the belly. She screws her eyes tight shut, opens them, looks again and yeah, it's him, it's fuckin' him. Without a shadow of a doubt. That jacket, that stupid pimp roll swagger, that same stupid sneer plastered across his gob. Four months it's been, no, not even four months and here he is with his new bird, not Zoe, his new bird who he's dressed up to look exactly like Zoe, walking round Hull Fair, strutting about among normal decent people like he's fit to be a part of the human race and not just some piece of murdering fuckin' dirt scraped off someone's shoe.

That bastard.

That fuckin' horrible murdering little bastard.

Kerry can hear herself breathing, and it's like her heart's a tennis ball and someone's got their hand round it, squeezing hard, making the blood pound straight to her head and before she can stop them her feet are taking her after the pair of 'em, quickening her pace, till she's right behind 'em, right on their shoulder.

– Now then wanker. You don't fuckin' hang about do yer?

He glances behind him quick and yes, thinks Kerry, it's me, motherfucker, keep fuckin' walking cunt. But he doesn't, the little shit, he stops and turns to face her, palms up.

– Kerry, mate, he says.

– Don't fuckin' mate me, you little piece of shit.

– Kerry, this int the time or place, he says.

– Why, what's the matter Darren? Frightened I'll show you up in front o' yer new bird? Scared I'll tell her what a pathetic cowardly little bastard y'are?

This bird's giving Kerry the evils, big-time. She's a fuckin' hard-faced cow this one. How could Kerry have possibly thought she looks owt like her Zoe? She's nowt like Zoe, nowt like her at all, she's just copied her hairstyle and the way she dresses. But she's not her. She could never be her. No one could, never, not in a million years.

– Darren, what the fuck is going on, she says.

– S'alright Shell, he says – Look, Kerry, I know you're . . .

– You know fuck all mate, Kerry says, and she's backing him off, her finger jabbing in his chest. He goes to grab her arm but she twats him away and knocks this lass's tray of chips clean out of her hand.

– Ey bitch, she goes, and steps right to her, but Kerry cracks her one clean across the face and then goes for the lad, goes for his evil murderer's eyes with both sets of nails, but he's ducking out the road and then Barry's right between the pair of them and he's got hold of Kerry's wrists.

– Alright, Kerry, he says, – that's enough now, pack it in!

– She's off her fuckin' head, this lass shouts, and Kerry's spitting and kicking but Barry's picking her up and turning her round, carrying her away. Kerry yells back at the lass from over Barry's shoulder.

– CAREFUL HE DUNT CHUCK YOU OFF THE BIG WHEEL LOVE!

Barry pins Kerry up against the side of this chip van. She's bawling her eyes out now. Barry keeps her there, an arm on either side of her. People walk past, but hardly anyone takes any notice. Kerry can see her residents through a blur of hot tears and passing bodies: Gail ashen-faced, Gordon clutching onto her, terrified, Pete, his arms folded in sour-faced judgement. Christopher's got his back to all of them, staring up at this massive grinning skull.

After a bit Kerry manages to calm down and get herself together. She says sorry to everyone for losing her temper and showing 'em all up and says that they really have to be getting back to Lime Tree Lodge now, cos Sandra'll be getting the tea on and be wondering what Kerry's done with 'em all. Gordon asks what they're having and Kerry tells him it's chicken burgers, beans and chips. Pete Craven sets off ahead without waiting for them. Gail links her arm through Barry's and Kerry takes Christopher's hand and leads him away. They set off back in the direction of Walton Street.

Kerry asks Christopher if he's alright and if he's had a nice time at Hull Fair. He turns round and points back at the Ghost Train, up at the skull and all the smoke blasting up into the sky.

– The Devil lives here, he says.

Hull Fair: 4.46pm
Darren, the big puff! He's only frightened of the bloody Ghost Train! Michelle can't believe it. She's trying to drag him on, but he's not having none of it.

– It's a load of shite, he says. – Complete waste of money.

– What's up, not frightened of ghosts are yer?

– Yeah, right. Fuckin' ghost. It's a bloke dressed up in a sheet.

– No! You're joking! And here's me thinking it was real! You'll be telling me there's no Father Christmas next!

After a bit he lets her get him into a carriage and off they go, this mad cackling laugh sending them banging through the double doors and into the darkness. Darren's got his arm wrapped round her, squeezing her dead tight as the train lurches about from side to side. Michelle clamps her hand over her mouth to stop herself laughing out loud. She's been more scared walking down Spring Bank on a Saturday afternoon. There are a couple of dodgy moments: invisible fingers brushing over faces, weird cackling, all that type of sketch. At one point they bang to a halt and this big Frankenstein's monster is lit up right next to them, red eyes blazing, this horrible groaning. Darren squeezes her tighter into him.

A little lad in the carriage behind them starts roaring his eyes out. His dad's telling him it's alright mate, it's only a model, but this little lad's in floods, inconsolable. Then his dad starts losing his rag and telling him to pack it in and stop being a fanny, that he'll be going straight home if he carries on like that. What a complete wanker, thinks Michelle. What did he expect, bringing a bain on a bloody Ghost Train? His voice is slurred, like he's half pissed up. Michelle turns round to give him evils, but she can't see them in this dark.

They swing round a corner and this bloke in a day-glo skeleton costume steps out of an upright coffin, reaches out to touch Michelle's head. He ruffles her hair and then they're out the exit doors and back into the light and noise of Hull Fair.

She looks at Darren and he's got his eyes clamped shut, the big puff!

They decide they've had enough of Fair. It's getting dark now, and the big hand is pointing to pub o'clock. Darren wants to get some chips so they stop at this van. Michelle's ragging him to bits for being shit scared of the Ghost Train. He reckons he was only pretending to be scared, but Michelle knows the score. She tells him it's alright, she doesn't mind, she admires a man who isn't afraid to show his sensitive side and he laughs and tells her to fuck right off.

What happens next happens so quick Michelle barely has time to take it all in.

They set off walking back towards Walton Street when this lass comes up behind them and starts mouthing off, giving it all fuckin' bastard this and wanker that. For a second Michelle thinks it's some kind of joke, that it's some old mate of Darren's, but his face is telling a different story. He looks like he's seen a ghost, and a proper one this time. This lass, she looks half demented. She gives Michelle a look like she wants to rip her limb from limb. Darren says something to her, calls her by name, Karen or Kerry, but she's snarling right in his face, backing him off, giving him big digs in his chest. He goes to grab her arm and she swipes out at him, knocking the tray of chips out of Michelle's hand. Michelle goes to get hold of her, and all of a sudden her head's ringing like a bell and the side of her face is stinging red raw.

Next thing Michelle knows this bloke has appeared out of nowhere and he's dragging this mad bitch off Darren. She's spitting and kicking like a lunatic, scream-ing her head off as this bloke picks her up and carries her off. She points at Michelle and shouts something about the big wheel, getting chucked off the big wheel, Michelle thinks she says.

Michelle's fuckin' fuming now and she goes after her, but Darren's got tight hold of her, telling her it's not worth it, people are looking. Michelle tells him she doesn't give a fuck, the lass is getting her face tanned and that's that, whoever the fuck she is, but Darren won't let go and Michelle's being pulled about like a rag doll.

– Get the fuck off me, Darren, she tells him.

– Not till you calm down, he says.

– Get yer hands off me! Now!

This woman comes over and asks Michelle if she's alright.

– No, she tells her, – no, I'm fuckin' not.

The woman looks back at her husband who's stood a few feet away. He takes his hands out of his pockets and starts walking over.

– I think you should let go of her mate, this woman says to Darren.

He lets go and Michelle walks off, pushing her way through the thickening crowds. The side of her face is throbbing and her eyes are swimming hot with tears. People are looking, she can see they're looking, but their faces are all a blur.

She can hear Darren's voice somewhere behind her.

– Michelle! he says. – Michelle, hang on . . .

Boothferry Estate: 5.05pm
Trevor always liked Boothferry. A good estate. Or at least it used to be when he was last knocking about

52

round here. Penshurst Avenue, where Bald Arnold used to live. Trevor counts the houses down, 33, 31, 29, til he comes to it: 27, red door, just like she'd said. He can hear whimpering and scratching at the other side as he turns the deadlock then the Yale.

Dogs, she'd said. Two of 'em. A lad and a lass.

Trevor doesn't mind dogs. They jump up and bark as he comes in but once he's put his bag down and ruffled their lugs and made a bit of a fuss of them they calm right down. They stand there side by side, panting and looking up at him.

– Alright kids. I'm looking after yer for a bit. That alright with you?

One of 'em, the black and tan Collie, she barks once in reply. Her mate, the Shar Pei, just squints up at him. He was expecting this one to be one of them comedy wrinkly-skinned fellers. He thought Shar Peis were the ones with that baggy pelt on 'em. This one though, he's just got a few creases on the back of his neck and underneath his chops. Trevor gives him a pat on the top of his big grey-blue head. He's got these little slitty eyes caked in weeping yellow snot. A dog with conjunctivitis, thinks Trevor. No wonder he looks a bit peed off. Sturdy-looking bugger though. The Collie starts bounding up and pawing at him again.

This house, it belongs to some old couple that Janice knows. Or she knows their son. Anyroad, they're music teachers. Or one of them used to be a music teacher, Trevor thinks she said. Retired couple, from the look of the gaff. It's the standard sort of council house for round here, two downstairs rooms knocked through into one big one, kitchen out the back, small backyard beyond that. Nice, cosy, non-descript little place. Shelves round the gas fire full of chintzy little ornaments and various books. The owners' preferred reading matter seemed to be local geography, music, dogs and the tales of Catherine Cookson. Three-seater couch and a battered old armchair in the prime telly spot; obviously the old feller's throne. Remote to hand on nearby footrest. There's one of them big organs as well. Big fancy professional-looking job that takes up nearly all the back wall. Impressive-looking thing – two keyboards, rows of chunky buttons and switches. A line of foot pedals on the floor. Wow, thinks Trevor, space age, man. Or what probably passed for space age in the seventies.

He switches it on and a low whirring noise starts to rise up from the floor. Like it's filling up with warm air. He sits at the thing and presses a few keys down. Trevor can't play the organ. Makes a great noise though, sort of deep and mournful. Like a giant waking up and groaning from a bad dream. The red and black buttons to the right of the top keyboard say things like JAZZ, SLOW ROCK, COUNTRY and GOSPEL. He presses the GOSPEL and it lurches into a slow swaying drumbeat, electronic handclaps and what sounds like a choir of voices singing. No, not singing. Like a humming. Voices humming in unison. He presses a few keys and the voices move up and down in pitch.

Nice.

He sits and larks about with it for a bit till the Collie starts to whimper and paw at his leg.

– Hungry, kidder?

Trevor turns the voices off and goes through to the kitchen. There's a note on the table:

GRAHAM — THANK YOU FOR LOOKING AFTER JESS AND CHARLIE FOR US — THEY BOTH NEED WALKING FIRST THING IN MORNING AND AGAIN AFTER TEATIME — FOOD AND BISCUITS UNDER THE SINK — FRESH WATER EVERY DAY. THEY WILL LET YOU KNOW IF THEY NEED TO GO OUTSIDE FOR TOILET. HELP YOURSELF TO ANYTHING IN FRIDGE, BACK DOOR KEY AND MONEY IN TEAPOT IF YOU NEED ANYTHING — THANK YOU, JEAN AND ARTHUR.

Trevor opens the back way up and has a quick skeg outside. Neat little square of lawn, a few flowers in the beds and a fairly new-looking tool shed. Nice. The dogs squeeze past him and trot around outside. Charlie sniffs up the side of the shed, cocks his leg and pisses.

He fills the two bowls up with dog meat and multi-coloured biccies and then has a gander in the fridge.

Four cans of Heineken.

Superb. That'll do him.

He cracks one open and goes back through to the living room. Gets himself comfy in the Head Of The Household chair. He fires up the telly and scrolls through the options. Sky Sports. Some lasses on a beach in America playing volleyball. Marvellous. Trevor watches 'em jump and jiggle about as he sups his beer. There's a snuffling from the kitchen, then noisy lapping at the water bowl. Trevor finishes his can and goes back through for another. The dogs' bowls are licked clean.

Flippin' heck, the greedy buggers have polished the lot off!

– Hit the spot, kids?

Trevor shuts the back door and goes back into the front room. The dogs trot through after him. Jess jumps up onto the couch and gets curled up. Charlie, the ignorant bugger, he parks himself squarely in front of the box. Right in Trevor's line of vision.

– You can sod right off.

Trevor snaps his fingers and points to the couch. Charlie just stares at him through them caked-up little piggy eyes. Breathing all heavy through his snout.

– Come on lad, play the game.

Charlie's not shifting. Trevor gets up and moves over to the couch. He sits on the arm and pats the space next to Jess.

– Come on then Charlie, up here with your sister.

Jess lifts her head and looks up at Trevor. She whimpers. Looks at Trevor then Charlie.

Charlie doesn't move.

Trevor laughs.

– Bloody stubborn bugger you aren't yer, he says. – Alright, let's go for a walk then, eh? Shall we have a walk? C'mon on then, the pair o'yer . . .

Trevor goes into the hallway and the two dogs immediately follow on his heels. He finds two leads hung up and once he's put them on they leave the house and set off down the road, up towards First Lane.

Hundred quid he's getting for this. Supposed to be their Graham's job. A weekend of dog sitting and dog walking. No bother to Trevor. First day he got out of Lindholme he walked and walked and walked. Walked all the way from Orchard Park to Walton Street, once round Fair, down Anlaby Road and on to Janice's at the top of Lymington Garth. He walked his time away in Lindholme too. Round and round that bloody yard every dinner time and evening. Used to do his nut in to just sit on his arse out there. Nowt to look at. Just high grey concrete and razor wire. Might as well stop in his pad and stare at the walls. Other blokes would just lounge about, smoking on the benches and what have yer. But Trevor liked to keep a move on when he was out in the yard. To him, it was frustrating, being out there like. Like you was outside but not outside. He kept his eyes on the sky above and did lap after lap after lap. Used to watch birds flying overhead he did. Used to count how many went over him and try and imagine where they were off to: Africa, Canada, China even. Trevor flew all around the world from that yard, from behind those tall concrete walls.

Got to him a bit, his last stretch. He doesn't mind admitting it. Before, his other two times, he didn't give a bugger. First time, detention centre in Donny, he was full of piss and vinegar. Cocky little bugger he was. Got in with a right load of flippin' idiots. Made the mistake of staying in touch with a few of 'em an'all. Which led to his second spell. So when Trevor ballsed up again he said to himself that's it, keep meself to meself. Don't get involved with no bugger. Just do the time and get out. Which isn't always easy in there. But Category C in Lindholme? Piece of piss mate. Most of the blokes in there were trying to get on Cat D and didn't want no shenanigans. All you had to do was avoid the daft lads and keep your head down.

Or, in his case, up.

So when Trevor got out and Janice said how do you fancy doing some dog walking, he thought yeah, no problem. It was good of her to put him onto it. It was obvious that their Graham'd agreed to do it and then regretted it, what with these people being friends of Janice's and all that. Felt a bit awkward, probably. Trevor feels sorry for Janice. Fifteen years of marriage, three bains and then Graham just goes and leaves her for some young lass he meets in pub. Ugly little bitch an'all, by all accounts. She's sound, is Janice. How she's put up with that nasty arrogant bastard all these years is beyond Trevor. He doesn't care if Graham is his brother. I can't be looking after no bloody dogs, that's what Graham had said on the phone. It's a bad time for me, he'd said. Aye, said Trevor, I hear you've got enough on with your own dog.

This Shar Pei though, this Charlie, he's a right strong bugger. Jess gets a nice lively trot on, stopping now and then to snuffle on the deck or piss by a hedgerow. But this Charlie Chan Chinese Fighting Chappie, it's like he's ploughing a bloody field. He's nearly pullin' Trevor's arm out of its blinkin' socket as the three of them set off at a rapid pace into a lively head-on wind, down Penshurst Ave and onto First Lane. Trevor's trying to keep 'em both on an even keel, trying not to get the two leads all taffled up as Jess stops and starts and Charlie stomps on relentless. Shoulder muscles on the bloody thing. Like a miniature bloody bull. Trevor staggers after his two new charges as they turn off the main road and head into Bethune Ave.

There's a strip of shops up at the end of Bethune,

as he recalls. A beer-off and a newsagent and that. They go past Mermaid, or rather, where Mermaid used to be. Looks like they're building some new houses now. You turn your back for five minutes and everything changes. He used to have some good nights in Mermaid.

Trevor ties the mutts up on the bike rack outside the newsagents.

– Sit!

Do they hellers like though. Just both stare up at him expectantly. Charlie's chops are blathered in foamy snot and the wind has brought his eye gunge out in long stringy globs. He's a flippin' looker is this Charlie.

– Stay!

They both bark their heads off as Trevor nips in and gets some bacca and cig papers. Two Mars bars and a night paper for after. He rolls himself a tab outside, lights it and sticks it in his trap before setting off again. Smokes it non-handed. He tries and takes a drag but it's jerked out of his gob when Jess starts leaping about. Burns his lip, showering sparks everywhere in the wind.

Flippin' bastard hell!

Right, bollocks to this. Pair of awkward bloody buggers. Once round the block and then they're off back to their pad.

Clumber Street: 5.16pm

Six pounds she's got, six pounds and thirty-seven pence actually, which is nearly seven pounds cos Grandad gave her a five-pound note and her Auntie Norma gave her a pound coin (which is the gold one) and she added that up to the money she already had hidden in her den and Heidi helped her count it all up and it's six pounds and thirty-seven pence and she's going to spend it all on rides and goodies at Hull Fair, which is tonight!

Yes!

Her friend Keavey's already been to Hull Fair twice, once with her dad and once with her mam and her nana but she's just showing off. She went on the Jumping Jacks and got a *High School Musical* top and some pink and green candyfloss but she didn't eat all of it cos her mam said it would rot her teeth away and anyway Billie's already got a *High School Musical* top and a sticker book and loads of stickers and she could even get loads more if she wanted but anyway she's saving her pennies up for Hull Fair.

CBeebies is for babies. Imagine . . . imagine . . . imagine a story. Billie likes Blue Cow though. Blue Cow, blue blue cow. Blue Cow is real good. Billie likes her voice. Moo-er! But all the other bits are for babies. Benji likes it, but that's cos he is a baby. They have to have it on while they're waiting for their tea or else Benji goes mad. Benji is three. He's a total ming mong. He only goes to nursery, he doesn't go to big school yet. Billie goes to big school and she's in Mrs Johnson's class. She used to be in Miss Graham's class but Miss Graham left cos she's having a baby, not a baby like Benji, a proper little tiny baby who can't talk or eat or owt like that, one that just cries and poos. Billie asked Mam if they could have another baby but Mam just laughed and said yeah right.

Billie hopes it's fish fingers for tea. Fish fingers and chips and beans and not them yakky green trees. She puts loads of red sauce on her green trees. Benji just spits 'em out and Mam goes mad. He can't have a pudding if he doesn't eat his tea and there's some lollies in the fridge. Billie knows, cos she saw her mam get 'em from shop yesterday on the way home from school. There's red ones and purple ones and yellow ones and Billie wants a yellow one.

Blue cow . . . blue blue cow . . . today at school they did about China, which is a foreign country. In China the colour red is a lucky colour and the number seven is a lucky number and Billie can even say something in China which is Gung Hay Fat Choy. That means Happy New Year.

One of her teeth is wobbling, one of the front ones. She can move it backwards and forwards with her tongue. She keeps daring herself to waggle it right out. All day yesterday Billie was hoping it was going to fall out before the last sleep before Hull Fair so she could get another gold coin for the rides when she woke up. Keavey reckons the Tooth Fairy isn't real but the gold coin is really real though.

Mam shouts Billie Benji tea and they go through into the kitchen and ugh yak it's shepherd pie and they even had that last night an'all. Benji starts moaning and Mam tells him off and then she tells him to get it eaten else he won't grow up big and strong. Benji is acting like a total loser. Billie doesn't say owt, even though she hates shepherd pie cos if she says she doesn't like it then her mam will say they aren't going to Hull Fair even though Billie knows they are really. Benji doesn't even know what Hull Fair is cos he can't even remember going even though they both went with their dad last year. Benji doesn't even remember their dad either. Billie asked him one day what colour hair Dad had and he didn't even know. He said it was brown. But Dad didn't even have brown hair, he had blonde hair like Billie.

Mam isn't having any tea, she's having a cup of tea and looking at her magazine full of ladies. Mam wants her hair cutting like one of them ladies, Billie can't remember which one, but she doesn't want her to cos she heard her saying to Heidi if she had her hair done she might get a new bloke which means a new dad and anyway Billie doesn't want a new dad.

When Dad went to live in the sky with Jesus Mam cried loads and Benji cried for a bit but Billie only cried twice, once with her nana and once in the playground over near the bins where nobody saw her.

Billie's a big girl. She's six after Christmas.

This is the order it goes in, starting from now – Hull Fair, Halloween, fireworks night, then Christmas then her birthday. She wants a Nintendo DS for Christmas but Mam says wait and see, which means no she can't have one. Keavey's got a Nintendo DS and even Molly and Caitlin have. Molly let her have a go on hers when Billie went to her house, but Billie kept getting dead but if she had her very own one then she could get real good and not die as much.

They have their tea and Mam puts the pots in the sink and then they get wrapped up tight in their big coats cos it's cold outside. They get Benji in his pushchair and Mam rings Heidi up on her phone and says they'll meet her at the top of Walton Street, which is where Hull Fair starts. She asks Billie where her money is and Billie shows her and Mam says she'll put it in her purse but Billie wants to be in charge and Mam says no but then she says alright but if she loses it then it's her own fault. Billie promises she won't lose it and she really definitely won't.

Billie gets her five-pound note and her gold coin and her pennies tight in her hand, puts her hand in her pocket and off they go! Yes! Hull Fair! Hull Fair, Hull Fair, Hull Fair!

Hull Fair is real good!

Princes Avenue: 5.35pm

They're sat in Linnet and Darren's telling Michelle about this Kerry bird, how he went out with her sister for a bit and finished with her, and how this Kerry took it all personal, decided to start a vendetta against him. Then he tells her that this Kerry isn't right in the head, that she's been sectioned twice and now she lives in some mental home up Cottingham Road.

– Complete fuckin' screw loose, he says, tapping the side of his head.

– How come she's allowed to walk round the streets if she's mental?

He shrugs.

– Fuck knows. Care in the community innit.

Michelle finishes her WKD and points to the bar. She needs a drink. She needs several drinks.

Michelle is weighing up what Darren's said as he's getting served. She so badly wanted this one to be hassle free. No head stress, no complications. And certainly no mental bitches with attitude kicking off in public. Michelle looks round the pub, half expecting her to come flying through the door. She'd be right at home in here. This is a proper old-style boozer, not like the rest of these cafe bar places that have sprung up on Prinny Ave. No ciabattas or three-piece jazz bands in here. This is a strictly Sky TV and Stella type gaff. There's hardly anyone in at this time though, just a couple of old timers, a few blokes in work clothes playing pool, two baseball-capped youths on the bandit and the landlord sat up at the bar reading the *Hull Daily Mail*.

Darren comes back with the drinks.

– Michelle, listen to me, he says, but she's not in the mood for fairy tales.

– No, she says, – you listen to me. What did you do to upset this lass?

– What?

– Yer ex, this . . . what was her name again?

– Zoe.

– This Zoe. What did you do to her?

– I dint do fuck all!

– So is she another loony tune then? Is it an entire family full of 'em, or what? Am I gonna go round Town and get me face rived off by another mentalist?

– No, course not.

Neither of them say anything for a bit.

These two old fellers in the corner, one of 'em looks a bit like Michelle's Grandad Bill. Or at least how Grandad Bill used to look before he got real badly. Then Michelle remembers he's off back into hospital tomorrow. Or is it the day after? That's what I should have done this afternoon, she thinks, I should have gone to see me grandad. Might not see him again in his own house.

Her mobile vibrates in her pocket. She digs it out and MAM is flashing up on the display. Michelle dumps the call. Bollocks to that, she thinks, I'm not in the mood for her right now.

– Why did you finish with her? Michelle asks him.

– I . . . I just did.

Darren starts gnawing on his thumbnail and spitting bits onto the carpet.

– Why though?

He says summat that sounds like she was doing me head in, but he's muttering and Michelle can't make him out properly. She takes his hand away from his mouth.

– How long was you seeing her for?

He shrugs and picks up his bottle of Becks, starts peeling off the label.

– Not long. Six months, summat like that.

Michelle thinks that there's something not right here. He's got this desperate, hunted look about him. Like he's about to either kick right off or burst into floods of tears.

– Well there must have been a reason why . . .

He slams his bottle down on the table.

– Look, just fuckin' leave it, alright? It's over with! It's finished! Alright?

The landlord looks up from behind his paper. The two baseball caps spin round for a quick nosey, then go back to feeding coins into the bandit.

– Alright, she says. – Bollocks to it. Let's just forget it.

He takes both of her hands in his and pulls her round to face him.

– Michelle, listen right, whoever I've been with in the past or whatever's happened, it means nowt to me. Alright? It means absolutely fuck all. Cos I'm with you now. I'm sat here with you. And I'm into you big time. Yeah?

His jaw clenched, he looks so intense, almost like he's pleading. Them blue eyes. They burn like torches. They make Michelle melt.

– It's me and you now, he says. – And no one else. Yeah?

She nods yes.

– Yeah, she says. – Yeah. Totally.

She lifts his hands up to her mouth and kisses them. Her mobile's buzzing in her pocket again.

She doesn't bother reaching for it.

Lime Tree Lodge, Cottingham Road: 6.19pm

Kerry wipes all the tables down after teatime while Gary sorts the kitchen out. Sandra's in the telly room doing the ironing. She didn't ask where they'd all been when they got in, just made a bit of a fuss about Gordon having no coat on. Kerry thought she'd properly kick off, but she's said nowt up to now. Not to Kerry, anyway.

Kerry stacks all the chairs up on the tables and runs the Hoover round. Then she goes and helps Gary in the kitchen. He's got his iPod on, filling up the dishwasher and singing away to himself. Kerry waves her hand about in front of his face and he pulls one of the earphones out, raises his eyebrows. Kerry asks him if Sandra has said owt to him about her.

– You? No, why? What yer done?

– Nowt, I ant done owt. Just wondered if she'd said owt.

Gary tries pressing Kerry for details, but she just clams up. Probably said too much already. She doesn't want him repeating all her personal business with everybody in the house and especially not to his mother. Kerry once heard Barry say there were three ways to send a message in this city – telephone, telegram and tell Gary. Sandra's bound to find out where they went, cos Pete Craven will tell her, or she'll hear it from one of the others. Kerry's already heard Gail romancing to Joanne and Alec Nelson about Barry taking her on the Waltzers and winning her a big teddy, even though he didn't. So everyone's bound to find out where they've been. All Kerry's bothered about is Sandra being pissed off at her cos she didn't tell her before she took 'em out, and then Sandra telling Maggie. Kerry can't afford to lose this job.

She helps Gary fill the dishwasher, wipe all the sides down and put the big pans and bread boards away. Then she goes through to the telly room to see Sandra. Might as well get it over with, thinks Kerry. If she's got owt to say to me then she can say it now. And if she starts getting clever Kerry'll just have to remind her that she isn't her boss, Maggie is, actually, and Maggie never said nowt about not being allowed to take the residents out. Like Barry says, they're not prisoners.

But Sandra's good as gold with her, absolutely fine. Doesn't say a word about Hull Fair or kicking off with lasses or anything. Just says thank you for Kerry hoovering up and that she'll get through this ironing and then make everyone a brew. Kerry offers to finish off the next load for her, but Sandra tells her there's no need, she'll soon whip through it then they can all sit down and relax in front of the telly. Kerry empties all the ashtrays and wipes the surfaces and then she sits herself down next to Frank. You have to keep an eye on Frank, make sure he doesn't drop any lit tabs down the side of his chair. Sandra puts the ironing away and then goes off to make the brews.

– She's a good lass, int she, says Frank.

– She is, says Kerry.

Princes Avenue: 6.24pm

It's cold outside and their street is all dark except the lights on the big tall lamp-posts and the square yellow windows in the houses. Billie's mouth makes smoke like a dragon. All the cars are dark when they swoosh past and unless they're white or silver you can't tell what colour they are till they go under the lamp-posts. Benji likes cars, he says blue car green car red car as they go past. Billie holds on tight to the handle of his pram and Mam's phone goes beep beep. She looks at it as they're walking along. Cheeky cow, she says, but she's not talking to Billie she's talking to her phone.

There's loads more people when they get to the top of their street and onto the big road. Billie likes being out late on a night. All the shops are lit up and there's nice food smells from some of 'em like fish and chips and spicy stuff and it all mingles in with the cold wind and the smell of petrol from the cars. Food is good for you cos it gives you energy and helps you get big and strong but petrol is bad for the planet. They go past a shop with Chinese writing in the window and

68

there's Chinese people in it stood behind the counter. Billie waves to 'em and says Gung Hay Fat Choy, but they can't hear her cos they're behind the glass.

They get to the big Jackson's shop and Mam says we just have to nip in to get Heidi some cigs but Billie doesn't like that cos cigs are bad for you like petrol and they make you cough and even die. Callum's grandad died cos he had to keep smoking cigs. Billie's mam smokes cigs and Billie tells her off but she doesn't listen to her. One day Billie even made a poster and put it up in the kitchen but her mam still smokes cigs. She's a right ming mong sometimes.

Soon as they get in the shop Benji starts asking for crisps and goodies and Billie's mam tells him they're going to Hull Fair so button it and I want never gets. Mam always says that so Billie starts thinking that means if she wants to get summat she has to not want it. That's real mad. She asked Mam if she would get a Nintendo DS if she didn't want one and Mam said don't be clever Billie. Benji starts whining but he's only three and he can't help it. He doesn't know that when they get to Hull Fair there'll be loads of real good stuff there for him like pink nougat and candyfloss and toffee apples. Last year Billie got a toffee apple and it lasted her nearly all week till it went brown in the fridge and her mam pelted it in the bin.

There's loads of people in the queue so they have to go up one bit and then down another to get Benji's pushchair through, and he drags a load of comics off the shelf as they go past. Mam chows at him and bends down to pick 'em up and put 'em back on the shelf and then as she stands up and goes to push the pram again there's loads of shoutin' and bad swear words and stuff crashing about, and these two misters are dancing with each other near the bit where the tills are. One of them is the big mister with the black jumper on who never smiles at you when you go in, and he's got the other man held tight to him but facing the other way. Then Billie sees this other man pointing a pen at both of 'em. He's shouting and he looks real angry.

Billie's mam grabs hold of her and pulls her real tight to her but Billie isn't even scared. Benji is scared though and he starts screaming real loud. Mam shushes him and tells him it's alright and that the misters are only playing. The mister in the black jumper looks at Billie and Benji and then he pushes his friend away and him and the man with the pen run out the shop real quick.

Mind the glass says a lady and there's glass and purple stuff all over the floor. Mam gets Heidi's cigs for her and Benji stops crying and they go back out of the nice warm shop into the cold again.

There's loads of people going to Hull Fair and coming back as well. There's dads and mams and little kids with balloons and toys. As they get further up the road Mam makes Billie hold the pram handle real tight and she says to keep close next to her and don't go running off. Billie sometimes gets tired legs if she has to walk real far, like when they go round the shops in Town on a not school day, but Billie's that excited she could walk and walk all night and even run if Mam would let her. She can see bright lights bobbing about in the sky now, they look like fairies flying and there's shouting and screaming and music. Billie asks her mam if that's Hull Fair and she says yes. Look Benji, Billie tells him, look up there, that's Hull Fair! We're nearly there!

Then they go round the corner and Billie's heart goes boom boom boom in time with the music and the screaming and she starts giggling and getting all butterflies inside cos she can see the prancing dancing horses and the roundabout going round and round and the spinning teacups and the Helter Skelter stood up straight, and the big white and yellow wheel all lit up in the distance far away, turning above everything, bigger than the world, bigger than the Humber Bridge even, and that's Hull Fair!

Princes Avenue: 6.24pm

This one here, this scruffy little get. He must think Brian fell off a bleedin' Christmas tree.

– Alright mate, he goes, as he slips past him down aisle one. He glances back over his shoulder and kneels down near the nappies, big grubby anorak billowing out around him.

But Brian's onto his lark, and instead of following him down the aisle he's wheeled round and he's right behind the other one, his mate who's darted in behind him and shot straight down the end aisle to the wine display. Thinks Brian hasn't clocked him as he slips a bottle of red down his trackie bottoms. Thinks he hasn't seen this stunt pulled a million times before.

He turns and walks straight smack-bang into Brian's big uniformed belly.

– Sorry mate, he goes, and tries to sidestep him, but Brian parks himself back in his road and gets a grip on his arm, his skinny thieving little arm. Feels like a pipe-cleaner, thinks Brian. Bet it's got more holes in it than a flute.

– Just owld on a minute, Brian says, but before he can do owt the kid's yanked himself free and he's off for the door, off like a robber's dog. He drags a load of beans and soup off the shelf behind him as he barges respectable paying customers out the way, but Brian's right behind the bastard, and as he tears round the corner he gets hold of the back of his jacket. They both go flying into a shelf full of shampoo, and the bottle of vino slides down the kid's leg and shatters on the deck, glass crunching underneath Brian's boots as he nearly goes over with him, but he stays on his pins and drags the kid upright, pushes one arm up behind his back. He's shouting and thrashing about, but Brian's got the little bastard.

– FUCKIN' LEAVE HIM CUNT!

It's his mate. The scruffy little get in the anorak. He's got a needle in his hand and he's waving it under Brian's nose. A syringe. The barrel's black, full of blood.

– LET GO OF HIM RIGHT NOW, OR THIS GOES STRAIGHT IN YOUR FUCKIN' NECK!

He's sweating like a bastard. Brian can smell it coming off him. Sneering little freckle face, but he's shitting himself. Brian can see his bottom lip going. Ugly little twat he is; greasy white skin, scabs all round his mouth, teeth like broken chocolate. Typical fuckin' smack rat. Only about fourteen. Fifteen at most. Brian's got two at home older than him.

There's a lass at the end of the aisle, a young lass

with two bains, one in a pram. She stops dead, frozen to the spot, pulls the eldest bain tight to her side. A little blonde-haired lass with pink slides in her hair. Pink slides shaped like butterflies.

This smack rat, his arms shaking like fuck. The needle starts to bob up and down. I could grab that arm right now and snap the bastard in two, thinks Brian, snap it like a twig before he even had time to blink.

– FUCKIN' LET GO, CUNT!

. . . one . . . two . . . three . . . four . . .

The bain in the pram starts crying.

– It's alright Benji, says his mam. – It's alright. The misters are just playing.

Brian lets go of the lad, pushes him towards this little scabby-faced mate, and they both nearly knock each other over in their hurry to get out. An old woman nearly gets put on her arse as they barge past her and bolt down the road. She's clinging onto the doorway, the contents of her shopping basket scattered all over the deck.

Brian helps the old lass up. A couple of young lads and a lass help her collect her gear. She's alright. Just a bit shook up, like. She leans on the chest freezer while she gets her breath back.

– Little bastards, she says.

Bloody glass and red wine and shampoo everywhere. Kafi goes to get a mop and a bucket. Brian follows her through into the back. Gets his inhaler out his coat pocket. Sits down and has a good blast.

– Are you OK, Brian? she asks.

– Aye, just gis a minute.

His heart's going like a bloody jackhammer.

He sits there for a bit until his breathing gets back to normal. Then he goes back out and helps Kafi clear everything up.

Five pounds fuckin' thirty-five an hour he gets for this.

Lymington Garth: 6.45pm

Their Janice looks shattered. She's trying to carry on as normal since laughing boy slung his hook, but Dave can tell she's had some heavy days and nights. He can see them in the black shadows smeared under her eyes and in the way she drags hard on her cig. Like it's the only bit of comfort left to draw on. She said she was going to try and pack 'em in last year, go with Denise to the support group. For extra support, like. But there's no chance of that just now.

Their Janice is the only one out of his family that Dave really bothers with now. Out of all of 'em, she was the only one who was there for him last year. Wasn't always the case though. All them years he was unhappy and confused, he never really had owt to do with her at all. Mind you, she was all wrapped up with Graham, living love's young dream. He used to resent her a little bit, if he's being truthful. Look down in judgement even. Janice and Graham with their nice semi-detached house in Hessle and their three beautiful bains and their new cars and their two holidays abroad every year. Janice and her coffee mornings with her stupid pretentious friends and Graham with his fancy office job, his divvy golfing jumpers and his shite eighties record collection. They stood for everything Dave sneered at – home improvement, Sunday dinners, drives out to the seaside with the dog. Mr and Mrs Suburbia. Dave used to do a lot of sneering back then.

But when his marriage collapsed and the shit hit the fan, Janice was the only one to stand up for him. Stood up loud and proud, in fact. The only one out of the entire family. The rest of them reacted more or less exactly as you'd expect – equal parts shock and embarrassment, with a side-order of taking the piss. But not Janice. She didn't stand in judgement. Didn't ask for an explanation, even. She just showed a bit of human decency and compassion. Even stood up to his mam after she called him – what was it again? – oh aye, 'a filthy piece of perverted scum'. Nice eh?

So even though Dave lost virtually everything – his wife, his house, his fuckin' mind nearly – he found a friend he never even knew he had. Most of his mates gradually melted away, the rest of the family more or less disowned him and then Janice was the only one there. She was the one who held him when he was pissed up in his dressing gown on a Monday afternoon, sobbing like a bain. She was the one who was on the end of the phone at half three in the morning when he couldn't sleep cos of the nightmares. She was the one who cleaned the blood off his bathroom floor and sat with him in hospital.

And then, just as he's getting to the point where he's feeling comfortable in his own skin, getting a bit of self-confidence and what have yer, Janice gets to the wrong side of forty and it all turns to shit for her. Golden Boy Graham has a mid-life crisis and takes off with some daft young tart from round Town. Gets her up the stick, moves in with her, the full nine yards.

75

And on top of that, their mam got diagnosed with cancer, in and out of hospital for the last three months. So Janice has had all that to deal with on top of everything else. Dave's younger sister Cath, she's no use. And his brother John, fuck knows where he is.

So now it's Dave's turn to provide the shoulder to cry on.

There's no point going over it all again, so he tries to keep it light and not mention the dreaded G-word. And to be fair, Janice doesn't either. But she starts going on about their mam, which is nearly as bad. She tells him the cancer has spread to her liver, which is Goodnight Vienna, really. They've moved her into Dove House Hospice, she says.

– She dint wanna go. She knows they can't do owt for her now.

Dave really doesn't want to talk about that demented old bitch, so he changes the subject. They talk about her bains and how they're doing at school, he tells her about Lindsey starting her final year at art college and their vague plans to get a house together when she finishes her degree and gets herself a proper job. They have their chips and two cups of tea each and then it's nearly time for him to get off, get to Fair.

Dave thinks he's managed to get away with it, but then he mentions that Linds is on about getting a dog. Janice tells him Graham's brother Trevor is looking after some dogs for some friends of hers on Boothferry who've gone away for the weekend.

– Another bloody responsibility he's shirked. She grinds her tab into the ashtray and immediately sparks up another. – That useless twat was meant to be doing it, and then he suddenly remembers he's got summat else he has to do. So I had to ask their Trevor. I must be crackers. Half the bastard house'll be missing when they get back, you watch. Or burnt to the bloody ground.

– I'm sure it'll all be fine, he tells her.

– Will it? How will it?

Dave hasn't got an answer for that.

They don't say owt for a bit.

Dave has to get to Fair to see Lindsey, and he's starting to want a tab, so he tells Janice he has to get off.

They both stand up.

– You need your roots doing, she says to him. – I'll get Andrea to come round with all her gear. She's gone mobile now, y'know.

She looks at her reflection in the window and pats her hair.

– Get her to do mine an'all. Might as well start making the effort, I suppose. I aren't ready to turn into me mother just yet.

Dave gives her a big hug on the doorstep and tells her to look after herself.

– Sisters, he tells her. And he holds his little finger up.

She smiles, and hooks her little finger round his.

– Sisters, she says back.

Hull Fair: 7.05pm

Billie's let go of the pram handle but Mam's got tight hold of her wrist and there's Heidi near the horses with some chips and she gives Billie's mam a hug and a kiss and then brings her face down to Billie and Benji. Are you both excited she says and they both nod yeah. Mam's face bobs down next to Heidi's and she tells them they've got three rides each and one toy and that's it so have a think about it and don't just ask for the first thing they see. Billie can see the teacups behind her whizzing round and round. Teacups! she says and Benji says teacups an'all but he's just copying cos he's a double loser.

They wait till the ride stops and the other kids get off then Billie and Benji pile into a big green teacup and the mister straps them both in. Billie gives him her five-pound note and he gives her three gold coins back out of his belt. Hold onto your brother Mam shouts, but Benji wriggles like a wriggly worm so Billie doesn't hold onto him and anyway he's strapped in tight, and off they go! The mister spins them round every time they go past him and all Hull Fair goes round and round and round and Billie can see Mam and Heidi waving and Mam pointing her phone at them to make a video. Benji makes an O shape with his mouth and howls like a doggie, but anyway it's not even going that fast. It's a baby ride really.

The teacups don't last long enough. Benji wants to go on the other ride next to 'em, the one with elephants and hippos but Mam says don't just go on the first things you see so they all set off down Walton Street, Mam and Heidi smoking cigs and Billie blowing smoke out her mouth like a Chinese dragon. They go past the mucky pub and the policemen who are there to look after everybody with their shiny yellow jackets and crackly walkie-talkies. There's loads and loads of people walking towards them now and behind them and around them. Stay tight close together says Mam and Billie holds tight onto Heidi's hand cos Mam is pushing Benji in his pram. They have to go slow then quick then slow again. It gets real crowded and Billie can't see Hull Fair any more, just people's legs and coats and prams and she has to tilt her head back and look up at the sky to see the lights. This is doing my head in says Heidi and Mam says look let's go between these and she swivels the pram round and they go through a gap between two chip vans and then they're in proper Hull Fair!

There's tons of stuff everywhere you look, rides and games and roundabouts and everything. The Fair looks ace all lit up in the dark, like a big massive spaceship with flashing colours and whizzing lights. Billie can hear screaming from up in the sky, and she tilts her head back and there's people flying over their heads, holding on tight as their legs kick the air. Billie can't go on that ride cos she's too little. But there's loads of kids rides and a Hook-a-Duck over there with some big fluffy doggies, brown and white with big floppy red tongues. Billie wants a doggie and she's tugging on her mam's hand but her and Heidi have stopped to talk to these misters with caps on and Mam tells Billie to just hang on.

Benji is singing in his pram and Billie rocks him for a bit till the misters say ta-ra and then she pulls her mam over to the Hook-a-Duck. The lady behind the counter gives Billie a big pole but it's too big for her and Heidi has to help her hold it. She kneels her up on the counter and stands behind her as the pole waggles about over the ducks' floaty heads, but Billie can't hook one up properly. They just bob about as she biffs and bashes 'em with the end of the pole. Billie's getting all mad and hot in her eyes when all of a sudden one little ducky catches on the hook and Heidi cheers and lifts the pole up and the lady pulls it off and says anything from the bottom row. Billie wants a big brown and white doggy but Mam says she can't have one of them and points to the toys in the boxes on the floor behind the counter. There's a plastic sword or an aeroplane or a little doggy or a princess crown or a trumpet or a keyring. There isn't any Nintendo DSs though, so Billie has the little doggy and she calls him Bruno. Then Benji starts shouting that he wants a doggy an'all so they have to have another go and Mam is saying it's two pounds for a bit of tat.

They carry on some more and Billie's holding Bruno. He's a real good dog. He barks at people passing by then he barks at a load of big kids stood round this big ride. It's spinning round like mad and the mister in the middle has got a microphone and he's shouting here we go now and scream if you wanna go faster and everybody screams and the other misters stood at the edges spin the people round faster and faster. Heidi says the ride is called the Waltzers and Billie says I wanna go on the Waltzers but Mam just laughs and says no way Billie and they go on the Dodgems instead, her and Mam but not Benji cos he's too little. Heidi stays with him and Bruno and watches Billie and Mam as they go bombing round bumping into everybody. Mam likes this ride, she's screaming her head off laughing and Billie is too but then these big kids bang right into the side of them, sending them all spinny.

Mam gets real mad and shouts at 'em to eff off and Billie tells 'em to eff off an'all but only inside her head and anyway she does give 'em a real mucky look and make the L shape with both her fingers cos they're total ming-mong double losers.

Boothferry Estate: 7.14pm

Rose took Bella out for a walk after teatime and she's back in her basket by the time *Emmerdale* comes on. Rose sits and watches the telly with a cup of tea and a couple of biscuits but she can't seem to settle. Before the programme's finished she's up in the back bedroom and logging onto the site. She can't see Leo anywhere on the screen but then she gets an invite to a private chat from someone else. Someone she's not spoken to before. Rose refuses it twice but he keeps persevering, so in the end she clicks on YES.

Yorkshire_Rose: Hello.

JackSparrow: asl?

Yorkshire_Rose: F 59 UK. You?

JackSparrow: wot u into?

Yorkshire_Rose: I like local history and keeping fit (dog walking etc). Music, I like Frank Sinatra and Dean Martin, all the old singers. Cooking. And yourself?

JackSparrow: fuck that, what gets u hot?

Yorkshire_Rose: I beg your pardon?

JackSparrow: i've got a 9inch cock thick as well

Rose slams the lid down and pushes herself away quick from the table, so quick she knocks her cup of tea all over the shop. She pulls the plug out of the laptop and whips it up out the way before the spilt tea spreads all round it. There's a towel drying off on the radiator. She chucks it over the table, soaks up all the mess.

Bloody bloody hell!

She goes downstairs, puts the laptop on the kitchen table and makes a fresh cup of tea.

Her hands are trembling.

They're not real people, she tells herself. Just made-up names on a screen.

She takes her cuppa through to the front room and puts the telly on, has a flick through. Nothing worth watching, just the usual game-show rubbish, people shouting and screaming. Why do they all shout on telly nowadays? They're either shouting or arguing. She picks the *Mail* up from the coffee table. The telly guide says there's a film on at eight o'clock. Something about a married couple in America caught up in some mystery. That Richard Gere. Rose doesn't mind him, he takes a good part. He was good in that one about the Air Force.

She'll have a go at this crossword till eight o'clock, watch the film and then that'll take her up till bedtime.

Lime Tree Lodge, Cottingham Road: 7.32pm

Alec Nelson's sat right next to the telly, muttering away to himself. The rest of the residents are trying to watch *Coronation Street* but all they can hear is Alec. A couple of them are starting to get a bit upset. Kerry asks him to be quiet please but Alec takes no notice. Then Joanne tells him to shut up, she's trying to watch the telly, and this gets his proper doe down. He starts going on about this being as much his room as anyone else's and how he has his human rights and Maggie is a very old friend of his family and he'll be seeing her tomorrow about sorting all this lot out oh yes mark his words, etc. etc.

Joanne picks a magazine up and holds it in front of her face as if to shut the noise out. Kerry can tell she's close to the edge. Joanne's knee is bouncing up and down and her fists are trembling as she grips the pages.

Sandra tells Alec if he wants to talk to himself he should go in his own room, but he's not taking any notice. If anything it just agitates him more, makes him raise his voice even louder. The residents all start looking at each other, looking at Sandra. Waiting to see what's going to happen. They've got some woman giving her bloke a piece of her mind in the Rovers Return on the TV screen and Alec rocking backwards and forwards in front of them, banging on and on and on. He's like a machine, he doesn't even pause for breath:

– I don't have to put up with this I have money you know oh yes I don't have to stay here with all these morons bloody rubbish on the telly call that entertainment just people arguing, load of morons they are bloody imbeciles don't know what day it is half of this lot oh yes I will be having words in the morning and another thing

– FOR FUCK'S SAKE SHUT THE FUCK UP!

Joanne stands up and hurls her magazine at Alec. It misses his head by about an inch and hits the mantelpiece behind him, sends half the ornaments flying. Alec leaps up and charges out the room, shouting and bawling about calling the police and pressing charges. They hear him go pounding up the stairs. Kerry gets up to go after him but Sandra says no, she'll go. Joanne's fuming. She paces round and round in a circle, once, twice, three times; sits back down and then gets back up again, strides out after Sandra. Kerry waits for her feet to go flying upstairs an'all, but the front door goes instead, nearly slams off its hinges. No one says a word, apart from Frank who starts laughing his head off.

– By 'ell! Fun and games tonight eh? Better than the telly! By 'ell!

– Alright Frank, says Kerry.

She picks the ornaments up off the floor. One of 'em's shattered into pieces, this little girl in a bonnet and an umbrella. She collects all the bits up carefully and wraps 'em in the magazine. Best put that in the big bin out back, she thinks, so no one cuts theirselves.

Christopher's sat in the dining room at one of the tables. He's breaking up all the tab ends he collected at Fair into a big pile in front of him.

– Christopher, them tables are for eating off, Kerry tells him.

He looks up at her as she walks past him and out the back door.

– Have you got any cig papers, he says.

Admiral View, Hessle High Road: 7.35pm
Bill lost his bloody glasses yesterday. They're not in any of the usual places. Not down the back of the couch or in one of the drawers or owt like that. So he's having to make do with these, his second pair. And they're more for looking than writing. Took him half an hour

to find a pen that worked, and now he can barely see the page in front of him.

He's in a right bloody pickle.

This is what happens when he breaks his usual routine. There was a programme on last night about Muhammed Ali and instead of getting in his bunk at nine bells like he usually does, he thought, aye, I'll stop up and have a look at that. He was going to watch it in his galley on his little portable but then his head started banging again so he thought he'd watch it on the big set in the main room. Bigger screen, y'know? Have a lie down and that. He must have bobbed off, because when Bill woke up the programme had finished and he couldn't find his bloody glasses.

Bill knows where everything is in here though, here in his galley. Barometer, radio, portable telly, tea bags, milk in the fridge and his kettle on the side. Electric kettle, like. Plug-in job. Bill keeps all his logs in the wall cupboard. Dozens of 'em he's got, going back to the eighties when he came on shore for good. He used to use them little black notebooks from the newsagents near the old house, but since Madge passed away and he moved onto this new estate he's a bit nearer Town. So he hops on the bus and gets them big notepads from WH Smith. The ones with the rings down the spine, y'know? They're a bit easier to write in, now his hand isn't as steady as it used to be. Bit more room in 'em an'all.

The joke of it is, these days, even though Bill's got less and less to do, he writes in his log more than ever. He always keeps a record of everything, the day's events, the weather, local and national news, all his upcoming appointments. Everything. Old habits, he supposes. And anyroad, he thinks, you never know, do you? One day you might need to look back and refer to a piece of information. Chrissie takes the mick. She says he has a job telling folk what he did last week, but if you want to know the wind direction and rainfall from the last Sunday in May two years ago, then Bill Richardson's your man.

She's been worried about him has their Chrissie. More so than usual. Ever since she came in with Bill for the results of the third test and Kundu told him it was in his liver and his kidneys. Course, they all knew what that meant. Meant it's in his blood. That accounted for all the pain, because some days he'd been bloody racked double with it, y'know? Headaches mainly, but all over his body an'all, his arms and legs and what have you.

So Kundu tells him this and what stage it's at and what the next step is and how they'll do all they can and all the rest of it. And then he tells Bill that he's sorry and he shakes his hand. He's a decent chap is Dr Kundu.

Chrissie got a bit tearful when they got outside so Bill took her for a cup of tea in a cafe on Hessle Road. He told her to stop being so daft. He's seventy-four years old for Christ's sake. There's been about half a dozen occasions when he could have let go of the bloody rope. So Bill reckoned he hadn't done too bad, y'know?

He's had two spells in Castle Hill since then. As it's progressed, like. Not much to report from there. They pull and prod you about and fill you full of tablets, but there's not a great deal they can do except try and keep you as comfy as they can, like. Encourage you to rest, y'know? They do a marvellous job, though, them young lasses. There's people in there who are proper poorly, like. One guy in there had half his face eaten away. All in his mouth and jaw it was. Terrible to see, old chap like that with all his head bandaged up.

A lot of the fellers were in there due to smoking-related diseases. If it wasn't the old Spanish Dancer it was either lung disease or heart trouble. All through smoking, generally. John Taylor was in there. He used to be a bosun round about the same time Bill was doing trips. Triple bypass he'd had. Bill never recognised him at first till he said now then Bill. Shocked him, it did. Bill could hear him all through the night, wheezing away like a busted pair of bellows. Kept pulling this oxygen mask down and having a good suck on it, y'know? And the best of it was, he was still bribing his grandbains to smuggle him tabs in. Bill told him, he said maybe it's time you wanna think about chucking that Johnny Boy, but John said he didn't see the point. Only pleasure I get now Bill, he said. Terrible addiction, smoking. Bill remembers their Ronnie used to joke about it, used to sit in Rayners with the paper looking at the deaths. Just having a look to see who's packed in smoking, he'd say.

And there was Bill feeling all bloody chuffed with himself cos he chucked it twenty odd years ago. It was a Boxing Day, as he remembers. He'd brought a big packet of 200 home, one of them long sleeves. Peter Stuyvesants he thinks they were. Some fancy brand. Anyroad, the previous two days they'd had everyone round for their dinner and what have you, and course in them days the shops were shut all over Christmas. None of these twenty-four-hour garages or all night opening. So whenever any of them ran out of smokes Bill'd sling 'em twenty from this big packet.

Then on Boxing Day Bill's sat watching a film and he goes for a tab and there's none left. And he got himself in such a state he thought, hang on a minute, am I handcuffed to this bloody business? So he never bothered getting any more. And that was it. Madge still smoked, though. She said don't expect me to stop just because you have. She enjoyed a cigarette, did Madge.

Bill's off back in after this weekend. Castle Hill, like. Their Chrissie's coming for him first thing Monday morning, so he'd best get his kit bag packed. Best get a few things in order. He tried to get a few bits and bobs together this afternoon but he had to have a lie down about three o'clock. He managed a bit of shut-eye, like. Phone woke him up about half past four. He had a job finding it, cos the light had fast faded and he was lied there in the bloody dark. It was their Nathan, checking he was still alright for tomorrow and did Bill want anything fetching.

Nathan's stopping with his pal since their Joe and Marie got flooded out. They've got a caravan on the front but they can't fit them all in it, so Nathan's living somewhere round Anlaby way and their Michelle is stopping with her Auntie Chrissie. They were lucky down Chrissie's street, the water got as far as the doorstep but never came in the house. Their Joe's street though, Bill doesn't think there was a single family that didn't get washed out. Like a Gypsy camp down there now, caravans in every front yard. Terrible bloody business.

He'll never forget the day it all came down. A Monday, it was. It was siling down in the morning when he got out of bed, about seven o'clock, and it just went on from there, on and on and on. Relentless. Never seen anything like that, not on land, anyroad. Bill sat in his galley and watched it out the front window, listened to it all unfold on the wireless.

Be a long time till they get all that bloody mess cleared up.

Well, anyroad, it's behaved itself out there today. Bit more settled than it was yesterday. Blew a bloody gale yesterday it did. He thought them little saplings across the way were going to be uprooted and carried off across the Humber. They only planted 'em this summer just gone. Bill watched the lads come in a flat-back truck and bed 'em all in. He had a wander over when they were having their cig break and had a yarn with them. Nice lads. Said they were doing it as part of their community service. Bill didn't ask what they'd done. You could see they were rum lads. Could see the roughness in their faces, like. But it's none of his business, y'know? Speak as he finds, and all that carry on. They did a good job an'all. Bedded 'em in properly. They stood up to that wind, anyroad.

Bill has to stop writing now cos these bloody headaches are starting again. The light's getting worse in this kitchen. He thinks it might be the bulb. Must need changing. He'll see if he can get out tomorrow for a new pack. Have a walk up to Gypsyville, if that rain keeps off.

He made himself some supper but he didn't fancy it. A bit of smoked mackerel and some bread and butter. He'll put it in the fridge and see if he can tackle it tomorrow. Have a dram, have his tablets and go to bed. See if he feels any different when he gets up. Chrissie gave Bill a proper holder for his tablets, one of them that sorts 'em all out into little compartments. Two tablets in the morning, two in the afternoon and another slack handful before he goes to bed on a night.

It's a wonder I don't bloody rattle, he thinks.

Princes Avenue: 7.48pm

They go in Garbutts then Dukes then Lounge Bar then Pave. All the pubs are starting to properly fill up. It's always mad busy on Princes Avenue now. They go back in Linnet and head out the back for a smoke. There's this bunch of lads out there with a joint on the go. One of them nods at Michelle as her and Darren sit down at the next table. His face is familiar, she's not sure where she knows him from though. She thinks he might be a mate of Carl's, their Angie's bloke.

Michelle's telling Darren about her mam tearing into these builders today and he's cracking up laughing. She tells him about when the loss adjuster came round to sort out what they were claiming for on the insurance. He was Spanish, this bloke, and he's going through the list with Michelle's mam and dad and he says carpets and her mam says aye, and underlay an'all. This Spanish bloke looks at her all confused and says what is this underlay? Her mam starts getting all arsey with him, going you know, underlay, underlay, and her dad's helpless with laughter. Michelle's mam turns round to him and goes what the fuck are you laughing at silly bastard and her dad's going underlay underlay arriba arriba, like that Speedy Gonzalez, that cartoon mouse that used to be on the telly. Her mam's really losing her rag now and she goes running out to the skip and comes back with this lump of wet underlay and goes there y'are, look, underlay. Michelle's dad's crying with laughter and this Spanish bloke's just looking at the pair of them like they're completely mental.

Michelle tells Darren this and he's absolutely helpless. Nearly chokes on his pint.

– That is class, he says wiping his eyes. – That is absolute class.

Michelle likes making him laugh.

They debate going into Town but then decide against it. They've both had enough for one night and besides, they're off out round Town tomorrow night for a big one. So they get a carry out from Jackson's, then dive into a black cab and head back to his.

There's fireworks going off all over the sky. They watch all the different coloured stars from behind the glass. Two weeks till bonfire night, but the kids have been lobbing bangers and air bombs about for the last couple of weeks now. As the cab turns into Darren's street a gang of kids lob something into the road and it explodes in front of them, causing the cab driver to step on his brakes and jolt them forward. Darren grabs Michelle, stops her from being thrown forward out of her seat.

– Little bastards, says the driver.

They get into Darren's, put the fire on and order a pizza. A deep pan pepperoni and *Pirates of the Caribbean* on DVD. Darren rolls a couple of joints. It's skunk, which always knocks Michelle out and sure enough, before the film is halfway through she's bobbed off, her head heavy on Darren's lap.

Hull Fair: 8.07pm

After the Dodgems Billie has to decide what her last ride is going to be cos she only has one ride left cos Hull Fair is very expensive. Her legs are getting tired and she wants Mam to carry her but Mam says she's too big and she's getting fed up now cos it's getting late and it looks like rain and Billie can't decide which ride she wants to go on.

Then they go round a corner and Billie sees a little boy and a little girl bouncing up and down real high on the bouncy trampolines with the straps round their shoulders and yes! It's the Jumping Jacks! Jumping Jacks, Jumping Jacks she says to her mam and Mam stands and looks at it for a bit and then says no you're too little. But the little boy who's bouncing on it is the same age as Billie or anyway he's not much bigger than her and anyway her dad let her go on the Jumping Jacks last time they came to Hull Fair and then her mam starts getting really cross saying will you be said, Billie. But Billie won't be said cos first Mam says she's too big then she says she's too little so what is she on about and she's a stupid effing ming-mong loser.

Billie doesn't want to go on owt else she wants to go on the Jumping Jacks and it's not fair, but Mam is dragging her away and Billie knows if she starts crying Mam'll go real mad. But Billie can't help it and her eyes go all hot and she starts having a cry. My dad would let me go on them if he was here she says in her head, but she must have said it in real life cos Mam kneels down and clatters her round the legs and Billie starts properly roaring and Benji starts roaring even though no one's clattered him, and Mam asks her if she's happy now.

They're near the Helter Skelter and Mam says right this can be the last ride and then they're off home. It's not even the big Helter Skelter, it's a little baby one. Heidi helps Billie count the pennies in her pocket and she's got four pounds and thirty-seven pence and she says if she stops crying she'll pay for her to go on so she can save her pennies to get a balloon and a bag of candyfloss on the way home. She holds Billie's hand till the crying stops while Mam stands and smokes a cig and pushes Benji backwards and forwards in his pram.

Anyway, Billie wishes Heidi was her mam. Heidi pays the mister with two gold coins out her purse and he gives Billie a carpet to slide down on but first she's got to go all the way up, round and round the twisty turny wooden stairs. She has another little cry on the way up but when she gets to the top she can see all of Hull Fair stretched out and it looks real cool. She can see the Jumping Jacks and the Dodgems and she wants to stand there and watch all the colours and the lights whizzing about but then there's a boy clomping up behind her and he's waiting his turn so Billie sits down on the carpet and shuts her eyes and starts sliding down. She goes real slow at first but then she starts going faster and faster and she can feel her tummy going all whoosh and then there's a bump and she stops and opens her eyes.

Her mam and Heidi are stood talking to another mam with a pram. They've both got their backs to Billie. She shouts Mam but the music is too loud and they don't hear her. Benji twists round in his pram and smiles and waves. Billie waves back and jumps up and runs to where the Jumping Jacks are, her hand in her pocket wrapped tight around her money. She runs as fast as she can and she doesn't look back in case they can see her.

Princes Avenue: 8.17pm

About quarter past eight Brian goes outside for a cig and a yarn to Moz. Moz sells the *Big Issue*. He used to just beg, which they can't do owt about, not really, but then he started turning up pissed or off his head. Being aggressive with the customers and that. So Nick the store manager got him properly pelted: court order, ASBO, little picture in the window, the full lot. Then about three months later Moz reappears and does some more begging, but this time he's begging Nick for another chance. Explains how he's on some sort of rehab programme now and selling the *Issue*. So Nick, being a decent kind of bloke, says aye, alright then, takes the picture out of the window and gives him another chance. Brian wouldn't have done that. People don't change, in his experience. Especially not druggies. But fair play to Moz, he does seemed to have calmed down a bit and made an effort. He even looks like he's had a wash and a shave this week.

Brian crashes him a cig.

– Sold many tonight Moz? he asks, as he lights them both up.

– No, Bri, it's been shit. Everyone's off to Fair. Might do a few when pubs chuck out.

He nods over to Linnet. Looks like there's some sort of disco going on, windows flashing red and blue and yellow. Music thudding away. Indie night, it sounds like. Not Brian's cup of tea. He likes his eighties tunes. Bit of soul. Luther Vandross, Alexander O'Neal, all that type of gear.

It's the in place now, Brian considers, Princes Avenue. Never used to be. Used to be dead quiet on a night down here, when he first moved over to this end. Just the odd student and a few locals walking about. The only pubs was Queens at the top, Linnet, The Zoo and then that queers' pub, Polar Bear, at the top of Spring Bank. Botanic next to it an'all, but that was always a tatty old locals' pub, just old timers, piss-heads and paraffins. Couple of chinkies. And that was it. Oh, and Ray's Place, of course. They used to come down after work, all the door lads, and have a curry at Ray's. But that was about it as far as nightlife went. Now it's like middle of Town down here. Busier than Town, anyroad.

They did out that old car showroom into one of them big cafe bar things and that kicked it all off proper. Now there's about half a dozen more bars and cafes sprung up, along with a load of restaurants and take-aways – Thai, Italian, Malaysian and fuck knows what else. Like the United Nations down here now, thinks Brian. And all the bars get properly mobbed out on a weekend. Fuck knows where they all come from. They'll get bored and move on sooner or later though. He's seen it all before. It was Beverley Road before here, and Marina before that. Goes in phases. A spot gets more and more popular and then you get East Hull, West Hull, stag parties, hen nights and all the rest of it. Then the battling starts. There's already doormen on some of the bars down here. Two or three old faces from back in the day, but mostly young lads. Brian don't really know any of the young breed since he knocked all that lark on the head. But you don't get much bother down here, not really. Not yet, anyroad. There was a period where Moz was getting hassle off some young kids over some drug-related business. Every other night they'd come down and give Moz some grief: blacking his eye or scattering his *Issues* all over the deck. Nick the manager got proper sick of it, accused Moz of dealing. Moz protested his innocence, said these kids were after his prescription tablets, that they were singling him out cos they knew he was on a script and vulnerable. Brian never found out the proper ins and outs of it all, but he could tell Nick's patience was running out, so he put a stop to it all one night, dragged both the lads round the back way and panelled the pair of them. Never saw them again after that.

– Good 'un this week, says Moz. – Interview with the Arctic Monkeys.

He holds up his bundle of magazines. Some blank-eyed floppy-haired young lad on the front cover. Another fuckin' smackhead, Brian imagines. Bet he's got more money than me, though, he thinks. Definitely have more money than Moz.

Getting busier down here now. Last weekend of Hull Fair. Gangs of young lads and lasses heading for

Walton Street, and families coming back the other way, with bains and pushchairs laden down with tons of crap; all the usual shite, big fluffy animals and plastic toys and tat with flashing lights and bags of multi-coloured fuckin' candyfloss, coconuts, bags of chips from Bob Carver's, pink and white nugget and all the rest of it. Them big silver helium balloons bobbing about above them. Fiver each them balloons, someone told Brian. A fuckin' fiver! So that's a tenner if you've got two bains. Two bains round Fair, two goes on a ride at two quid apiece, two balloons, two bags of sugary shite, then two goes on the Hook-a-Duck to win two plastic pieces of tat worth about three bob apiece. Jesus Christ. Must spend a fuckin' fortune. Brian's glad his two are grown up now.

– Got any of them cards, Bri?

Moz has been collecting these little cards they've been giving away on the tills, part of some promotion they're doing. Some sort of bingo game. You're supposed to collect these little cards with pictures on 'em, bags of crisps, tins of beans, bottles of Domestos and what have you. You stick 'em on a board and match the pictures up, like. There's prizes for four corners, a line, full house, all that carry on. First prize is a holiday to Thailand. Most people just pelt the cards onto the deck when they get outside and Moz picks 'em up. Or he asks people if he can have 'em off 'em. He's obsessed with 'em. He asks Brian every night and every night Brian tells him the same thing.

– You've got to buy summat Moz.

– I only need a frozen chicken and a Fairy Liquid and Viennetta ice cream and I've got the top line.

Two lasses go clomping past in high heels. Moz holds his magazines up.

– *Big Issue*, ladies?

They don't even look at him, just march straight past. The two men watch 'em go up the road.

– Arse on that, says Moz.

– What's the most you've ever sold in one night then? Brian asks him. Moz looks at him sidelong like he's taking the piss. Takes a hard drag on his cig, blows out smoke and shrugs.

– Dunno. Twenny, twenny-five, summat like that. Mebbe thirty. But that's if I start at teatime and go right through till . . . *ISSUE* SIR?

The feller just marches straight past, shoulders hunched up, hands buried deep in his pockets, placcy bag full of take-away on his hip. Off home to his nice gas fire and his chicken chow mein and his Sky Plus telly.

– Thirty? That's quite good that, Moz. Where do you get 'em from?

– What, the *Issues*? Leeds.

– They send you 'em from Leeds?

– Do they fuck send you 'em, you've gotta go and get the bastards. Moz stamps his feet up and down, marching on the spot. Trying to keep warm. It's cold tonight. Looks like it might rain an'all. He's got a busted pair of trainers on, and this old anorak with half the lining hanging out the back.

– What, you've got to go all the way to fuckin' Leeds?

– Yeah. Piss-take, innit.

– How do you get there then?

– Get a lift off me mate, usually.

Brian never knew Moz had any mates. He's never seen him with anyone else, only on his jack.

– Do they set you targets, then? Give you like an incentive and that?

– Nah. They just give yer yer *Issue*s and let yer gerron with it . . . *ISSUE* SIR? MADAM?

A bloke and his lass, arm in arm, a bit pissed up by the looks of them. Moz smiles and waves a magazine at them as they go past. The lass looks at Moz and tugs on her bloke's arm – Buy a *Big Issue*, Chris, she says to him. He makes a big show of stopping and digging out a load of spare shrapnel from his trouser pocket, which he pours into Moz's outstretched hand.

– There you go my mate, keep the change.

Wow, get a load of Rothschild there, thinks Brian. Last of the big spenders. Just guaranteed his leg over, and it's only cost him a handful of sheckles.

– Aw, cheers blue, thank you very much, have a nice night now, says Moz, as the bloke and his bird saunter off up the road, him swinging his rolled-up *Issue* about like it's a silver-topped walking cane.

– Patronising get, Brian says. – He only gi'yer that to prove to her what a great bloke he is.

– Who gives a fuck, he bought one dint he? Moz sticks his fag in his mouth and counts the change in his hand. A ten-bob bit, two fives and a load of copper.

– Bastard! Twelve pence fuckin' short!

He looks at Brian, shakes his head, outraged.

– Cheeky cunt, slinging money at me like I'm some fucking vagrant. I'm a licensed vendor, me.

Brian grins.

– No it's right though innit Bri? It's not the money, it's the principle of the thing.

– A man of principle eh Moz?

– Dead right. It's like me old man used to say: I am a man of very strong principles. And if you don't like them . . . I have others.

Brian laughs, slaps Moz on the back and heads back into the store.

Moz calls after him:

– 'ey, Bri . . . you ant got twelve pence have yer?

Hull Fair: 8.26pm

Billie can't find the Jumping Jacks. She thought they were behind the ride with the motorbikes and racing cars and the bus with the ding-a-ling bell, but now they're not there and she can't find them anywhere. She walks round for ages but they're gone. Then she turns round and goes back to the Helter Skelter but that's gone an'all, and then she starts to get a little bit frightened.

It's not fair.

Everything keeps disappearing from where it used to be.

There's a van selling chips and she stands near that and tries to see her mam. There's loads of other mams, some of them even with the same colour hair and the same jacket but none of them are Billie's mam.

Billie's not going to cry cos she's a big girl and anyway she's six after Christmas, which is after fireworks night which is after Halloween which is after this.

She's not going to cry.

Then she hears that mister with that microphone

shouting here we go hold on tight now and she runs over to where the noise is coming from and there's the Waltzers with all the big kids and then there's the Dodgems and so if she goes round this corner near here . . .

YES!

JUMPING JACKS!

There's a lady watching a little girl bouncing up and down, *doing – doing – doing*! Billie goes and stands next to her and watches an'all. The little girl is screaming but it's a happy scream and every time she doings up she twizzles her legs like she's riding a bike and her face is a big smile. Billie looks at the lady and she's happy and smiling an'all.

Billie gets her pennies out her pocket and holds them out to the other mister and he says are you going on and she nods yes. Come on then he says and he takes the money off her and looks at it and laughs but then holds the straps up for her and she climbs up on the bouncy trampoline. Her tummy is already full of butterflies. The mister lifts her up and straps her in and then he starts doinging her up and down, slowly at first, just gentle, but then Billie starts jumping down hard on the bouncy trampoline and kicking her legs up, and then she's flying upwards to the sky, higher, higher, a little bit higher each time and then she's REALLY flying up and down, and she holds tight onto the straps and the butterflies are swirling round and round in her tummy and it feels FANTASTIC.

She's *flying*!

She's bigger than a *giant*!

She's higher than *all* the rides!

She's higher than *all* of Hull Fair!

She can even nearly touch the stars in the *sky*!

Then Billie sees her dad. She see his blonde hair near the chip van and she waves at him, look Dad, I'm flying! And he looks and sees her flying and he smiles and waves back at her and Billie wants to wave some more but she daren't let go of the strap again in case she goes bouncing all the way up to heaven.

When it's finished the mister brings her back down to the ground and helps her out the straps but it still feels like her tummy is going up and down. She runs over to her dad and she says Dad Dad I can't believe you've come back and he just smiles and bends down and says what's your name and Billie says it's me Dad, it's me, Billie and he asks where's her mam and she tells him she doesn't know. He looks round and then says come on, come with me.

Hull Fair: 8.28pm

Lindsey's doing Dave's head in. She agreed to work all week for Camp Colin but now it's Friday night she's chomping at the bit to get away. This is absolutely typical of her, thinks Dave. Makes a commitment and then starts moaning and groaning. Why she agreed to work in a burger van in the first place is totally beyond Dave. Typical posh bird; likes the idea of hanging about at Hull Fair, slinging chips at the proles, but as soon as the grease starts to cling to her hair, it gradually starts to lose all its romantic appeal. She probably thought she was going to run away and become a trapeze artist. Instead she's sweating like a dray horse in a confined space, burning her hand on the range and getting lip off lairy young kids.

– This van is a bloody death trap, she hisses, shovelling chips into a tray and slamming it down on the counter in front of the bemused-looking lad in a baseball cap who's stood next to Dave. – There's hardly room to swing a cat and the ventilation is totally inadequate. One pound fifty please.

The lad hands his money over and starts applying dollops of ketchup from one of the scabby-looking squeezy bottles.

– Well what did you expect, says Dave, – did you think it was gonna be like The River Cafe? Did you think you'd be serving up mushroom risotto in an earthenware pot?

– I expected a modicum of cleanliness and at least some observation of basic health and safety!

Camp Colin is hovering near the tea urn. He fills a Styrofoam cup and hands it over with raised eyebrows. Dave gives him a sly wink.

– Yeah but look at it this way, Linds, you're getting invaluable experience in the catering industry. Look good on your CV.

– Catering industry? This is not catering, David, this is like feeding time at the bloody zoo.

The lad in the cap is holding up the ketchup bottle.

– This has run out love.

– Well put it in the bin then. Lindsey indicates the big black tub overflowing with rubbish at the end of the van. The lad walks over, jams the bottle in, comes back and stands there, expectant. Lindsey stares down at him with barely concealed disdain.

– What now?

– Have you got any more?

– More?!? *More?!?*

She points at his tray, the chips hidden under a thick blanket of red.

– You can't fit any more on! You'll be ill! Good God! What's the matter with you?

The poor kid looks at her dumbfounded and then at Dave, but Dave's doing his best not to collapse in a fit of giggles.

The lad shrugs.

– I only want some more red sauce.

– Well we haven't got any. You'll have to be content with what you've got. Now will you please move away from the counter, there are other customers to serve.

And there are, a bloke and his missus with about four little kids in tow. The lad picks his chips up, grabs a wooden fork from the tray on the counter and sticks it into the steaming red and golden mound.

– Fuckin' stupid stuck-up bitch!

He wanders off into the crowd.

– SILLY LITTLE WANKER! Lindsey yells after him, which does not go down well with the family man.

– 'ey! There's bains here!

Camp Colin tells Lindsey to go and put some more chips on and he takes the bloke's order: three trays of cheesy chips and a double bacon burger with extra onions. Dave gets out of their road and leans up at the end of the counter with his cup of tea.

Dave's never really liked Hull Fair. Not even when he was a kid. Too noisy, too dirty. And it's bloody dangerous. Not a year goes by without someone getting flung off a ride or battered half to death by a marauding gang of kids. Denise, she hates it with a passion. Lindsey tried to get her to come last year, but there was no chance of that happening. So him and Lindsey trudged round half pissed in the rain and had a row on the Big Wheel. That was their second ever date and their third or fourth row. It's been a tried and trusted routine they've stuck to ever since. He sometimes wonders why they bother. They're hardly a match made in heaven. Spend most of their time rowing. Dave thinks he should have chucked her off the Big Wheel when he had the chance.

There's someone waving at him, a little blonde-haired lass bouncing up and down on that ride over there. At first he thinks she must be waving at her mam, but there's no one stood watching her. The only other adult nearby is the bloke bouncing her in the harness. Dave looks round and then looks back. She's definitely waving at him. Shouting an'all, but he can't hear what she's saying cos the music's too loud. He smiles and waves back at her.

She bounces slowly to a stop and the bloke unfastens her from the harness. She runs straight over to Dave, all excited and out of breath.

– Dad! Dad! Dad! I can't believe you've come back!

Then she wraps herself round his legs and gives him a massive hug.

Dad? What the fuck is she on about?

He peels her off his leg and squats right down so he's on her level.

She's about five or six. Bonny little lass. Dave's trying to think where he knows her from. He doesn't really know that many bains, apart from his nieces and nephews, and they're not really bains any more. She seems very pleased to see him though. Delighted, in fact. Dave looks round for a parent, but there's no likely-looking candidates in the area. She seems to be totally on her own.

He asks her what her name is and she says her name's Billie.

He asks her where her mam is and she says she doesn't know.

Lindsey and Camp Colin are busy filling little white trays full of deep-fried shite, so he takes the little lass's hand and sets off to find a copper. There's usually a few at the top of Walton Street, so he heads up there. Fair's starting to get real busy now, and he has to keep a tight grip of this bain, who's prattling away ten to the dozen. Keeps calling him bloody Dad. It's a bit unnerving for him. He keeps his trap shut and doesn't answer her. Best not to encourage her, he thinks.

They get to the edge of Walton Street and she says she's tired and starts pulling herself up on his jacket, so he picks her up and carries her the rest of the way. Dave is far from bloody happy about this, but tells himself if her mam is looking for her – and surely to God she is – then she's got more chance of spotting her if he holds her up at this height than if she's trailing behind him in a crowd.

There's two coppers up near the pub at the top of the road with two young lasses. One of the lasses, the one with all the dark curly hair, she's going absolutely ballistic, pointing into the crowd and shouting and bawling. She looks mental, like she's going to chin someone. The copper is holding up his hand to try and calm her down as he turns away to yap into his radio. The other one, the little blonde one with the ponytail, she's being spoken to by a female copper, who has both hands on her shoulders. At first Dave thinks she's restraining her, but as he works his way closer to them he can see this other young lass is frozen, in complete shock.

The bain yells, – MAM! DAD'S BACK!

Ponytail-lass looks up and it's like she's been hit by an electric shock. She bursts into tears, flies towards them and grabs this bain out of Dave's arms.

Her mate is in his face straight away, giving it loads – where was she, who the fuck was Dave, where was he taking her, all that carry on. He's ready to give her a proper mouthful back, but the female copper takes her to one side and tries to calm her down. He gives the other copper his details. The copper radios his name and address through and asks him where he found the bain. When he's satisfied that Dave's not some weird paedo wandering round Fair trying to kidnap little lasses he thanks him and says leave it with him, they'll sort it all out now.

The two young lasses are fussing round this little bain and Dave's thinking aye, if you'd have paid her that much attention before she wouldn't have been wandering about Hull fuckin' Fair on her own in the dark. It's a good job it *was* me who found her, he thinks, and not some bloody pervert. And calling him Dad an'all. Weird. Mind you, the poor little bugger has probably had a different bloody dad every year of her life. No wonder she's confused.

He's walking back to the chip van but it starts raining so he decides to have a quick one in Brickies and then get off home. He can't be doing with any more of Lindsey's amateur dramatics just now, and anyway, they're off shopping tomorrow and then out clubbing tomorrow night. He'll see plenty of her then. They'll only end up rowing if he goes back there now.

It was a stupid bloody idea coming here in the first place.

He's in a right mood now, pushing his way through all these people. He gets to Brickies and decides to keep walking. He'll get himself home and crash out on the couch. A glass of wine and some shit telly. Relax and unwind.

Them young lasses. Them stupid bloody young lasses. A little kid like that, left to wander round Hull Fair on her own, not knowing where her mam is or even who her bastard father is. They shouldn't have them if they don't want to look after them. Disgusting, that's what it is. Absolutely fuckin' disgusting.

Some people, thinks Dave.

They shouldn't be allowed to breed.

Hull Fair: 8.35pm

Billie's hand goes inside the man's big warm hand and they walk off through all the people, past the Dodgems and the Waltzers and all the vans. They go past the Hook-a-Ducks and the Hoopla and all the Big Furry Doggies dangling down, under the kicking legs as the spaceship flies over their heads. She says Dad I'm tired, I can't walk any more, so he picks her up and she can feel the ground moving beneath them like the Funny

House they both went in last time they came to Hull Fair. The Funny House with the wobbly mirrors that made you look massive and then little again, and the floor that moved under your feet and Billie had to hang onto her dad like she's hanging onto him now. The ground moves below them and he carries her back through the people, more and more people coming towards them now and they're going more slowly, they're going out of Hull Fair, back to the top of the road.

It starts to rain a bit, Billie can feel the raindrops starting to plop onto her face and then she can see the mucky pub and the policemen with their shiny yellow jackets and one of them is saying something into his crackly radio and then Billie can see Heidi pointing and looking really mad. The other lady policeman is talking to Billie's mam who looks like she's crying. Billie says don't cry Mam cos Dad's back and then Mam turns round and sees Billie and flies towards her, pulls her out her dad's arms and nearly crushes her till she can't breathe, she hugs her that tight. Billie's trying to smile back at her dad, saying look Dad, it's Mam, but he's busy talking to Heidi and the other policeman and the lady policeman asks Billie if she's alright and she says yes she's alright and Mam is crying and going Billie Billie Billie and nearly squeezing her till she pops. You're hurting me Mam she says and Mam puts Billie on the floor and brings her face down to hers. Mam's eyes are all red and with black lines running down her cheeks and she says oh Billie you gave me the fright of my life.

Billie twists round to try and see her dad but he's

walking off now and she can feel the rain starting to go plop plop plop on her head and the tears getting all hot in her eyes and then it starts to pour down and her mam spins Billie round and pulls her hood up and zips her jacket up tight to her chin. She grabs Billie again and whispers into her ear Billie Billie my baby, don't you ever do that to me again, don't you ever leave me again.

Lime Tree Lodge, Cottingham Road: 8.48pm
Barry's left all his drawings out on the table in the other room. He's added a bit more to his merry-go-round. It looks real good now, like it's almost spinning off the page. Could do with a bit more colour in it though. Kerry's no good at drawing, but she's good at colouring in. She knows what colours go with each other, got a proper eye for it. Bit of red, she thinks, for the horse's bridle. Or orange, maybe. Yeah, orange. And do the horses different shades of brown. A black and white one an'all, what are they called? A piebald?

Kerry sits down and has a root about in Barry's pencil box, finds a real nice deep orange and sets to work.

Her Zoe had always wanted a horse. One of her mates used to have one in a field up near Sutton. Massive thing it was; well it was massive to them at that age. Kerry would have been about twelve, thirteen, which would have made their Zoe about nine. Kerry used to go with her sometimes. She had to pretend to their mam that they didn't ride it, that they just went to muck it out and groom it and that, or she wouldn't have let them go. It wasn't a total lie, cos Kerry never did ride it. You wouldn't have got her up on that bloody thing. But Zoe, she used to love it. Kerry's heart used to be in her mouth every time Zoe climbed up into the saddle. She looked so little, bobbing up and down on top of this big brown horse. Kerry always had visions of her falling off and getting trampled underfoot. They stopped going after a bit, Kerry seems to remember they fell out with this lass, probably over summat daft, like you do at that age. But their Zoe, she wanted a horse big style. Obsessed with 'em, she was. Until she got older and got into lads.

Kerry never really got on with any of the lads Zoe went out with. That lad she knocked about with through school, that Lee, he was alright. But most of the others were dickheads. Zoe had proper shit judgement when it came to lads. She could have had her pick an'all, she was that bonny. Had lads swarming round her she did, especially when she started going round Town and that. Always had lads asking her out and ringing the house up and that; some of them decent blokes an'all from good families with good jobs. But Zoe always seemed to gravitate towards the arseholes.

And that Darren, he was the biggest arsehole of 'em all. Marked that bastard's card as soon as she laid eyes on him, Kerry did. Course their stupid bloody mother thought he was wonderful. Thought butter wouldn't melt. But Kerry'd seen what he was like, especially when he'd had a drink. Bullying gobshite he was. No way would Kerry have let their Zoe go on holiday with him. She wouldn't have let her go to the end of the street with that bastard, let alone a place like Zante, and especially not with all them head-bangers he knocked about with.

I should have gone with her.
I should have been there to look after her,
I should have . . .

The point of the pencil crunches down, hard, skids across the paper.

Oh shite.

She's scrubbed right through the paper. Rived a big hole in this horse's neck. Kerry licks her finger and tries to smooth it all out, make it better, but it's no good. It's completely ruined. If owt, she's just made it worse. Damp orange crumbs smeared all over Barry's ace drawing, and this big bloody rip right in the middle.

Oh bastarding hell.

He's gonna go proper mental.

Lime Tree Lodge, Cottingham Road: 9.04pm

Barry comes down the stairs in trackie bottoms and T-shirt, his hair all wet and pulled back in a ponytail. He's got a dab of tissue spotted red on his chin where he's cut himself shaving.

Kerry's waiting for him in the hallway.

– Alright Kerry? he says, but he can tell that she's not.

– I shunt have touched it, says Kerry.

– What you on about?

She takes him through into the front room and shows him his drawing.

– I'm real sorry Barr, she tells him. – I was only trying to finish it off for yer.

He doesn't say owt, but he doesn't need to. It's written all over his face.

– I'm really really sorry Barr, she tells him.

He picks the merry-go-round up and rips it in half; one, two, three, four times.

– Barry, she says.

He chucks all the bits up in the air and he's out the door before the last one flutters to the carpet.

Princes Avenue, 9.14 pm

Colin Power rings in about ten past nine to say he's badly and can't come in. Immaculate timing – he's due to take over in less than an hour. Brian's in Nick's office on the phone to his gaffer at Lockings but he's telling Brian he can't get hold of anyone else and can Brian stay till six. Six in the fuckin' morning, and he's already been there since two this afternoon. After about ten minutes of arguing the toss Brian calls him a useless twat and puts the phone down.

He goes and sees Carol, the staff supervisor, explains the situ. She looks harassed enough already. The place is getting proper busy, people in their going-out gear queuing up for cigs, lads with baskets full of carryouts, people wanting papers and bars of chocolate, pints of milk and lottery tickets.

– Well what are you doing then, are you staying or what? she says.

There's a bellow of laughter from down near the fridges an' some young lass is telling someone to fuck off and stop being a wanker. Carol looks down the aisle and then back at Brian.

– I can't be left with no security on a Friday night, Brian.

– I'll stay, then.

– Thank you, says Carol. – I appreciate it.

He goes and stands near the Lottery, right near the doors. Kafi and Ahmed and Yasmin are on the tills. The queue is getting bigger, snaking back down past the wine and beer display. Yasmin presses the buzzer and Terri comes out the back and goes on the end till, the one nearest Brian. She gives him a smile, says hiya and shouts next please.

It's not a bad crack, actually, this Jackson's job. Better than being sat in a prefab on a building site. Or wandering round an empty factory with a torch in the middle of the night. That last job Brian had was a right pain in the arse – a fish factory on Hessle Road. As soon as they started ripping it out, every tatter and gyppo in West Hull and beyond was all over it like a swarm of ants, looking for lead and copper and owt else that wasn't nailed down. Fuckin' murder it was. Like cowboys and Indians. Brian had to leather one of these gyppo cunts one night when he caught him hanging off some barbed wire at half two in the morning. Gave him a twatting and slung him back over the fence. They still come back the next night, though. They had to get dogs in the end.

But this security lark is alright, all things considered. Better than the doors. The shop work is definitely best though, no doubt about it. For a start, it's warm. And there's not that much hassle, to be fair. Not proper hassle, anyroad. You get the occasional bag-head on the rob, like them two earlier on; generally after stuff they can shift quick, like deodorant or coffee, shampoo and razor blades. Nick put most of it behind the tills, out of reach. You get the odd nasty bastard like that little rat earlier with the needle, but they're usually fairly easy to turf out. Half the time they're rattling that much they drop most the gear before they get to the door.

The main hassle you get is off people coming out of the pubs and clubs. There's a wave of 'em about half eleven, midnight, and then again about three or four in the morning. The half-eleven mob are usually the worst, pissed up and aggressive, shouting and bawling. The ones coming out the clubs, yeah, you get the odd one or two, but most of 'em are usually too out of it to be any proper bother. They're just after goodies and cold drinks, usually. Brian thinks some of 'em are just attracted to the shop-front lights. Like moths. They stop the taxis and float in, all wide eyed. You'll follow a bunch of sweat-drenched lads swaying and bumping round the aisles and find 'em in the cold section, giggling at the cheese.

— Now then Bri!

A punch on his shoulder and it's Steve Lodge, all suited and booted. Big Lodgie. Brian used to play rugby with him years ago, for Dockers. Good prop, was Steve. Good laugh an'all.

— Now then Lodgie. What you doing round here? Thought you never crossed the border. Have they finally spragged you out of Crown?

— Just come for a meal at that Boars Nest. Anniversary innit. Mind you, I've just looked in the window at the prices, I think I'll take her to fuckin' KFC.

He looks Brian up and down. Brian knows what he's thinking; he's thinking fuck me, he's turned into a right fat cunt. Yes Lodgie, he thinks, and when you finally stop whacking up the steroids you'll go exactly the same way, pal.

— How long you being doing this then? Lodgie asks.

– Couple of years.

– Where you livin' now?

– Just up near Orchard. Bought an 'ouse up there.

Lodgie greets this astonishing revelation with raised eyebrows. He thinks you need injections and a passport to leave East Hull.

– Thought I ant seen yer round Town for a bit. Don't yer do the doors any more?

– Nah. Had a heart scare. Our lass played up fuck, made me get a proper job.

Lodgie laughs.

– Bollocks, you ant got a fuckin' heart.

He claps his hand down on Brian's shoulder again.

– Anyhow, good to see you Bri. I'm just gunna get some tabs.

Lodgie gets in the line. He's about a foot taller than anyone else. His big grinning head on them big square shoulders, towering above the rest of the queue.

Brian can feel Lodgie's eyes still on him, so he has a slow saunter up Aisle Two. The magazine rack has been ragged all over, bains pulling the comics about. He squats down and rearranges 'em all. Gets 'em all in order, like.

That new lad, Dougie, he's filling the shelf with Jaffa Cakes further down, his gob hung open like he's catching flies. Been here two nights and Brian doesn't think he's said one word to anyone yet. It's like he's in a trance.

He looks down at Brian. Brian nods at him and he nods back.

Brian looks at his watch. Nearly half nine. Another eight hours of this shite.

Colin Power, you absolute fuckin' tosser.

She's massive now, Ange. Absolutely huge. Two weeks
to go. She spreads herself out on the couch with her
duvet and her magazines and her Diet Coke and the
remote. Carl sits up the other end, trying to ignore
the utter garbage on the box. That American bitch
who looks like a horse, notes Carl. Her and her mates
are sat in a cafe, yapping on about dresses or shoes or
the size of their blokes' cocks. Shane told him it was
written by queers, this. Carl can quite believe it.

He gets his tray from under the couch and knocks
one up. He's down to his last teenth. He'll have to go
and see Gibbo tomorrow. He said there's a bit of a
drought on. Best get a full ounce. Don't wanna be
caught on a dry shore with a new bain in the house,
his nerves'll be shot to fuck as it is.

– Go outside and smoke that, she says.
– I'll go in the kitchen.
– Go in the backyard with it. Bloody stinks.
– I'll open the window.
– Don't be opening that window. It's bloody freezing.
– Is that boiler still not come on?

Angie puts her magazine down and gives him a look.

– Oh aye, yeah. It came on. Then it went off again.
Then it came on for about half an hour and then guess
what? It went bloody off again.

– Fuckin' thing.

He twists the end of the spliff and gives it a shake.
Rips a bit off the Rizla packet and rolls a roach. Slides
it in gently.

– When are you gonna get it sorted out? she says.
– I'll have a look at it tomorrow.

– Why can't you have a look at it now?

– I'll have to dig the manual out.

– Why can't you dig the manual out now?

– Cos I don't know where it is.

– Why don't you look for it?

Fuck's *sake*!

– Look, I'll do it tomorrow, alright? Jesus fuckin' Christ. It's not even that cold, what's up with yer?

– What about hot water for a bath?

– Have a shower.

– What about the bain's bath?

– Why can't she have a shower?

– She dunt like it. Says the water gets in her eyes.

He stands up and feels in his pockets.

– Have you seen me lighter?

– No.

He gets on his hands and knees and looks under the couch. Nowt but dust and biscuit crumbs and bits of jigsaw. A couple of pens. Torn-off bits of Rizla packets. Her voice from above his head:

– And don't be leaving that lying about where Ella can find it. How many times do I have to tell yer?

Fuck's sake.

He gets up and has a root around on the mantelpiece. Not there.

– Did you hear me? I said don't be leaving . . .

– I heard yer.

Must be in the kitchen. He stops at the doorway, turns back and points at the telly with the spliff.

– And when I come back in here you can turn that fuckin' shite off.

– Fuck off. I have to put up with boring bloody

football morning, noon and night. This is the only thing I ever watch.

– You're not even watching it, you're reading your magazine.

– I am watching it.

– How can you do two things at once?

She gives a short sarcastic laugh.

– Practice, mate. Lots of it.

– I want it off by the time I get back.

He shuts the door behind him.

– Don't open that window, she shouts.

The drawers in the kitchen are crammed full of all sorts of crap, there's bound to be a lighter in here. But no, is there fuck, just bills, batteries, take-away menus, bits of Blu-Tack, bits of change. Must be about three quids' worth of copper in there. He scoops it all out, all ones and twos, and spreads it on the worktop. Few bits of silver an'all. He'll count that up and take it to Asda, put it in that machine.

No lighter in any of the drawers, not even a box of matches. At the very bottom of one of them he finds an old booklet:

NEATERHEAT RESPONSE 30KW
COMBINATION GAS BOILER

He has a quick flick through but it's all intricate diagrams and loads of technical jargon. A foreign language.

Fuck that. He'll see Shane tomorrow night. He knows a plumber.

He stuffs the booklet to the very bottom of the

drawer and covers it up. Then he goes in the hallway and feels in his jacket pocket.

Result! Red Clipper!

He opens the back door and sparks up, blowing the smoke outside. The nights are properly drawing in now. It's not freezing cold yet but there's a definite damp in the air. Hull Fair weather, as they say.

You can actually hear the Fair from here if you stand dead still. Distant shouting and screaming and that relentless muffled thud. You can see the yellow laser beams from the rides flashing over the rooftops and that big white spotlight moving slowly across the sky. There's the police helicopter hanging up there an'all, the red and white tail lights blinking on and off.

Carl feels sorry for them poor bastards who live down Walton Street at this time of year. He knows the council give them some money as a sweetener an' that, but still. All that mess and noise. Like a spaceship landed in your front yard and dumped all the trash in the known universe. Bet they're glad this is the last weekend, he thinks. He'd fuck off for the week if it was him. Come back when they've cleaned it all up.

The smoke is drifting back into the house so he moves away, out to the backyard. Good gear, this. He can feel his head loosening up. He'll get Ange back on it after the bain comes. Might calm her down a bit. She could do with it. Thing is, he remembers all this from before, from when Ella was born. The anxiety, the worry, the endless bickering. Only natural really. Him being out of graft doesn't help. Ange knows the score on that front though, he'll get a phone call off their Alan and it'll be all hands on deck again. Besides, he's still got a bit of a wedge from that last job away. It's not like they're skint. As soon as the bain comes he'll have a few more weeks off to help her round the house, and then he'll give Alan a bell and get summat organised. Everything'll be alright. They'll have a proper night out as well, the pair of them, once they've got into some sort of routine.

It'll all be sound.

The police helicopter turns and moves across the sky. The whirring of blades getting louder as it passes overhead, then tailing away. He gives it a wave, takes a last deep drag of his smoke, flicks the dog end into next door's garden and goes back inside.

Ange has turned the telly off and gone to bed.

He switches it back on and flicks through the channels.

Red Hot TV. Freeview. That bird who used to be on *Big Brother* laid out on a big double bed. Stockings and sussies, the lot. Looks a bit like Angie's sister, Michelle. Same hairdo.

Carl reaches under the couch and gets his tray out again.

Clumber Street: 10.14pm

Heidi came back to theirs for a cup of tea and she sat with Billie while Mam put Benji to bed. Billie got into her jim jams and her and Bruno and Heidi watched the *High School Musical* DVD. Then she has some biscuits and some milk and she brushes her teeth and Heidi goes home and Mam takes Billie up to bed. She reads her a story about Angelina Ballerina and then tucks her in and kisses her good night.

Billie can feel her tooth wobbling about when she pushes it with her tongue. It's really wobbly now. She asks Mam if she thinks it will fall out when she's asleep and she says no don't be daft it'll be alright. Then Billie asks her if the Tooth Fairy is really real cos Keavey says she isn't. Mam says course she is and shush go to sleep.

She sits there stroking Billie's hair for a bit. It feels nice. Then Billie says to her mam why did Dad just go away like that and her mam doesn't say owt for ages. Then she says I don't know Billie. I don't know, she says. But you've got me and Benji and Nana and Grandad and everyone and we're all here and we all love you.

After a bit she gets up, turns the light off and goes downstairs. It's quiet for ages then Billie can hear the telly being turned on. People laughing, then a round of applause.

There's lights outside her window. She gets out of bed and goes to have a look. The sky is all lit up in the distance. Hull Fair is still going on even though she's not there. There's a big white light swooping across the sky, up above all the houses. It goes from one side of the window to the other and then back again.

Billie stands and looks at it for a bit till she hears Mam coming up the stairs, then she runs back to bed quick and jumps in, pulls the covers up under her chin.

By the time Mam's feet get outside her door Billie's lied there in the dark with her eyes tight shut.

Lime Tree Lodge, Cottingham Road: 10.17pm

After she's tidied the front room up Kerry goes and checks on a few of the other residents. Most of them are watching telly in the front room, but there's a few up in their own rooms. Kerry gives Maurice's door a tap and looks in. He's sat on the bed reading the paper. Kerry asks him if he fancies coming down to watch a bit of telly but he says no ta he's alright there in his cabin. Calls it his cabin, thinks he's still at sea. He seems happy enough though so Kerry leaves him to it.

Gail's sat on her bed smoking. She looks like she's been roaring. Her eyes and nose are red raw and there's a soggy heap of tissues on the bed. Kerry asks her what's up and Gail says that Barry's mad at her for summat and she doesn't know what and she's sick of carrying on like this, she doesn't know where she is with him from one day to the next. Kerry tells Gail that it's her that Barry's mad at and tells Gail about the drawing, but Gail's having none of it.

— No it's me. He hates me. I went to his room to talk to him but he told me to eff off. That's no way to talk to your fiancée, Kerry. Sometimes he acts like we're not even engaged. I'm sick of it, honest to God I am.

She blows her nose. Kerry sits down next to her on the bed.

— It's just how blokes are Gail, she tells her, — don't tek any notice.

— I wunt mind, says Gail, — but I could have any bloke in here that I wanted. Always had blokes after me, I have. He dunt know how lucky he is to have someone like me.

And her eyes water up again as she pulls on her tab. The ash drops down onto her cardie. Kerry brushes it off, flicks it down onto the carpet. She'll have to run the Hoover round here in morning.

– Look, Kerry says to her, – why don't you come downstairs and I'll do us both a nice cup of tea eh?

Gail shakes her head.

– I'll just stay here out the way Kerry. I know where I'm not wanted.

She dots her tab out and lights up another one.

– Bastard wunt even win me a teddy at Fair either, she says.

Kerry goes up to Barry's room at the top of the house. He's got his music on loud and at first Kerry thinks he can't hear her knocking but then he opens the door.

– What? he says.

She tells him how Gail thinks he's mad with her and that she feels bad about it cos she knows it's her who's upset him, not Gail. Barry rolls his eyes, sighs and says hang on a minute. He goes and turns his music off and then Kerry follows him back down the stairs. He knocks on Gail's door and Kerry whispers that she'll go and make them all a brew. She passes Alec Nelson's door on the way down and thinks about popping in to see if he's alright, but he's still chuntering away to himself. Doesn't sound like he's calmed down much, so Kerry leaves it. Let Sandra sort him out after. She's better at dealing with Alec, he seems to respect her more than Kerry. Probably because she's older and been there longer.

Kerry goes in the telly room and asks who wants a brew. Surprise surprise, everyone does.

Ten minutes later Barry and Gail come down into the dining room. Barry says he's nipping out to the garage to get him and Gail some chocolate and does

Kerry want owt? Kerry takes this as an olive branch, which is a big relief to her. Barry's the last person she wants to fall out with.

Kerry pours the brews out and Gail helps her take them through.

– 'ey, Kerry, Gail whispers to her, – guess what? The engagement! It's back on!

Boothferry Estate: 10.24pm

This house smells of old age and old habits. Everything about it, from the yellowing photos on the shelves and walls to the hard yellow cake of soap on the washbasin upstairs. Trevor fills the bath up and gets in. Has a long leisurely soak. He stays in there till the water starts going cold then dries himself off in the back bedroom. The towel stinks a bit. He goes back into the bathroom and looks for some deodorant but all he can find is one of them ball roll-ons. It's got pale gingery hairs stuck on it. He puts it back in the cupboard.

Trevor finds the old boy's dressing gown hung up on the back of the door. A heavy maroon gown with a big letter A on it. He puts it on and goes back down-stairs. The dogs are in the kitchen in their baskets. Seems like they've turned in for the night.

He has a bit of a poke about in the living room. Opening drawers and sideboard doors and what have you. Old habits die hard. There's nowt of interest. Just envelopes and bills. Bits of string, scissors, Sellotape. Old forgotten bits and bobs. Feels weird to be wandering round somebody else's gaff. But legitimate, like. His bare feet on their carpet and his bare bits brushing against the old feller's dressing gown.

The stool in front of the organ is one of them ones with the flip-top seat. Full of songbooks and sheets of music. He flicks through a couple. Must be nice to be able to read music, he thinks. Entertain yourself, like.

Trevor sits at the organ and flicks it on. That deep slow groan swells up again. There's about two dozen different pedals on the deck. He larks about with it for a bit, making these low mournful notes. He bangs the GOSPEL button on. After a bit of buggering about he susses how to change the notes by pressing different pedals while the backing track's going. When you press a different pedal it changes the note. He picks three pedals out and presses them in turn. Gets this hypnotic slow sorta tune going, with these electronic handclaps and that. Tickles him how easy it is to get summat half decent out of this big machine. It sorta does all the work for you. Who needs music books? He gets dead into it. Makes him think of a church full of black fellers in purple robes, all swaying together from side to side and making this low humming.

Trevor's that absorbed he fair craps himself when he feels the hot breath on his bare leg. He looks down to see Charlie Chan's wandered through and has parked himself right down next to him.

– JESUS BLOODY CHRIST!

Charlie barks once, jumps up startled. Turns and bolts back into the kitchen.

Trevor goes through and the Collie is pawing at the back door. The Shar Pei looks up at him with them little eyes. They're badly gunked up. Poor bugger. That's an infection, thinks Trevor. Fancy clearing off on holiday and leaving a badly dog in the house. He gets some kitchen roll from off the side and tries to get hold of Charlie's collar so he can wipe his eyes for him. Charlie tenses up as Trevor gets a hold of him. This low rumble coming from his throat.

– Easy now lad, alright now, Charlie lad. Get rid of all that muck for you mate.

Charlie's not happy though. He's twisting his neck away from Trevor as he tries to get some of that weeping yellow snot. The growl in the dog's throat is getting louder. He plants his feet squarely on the lino and jerks his head away every time Trevor comes near his eyes with the screwed-up kitchen roll. Trevor can sense he's getting seriously peed off. He jerks his head from side to side. A big glob of eye gunge lands on Trevor's wrist.

So he leaves it as a bad job.

Trevor unlocks the back door and both dogs bolt into the backyard for a pee. Trevor wipes his wrist and then rolls a tab and smokes it, leaning up against the door as they do their thing out there.

After a bit his legs are getting numb with the cold so he shouts 'em back in and dots his tab on the doorstep.

– Time for lock up lads!

They both hit their baskets.

Back in the front room it's still The Reverend Holy Roller and His Songs of Praise as the organ keeps pumping out its automatic tune. It's staying on the same note though, like a needle stuck on a record, the same note over and over again. Trevor flicks it off and the music slowly dies, like it's being deflated.

He can never sleep properly the first couple of weeks

on the out. Throws him a bit. Eighteen months of the same routine. Lights out at the same time every night. The noises. The bangings and clangings. Sharing a pad with different blokes. The snoring and the screaming in their sleep and what have you. And now all of a sudden he can go to bed whenever he wants in a room where it's just him and it's dead quiet. Takes a while to get used to the peace. Trevor's bloody knackered. But there's no way he's ready for kip yet.

He scours the shelves for a decent read. There's bugger all here except women's books and standard old gimmer stuff. *Walks of East Yorkshire. How To Make Your Own Wine. Discover the Beautiful East Coast.* All that sort of stuff. Makes no difference to an ex-con insomniac though. Trevor'll read owt. It's a good way to pass the time. There's a few books about dogs an'all. One about Shar Peis. He gets it down and takes it onto the couch.

. . . Shar Pei were originally bred for fighting in China. Their wrinkles allow the dog to turn and bite an attacker if seized. The Shar Pei is extremely devoted, loyal and affectionate to its family, and will accept strangers given time and proper introduction. If time is not taken to properly train or socialise, it can become territorial and aggressive. Whilst this breed is gener-ally good-natured, it is also very protective of its home. A powerful dog that is willing to guard its family members at all costs. A common problem is a painful eye condition, entropion, in which the eyelashes curl inward, irritating the eye. This can cause blindness if left untreated . . .

North Bransholme: 11.30pm

Darren strokes her cheek until her eyes flicker open and then they both get off to bed.

Michelle's still half dazed when he starts pulling all her gear off, her head still swimming. It's only when she's climbing on top of him that she remembers they didn't get any johnnies out of the pub bogs.

– Condoms, she whispers to him, but he's already swollen hard and sliding inside her, his hands on her arse, lifting her slowly up and down.

– We'll be careful, he says.

But after a few minutes it's like her head's a balloon, filled with nothing but hot air, slowly detaching from her body, floating off up to the ceiling and she's away, she's gone, totally gone, lost in the moment, nothing else exists except this gorgeous rock-hard heat rubbing against her clit and she's leaning down, pushing hard, both hands on his chest and the room is shrinking, so hot, both of them locked together, slick with sweat and it feels like the centre of her belly is on fire and the heat is spreading slowly up to her chest and her neck and her head and oh fuck jesus yes yes yes, and then he's whimpering and moaning, tensing up below her and inside her and Michelle can feel he's about to come and she's thinking oh fuck babies babies babies and she tries to rise up off him but he's gripping fast onto her hips and pulls her down onto him, hard, harder, and he pushes up as he comes and comes and comes in floods, filling her up and oh jesus christ fuck . . .

Yeeeeeeeeeeeeeeeeeeeeeeeeeeeeeeeeessssssssssssssssssssssss sssss . . . .

She collapses on top of him and they lie there in

the dark, arms and legs wrapped around each other. Michelle's heart is banging ten to the dozen and she can hear his heart as well, his strong beautiful heart thudding deep in his chest, pumping the blood round his body, all his insides gurgling and pounding. The very centre of him. The miracle of life racing around inside of him. She kisses his belly and he strokes her hair and neck before he turns away on his side and Michelle snuggles up behind him, her knees lifted up into the backs of his legs.

The ticking of the clock and the occasional car swishing past outside.

A police siren shrieking somewhere in the distance.

Darren's breathing, gentle like a sigh.

Michelle starts to think about what she's going to do tomorrow . . . round Town shopping with Jennie . . .

. . . new top for tomorrow night . . . round Town with Darren . . . meeting him in Punch . . .

. . . nine o'clock, he said . . .

. . . maybe try and pop in and see her Grandad Bill . . .

. . . in the afternoon . . .

. . . maybe . . .

She's almost drifted off when she becomes aware of something else. A noise. It's Darren. She can feel his shoulders moving up and down, like he's silently chuckling away to himself.

– What's tickled you? she says.

He doesn't answer.

Michelle props herself up on one arm and shakes him gently.

– Darren! Oi, headcase! What you laughing at?

Then she realises he's not laughing. He's crying. Sobbing his heart out in fact.

– Oh Darren! Oh baby, what's the matter?

She strokes his head.

– Don't, she says. – Oh Darren, please don't!

– I'm alright, he says.

He rolls over onto his back and smiles up at her. A firework explodes outside and the room is lit up through the curtains, bright yellow for half a second. His eyes all shining wet with tears.

– I'm happy Michelle, he says. – I am so fuckin' happy.

Saturday 20 October

Newland Avenue: 12.03am
He's mashed by the time he gets upstairs and into bed.
Ange is curled up on her side. He slides in behind her
and cups one of her tits in his hand.

– Uuugh, she goes.

– Come on, he whispers in her ear. – Come on.

– Geddoff.

– Come on Ange. From behind.

Her hand reaches round behind her, pushes him
away.

– Come on Ange.

– Fuck off.

She gives him a back-heel, hard. Bunches the duvet
up around her.

He gets out of bed, gets a blanket out the airing
cupboard, goes downstairs and gets wrapped up on the
couch, his hands cupping his bollocks.

It's fuckin' freezing.

Lime Tree Lodge, Cottingham Road: 12.48am
Barry's gone to bed, Gordon and Pete Craven and
Maurice and Gail and most of the others have gone
to bed an'all. Frank went up hours ago. Joanne comes
back with a bag of chips. She seems to have calmed
down. She eats her food in the dining room and then

she gets off an'all. There's only Kerry and Gary and Christopher and Sandra still up, watching some daft film. After a bit Gary says he's off for a lie down in the other front room. Then Christopher wanders off and it's just Kerry and Sandra.

Sandra asks Kerry what sort of day she's had and Kerry tells her it's been alright but she worries some-times about the residents and how to handle some of 'em. Sandra asks her what she means and Kerry tells her about Pete and Gordon and that business with the money at Fair. Kerry mentions this on purpose to see what Sandra says, but Sandra doesn't bat an eyelid, just tells her that Peter can get into some right moods and he's best left alone when he's like that. Kerry tells her about Barry and the drawing and how Gail thought he was mad at her.

– Seems like every time I try and help someone I make a balls up, Kerry says.

Sandra laughs and says some people are beyond helping.

– But it's our job to at least try an help 'em, says Kerry. – It's our job to look after 'em an' see that they're alright, surely?

– Well sometimes that means leaving 'em alone, Sandra says. – And if they want to talk, you just listen.

Then Sandra starts asking Kerry about Zoe, but Kerry doesn't want to get into all that with her. Sandra's a colleague and, yeah, a mate, but some things are private. Kerry bats off every question with a don't know or can't remember. She picks up a magazine and starts reading an article about a woman who left her husband for another woman and adopted three orphan babies from Africa. After a bit, Sandra stops asking her and sits and watches the telly while Kerry reads the magazine.

Like Sandra said, some things are best left alone.

Boothferry Estate: 1.04am

Trevor wakes up with a jolt and for a second he hasn't got a clue where he is. One side of him is freezing cold and there's a taste like shite in his mouth.

Then he realises he's on the floor. He lifts himself up onto his elbow. The telly is on but there's no sound. The book on dogs is open and face down next to him. He twists himself round.

Charlie on the couch. His big blue-grey head. His hot breath coming down heavy between his paws. Those little slits for eyes.

Looking down on him.

Lime Tree Lodge, Cottingham Road: 2.27am

Kerry and Christopher are sat in the dining room having a brew. Christopher's telling Kerry that the floods were God's punishment for all the evil that goes on in the city. That God looked down on Hull and decided to send the rain to flush all the sinners down the drain, down into the sewers where they belong. Down into Hell where they're tortured for all eternity. This is what God does, says Christopher, he sends earthquakes to rip the earth open and giant waves to come crashing out of the sea and lightning to strike people dead. Anyone who's a sinner gets punished by nature, cos God's nature is good and it's stronger than human nature, which is bad.

Kerry asks him why God didn't flush that Darren away and Christopher says that soon God and the Devil are going to have a massive fight on Planet Earth and anyone who's proper evil will get rounded up and punished big style. That the Devil is only strong if he can get humans to do what he wants and if humans ignore him and don't listen to his tempting words then they'll be alright and God will save them on this special judgement day. But most humans are weak, says Christopher, and they listen to the Devil cos the Devil makes bad things sound normal, like good fun even, which is why people take drugs and drink and hurt themselves and each other, cos they think that's normal and that's how you're supposed to carry on.

Christopher tells her that human beings all came from another planet and that's why they believe in heaven, which is really just another word for the planet we came from and that's why we look up into the sky and talk about heaven being up there and we crashed here in a giant spaceship and the world was a paradise before we came and ruined it all with buildings and tellies and wars and diseases. He said when the space-ship landed it woke up the Devil who lived in the middle of Planet Earth and that's how he was let loose and started whispering in people's ears.

He goes on about other things, about Jesus fighting demons and the Holy Ghost living in a human body but after a bit Kerry stops listening to what he's saying and just stares out the window into the pitch black night outside. His voice is like a radio coming from another room, this low murmuring noise with no words that just goes on and on and on.

Lime Tree Lodge, Cottingham Road: 4.50am

Kerry wakes up to screaming, the sound of a woman screaming. She opens her eyes and for a few seconds she can't work out where she is. At first she thinks she's at home but then she sits up straight and she's at Lime Tree Lodge still, in the telly room and that's where the screaming is coming from, the telly, some sort of horror film, this woman being chased through a house by a maniac.

Sandra's asleep on the couch, head tilted back, snoring.

Oh Christ, thinks Kerry, this is no good. One of them is supposed to stay awake in case owt happens. If Gary knows they're both asleep on the night shift he'll go yapping straight to his mam.

Kerry gets up and turns the screaming off.

Where's that Gary?

She goes across the hallway and peers into the other front room. There's a blanket-covered shape laid out on the couch. It groans and turns over, so Kerry shuts the door to, dead softly, tiptoes back into the telly room.

It stinks in here of stale smoke. These ashtrays, full to the brim again. Kerry gets the bin and goes round emptying 'em all out, quiet as she can. There's a few mugs dotted about an'all, some of 'em half full of tea, gone stone cold. There's papers and magazines spread out on the floor, and a book fallen open next to Sandra's feet.

Kerry picks the book up, has a flick through. Looks like someone's diary, but it's in all different handwriting. She recognises Sandra's handwriting in there, and

Gary's an'all. Kerry reads a few entries. Stuff about the residents, what they've been up to and that. Like a daily report, what they had for tea, things they've said and done.

Maggie never said owt to Kerry about writing in a book. Never said owt about filling a report out.

She sees her name dotted about here and there:

Kerry is settling in nicely.

Kerry helped with all the hoovering.

Kerry went to bed at half past three in the morning.

Then this, on the last page filled in:

Friday 19th/Saturday 20th October (12.30pm – 8am)

Roast beef and mash veg for dinner, chicken burger, chips and beans for tea. Did all laundry and ironing. At tea-time Kerry, Barry, Gail, Gordon, Peter and Christopher went round Hull Fair without telling staff where they were going. It was Kerry's idea to go. While she was there she got into a fight with another girl who I understand was someone to do with her sister who died. Joanne got upset with Alec and threw a magazine at him for talking loud in telly room. Alec upset. Kerry ruined one of Barry's drawings, he was a bit upset but seems alright now. I talked to Kerry about her sister, she still seems to have some guilty feelings about this. She still likes to help clean up and help round the house with other residents. Most residents in bed by midnight, Kerry and Christopher stayed up til late. Sat and watched telly most of the evening. Christopher up all night but seemed calm. Rest of the night was quiet. – Sandra

Kerry slams the book shut, slings it back on the floor and goes down the hallway and into the dining room. Christopher's sat at the table pulling apart tab ends from an ashtray. He looks up at Kerry as she strides past him, through the back and into the kitchen.

– Can I have a cig please?

Kerry shouts hang on over her shoulder and then comes back out from the kitchen holding the fire extinguisher and drenches Christopher, a hard jet of water full blast in the face. Christopher screams and jumps up, tipping the table over, the ashtray full of dog-ends, full cup of tea, the lot, all over the carpet, the fuckin' carpet which Kerry stood and hoovered up. He throws his chair at her but Kerry's not there, she's gone, marching down the hallway, straight to the fire alarm on the wall, BANG! and the house is instantly torn to shreds with a shrieking ***WOOWOOWOOWOOWOOWOOWOOWOO WOOWOOWOOWOOWOOWOOWOO***

Sandra comes flying out the telly room and then goes flying backwards on her arse as the bottom of the fire extinguisher swings up and cracks her right under the chin. Kerry gives her a couple more on the deck for good measure, then goes in the telly room and empties the rest of it all over the couch, the chairs, the carpet, the telly, the fireplace, the curtains, the whole stinking lot and when the foam all sputters to a dribble and stops, Kerry goes to put it through the telly screen, but the fuckin' thing doesn't smash, just bounces off the screen, so she gives it another bastard but it still doesn't smash, so Kerry turns round to the window and lifts the fire extinguisher above her head and hurls it as hard as she can against the curtains, and SMASH! there you go, the glass explodes outwards into a hundred thousand tiny pieces, shatters and falls like hailstones onto the paving outside, shatters and falls like her sister did from that balcony in Greece, like Kerry's fuckin' life shattered and fell and is still shattered, still falling, guilty feelings guilty feelings, she'll give the bastards guilty fuckin' feelings and that fire alarm inside Kerry's head and outside her head, ear splitting, relentless *WOOWOOWOOWOOWOOWOOWOOWOO WOOWOOWOOWOOWOOWOO*

Kerry steps over Sandra and out the front door as the footsteps thunder down the stairs behind her. She hears Barry shouting her name and Christopher screaming like a wounded animal somewhere out the back and she walks away, quickly, outside, under falling sheets of rain and yellow pools of streetlight, past darkened houses and iron-shuttered shops, walking, then walking faster, then running, running faster, running as fast as she can until she's swallowed up by the dark, no streetlights or houses or passing cars, just her feet pounding on the pavement and the sound of her breath pounding in her head, all the noise and light faded away completely, shrank to nothing behind her.

Princes Avenue: 5.55am

Brian wheels his moped out of the back way and round onto Princes Ave. Straps his daft little piss-pot helmet on, and starts the bike up. He got this moped to save money on buses and taxis so it seemed a bit of a waste to get a proper expensive helmet. It's only a fuckin' runaround, he reasons, and besides, no cunt can see him when it's strapped on and he's on the move.

Hardly any traffic about.

He moves off the pavement and onto the road, and he's about to twist and go when he hears someone shouting his name.

It's Moz. He's capering about like a loon on the other side of the road. Waving his hand above his head.

– What? calls Brian.

Moz is pointing to summat he's holding in his hand, a tiny piece of card it looks like.

– What is it?

– Frozen chicken! Bingo! Yes! Fuckin' get in!

And the daft twat punches the air, like he's just won the Challenge Cup.

The Quadrant: 6.24am

Brian locks the bike away in the shed, hangs his water-proofs up and gets in the kitchen, makes a cup of tea. He moves the margarine and the loaf off the table and gets the paper spread out. Turns to the back pages. City away to Watford. He might have a bet this afternoon. Do a coupon. If he gets up in time, like.

He dots his tab, washes his mug out and puts it on the draining board, goes through to the living room and there's their Paul sparked out on the couch.

The place looks like a bomb's hit it. Bits of half-eaten pizza in greasy boxes, cans and bottles and over-flowing ashtrays everywhere. Pint glass half full of flat lager with three tab ends floating on top. Telly still on with the sound turned down. Trail of mud leading across the carpet. Stink of stale ganja smoke and sweaty feet hanging in the room.

Paul's snoring away, deep and heavy.

Brian pulls the curtains back, but it's still dark outside.

– Paul, he says, but Paul doesn't move.

Brian goes upstairs and brushes his teeth, washes his face and slips quietly into the bedroom. Julie's on her side, the duvet bunched up tight around her.

He gets in and tries to cover himself, but she's got proper hold of it in her sleep. She groans and rolls away. He reaches down and feels for his jumper on the floor where he slung it.

Wraps it round himself.

Tries to cover up best he can.

Newland Avenue: 7.24am

Carl's having a dream and in his dream he's laid asleep outside and it's pissing down with rain. The rain is battering against the side of his face, big heavy drops. He's trying to get up but he can't.

He can hear a voice and his eyes open.

It's Ella. She's got a biscuit in one hand and she's slapping him with the other.

– CBeebies! CBeebies Daddy!

– Say please.

– Please. CBeebies, please.

He gets up, puts the telly on for her and goes through to the kitchen. Some Marmite on toast for the bain and two cups of tea. He takes the toast back through for Ella.

– Don't get that all over.

Her eyes are glued to the box.

– Did you hear what I said?

She nods and stuffs toast into her mouth.

He takes the brews upstairs. He can hear the shower running.

– Cup of tea for yer, he shouts. He goes in the bedroom and put hers down on the bedside table. Carries his through into the bathroom.

He can see her shadow through the shower curtain, washing her hair. Big swollen belly, big swollen tits. He sits on the bog at the end of the bath and she glances over her shoulder, squinting through shampoo suds and steam.

– Made a cup of tea for yer. It's next to the bed.

– Ta. Hang on a minute, you can help me out of here.

She tilts her head back and rinses her hair through. The soapy water slides down her back, down the crack of her arse and the back of her legs before spiralling down the plughole. Fuck me, thinks Carl, from the back, you wouldn't even know she was pregnant.

Angie switches the shower off and turns round.

– What you looking at?

– Nowt.

– Pass us that towel.

He helps her get wrapped up and takes her by the elbow as she steps slowly out of the bath.

– Get Ella dressed, she says. – I don't want her sitting in front of that telly all morning.

– I'll take her in park.

Carl and Ella get their gear on and they go to the park. There's hardly anyone there, just a few alkies sat on the benches near the flower garden and a couple of early-morning dog walkers.

While he's pushing the bain on the swing he gets a text from Shane, who's just coming off the night shift:

LINNET HALF SEVEN BUGLE SORTED.

– Hold tight! he tells Ella. – Scream if you wanna go faster!

She grips onto the chains with her little fists and she kicks her legs up and screams.

Boothferry Estate: 7.45am

Rose and Bella are up and out on the park early doors, chucking a stick about. Rose could hardly sleep a wink last night. Proper shook her up, she must admit, that mucky article popping up on the site like that. First time that's ever happened to her, they're usually a good bunch on there. Local people. She doesn't understand what people get out of behaving like that. She can't imagine someone like that would get to meet up with many folk. Mind you, she supposes like attracts like. She'll just have to be a bit more careful about who she accepts for the private chats. Rose wonders if that was who that daft Gypsy meant, when she said that there was a man who had a gift for her? Well that's the sort of gift Rose can do without, thank you very much. And she shall certainly be reporting Mr Jack Sparrow to the admin, oh aye yes. An email will be sent, don't you worry about that.

Bella starts barking and Rose looks up to see Jean's dogs at the far end of the field, Charlie and Jess, coming out of the playground. She gives them a wave and Bella goes galloping over. As Rose gets closer she sees it's not Arthur with the dogs, it's some other chap, big fellow, unshaven, a bit scruffy.

Rose says hello to Charlie and Jess and has a chat to this man. Seems Jean and Arthur have gone away for the weekend. They've got a caravan up at Reighton Gap. They let Rose and Malcolm use it one weekend, years ago when the kids were bains. Nice spot.

Rose thinks there's summat a bit odd about this chap. Something a touch not right about him. Shifty, that's the word. He won't look her in the eye when she talks to him. And he's got tattoos all over the backs of his hands, little blue dots on his knuckles. Not the type of person she would imagine Jean and Arthur having much to do with. But she supposes he must be alright, or they wouldn't have trusted him with their dogs. Charlie, the Shar Pei, he's a beautiful animal. Him and Bella always got on with each other. Very clever dogs, Sharpies. Very perceptive. Good guard dogs. Rose thought of getting one herself before they got Bella. But she had Malcolm to look after her then.

Rose tells this chap to tell Jean to give her a bell when she gets back. She doesn't know if he heard her though. He just sort of mumbles a reply and starts dragging the dogs away.

Rose picks the stick up and slings it back towards the gates at the far end of the field. Best be getting back. There's pots in the sink still, and that back bedroom could do with a good tidy.

Boothferry Estate: 7.47am

There's hardly a soul in Gower Road Park. It's still too early for anyone but Trevor and Jess and Charlie and

the other dogs of Boothferry Estate. They pass a bloke
with a little yelping Jack Russell type thing. It's going
mental. The bloke bends to grab its collar before it gets
a chance to make a lunge. Trevor and the other bloke
drag their dogs away from each other, Charlie and Jess
nearly pulling Trevor off his pins in a fresh outbreak
of bug-eyed barking.

They head to the football fields.

A middle-aged woman throws a stick about at the
far side for a black Labrador. She sees them coming
onto the green from the concrete play park.

She waves.

Her dog clocks the other two dogs and comes belting
over. They seem to be old pals these three, cos there's
none of the instant aggression like with that other little
yapping bugger. They all bounce around each other,
trying to stick their noses up each other's arses. Trevor's
swivelling round with the leads like he's in a circus.

The woman eventually wanders over. Thick glasses.
Short grey hair. Early sixties.

– Hello Charlie! Hello Jess!

She bends down and rubs their heads and chests.
They crowd round her, two tongues slurping all over
her face. She screws her eyes up and laughs. Bloody
hell, thinks Trevor. She wouldn't be laughing if she
knew where Jess had had that tongue this morning.

She pushes them away by the collars. Straightens up
and gives Trevor the once over. She's still smiling, but
not with her eyes.

– Gone to the caravan?

– Caravan?

– Jean and Arthur. The caravan. At Reighton?

Trevor clocks her looking at his hands wrapped round the leads. The blue dots on the knuckles. He wraps both leads round one of his hands and sticks the other in his pocket.

– Yeah. Away for the weekend.

She nods. But he can tell she's not entirely convinced. She smiles down at the dogs.

– And you must be missing your mummy and your daddy! Yes you must be! You're lovely aren't you? Yes you are! Yes you are!

Trevor nods down at the Shar Pei.

– Never seen one of him before, not really. Not close up like.

– Beautiful dogs, Sharpies. Very loyal. Aren't you Charlie?

Charlie looks up at her, the wind whipping into them yellow-caked eyes. She rubs his neck and gives Trevor another tight-lipped smile.

– Well, tell Jean to give me a call when she gets back.

– Aye, alright.

– I'm Rose.

Then she slaps her leg and whistles at her dog. – C'mon Bella! C'mon girl.

And she walks off.

– I'm Graham, says Trevor.

But she can't have heard him, cos she doesn't turn round.

Hotham Road South: 10.02am

These razors are absolute shite, he's nearly cut his bloody leg off. Serves him right for getting the cheap ones he supposes. He tried that Immac, but it made him come up in a rash, sensitive bugger that he is.

You can't beat a good soak, he thinks. One of the few proper pleasures in life. He lays back in the bath and points one of his legs up to the ceiling. He's been blessed with good legs. The only decent thing me mother passed on to me, he thinks. The rest of him isn't up to much, but he has got decent legs. When they're not covered in razor nicks that is. He'll just have to put some dark tights on. Thank Christ he's fair-haired. At least he doesn't have to do his arms.

Bath's getting cold, so he sits up, gets a fresh razor out the pack and gives his face a good thorough shave. Considers doing his pubes again, but then dismisses the idea when he remembers the last time and how itchy it was growing back. Like having a live hedgehog wriggling about in your knickers. Not a nice feeling when you're sat on a forklift all day.

He gets out of the bath, dries off and wanders through to the bedroom. He gives himself a good going over with Oil of Olay and then has a root through his undie drawer. It could do with replenishing. If he's got time after they've been in Town, he'll nip down to Gwenap and have a look what they've got in. He selects and rejects various pairs of drawers till he settles on his Padded Hip and Butt Panty Shaper. No contest really, it gives him a proper shape, as does his Silicone Breast TransBra Plus – C Cup. He's got a D cup as well, but he's never really felt comfortable in it. Makes him look like bloody Jordan, which is *not* the look he's going for.

Tights next – Pretty Polly, the expensive ones from House of Fraser. So worth the extra cash, they're far more comfy than the supermarket ones. He has to get the extra large, else he's constantly pulling the buggers up. Another little lesson learnt. He stands with the wardrobe open for ages before selecting his trusty denim skirt and the new Warehouse purple polo neck that he got last week. It's really soft, feels gorgeous next to his skin.

Now for the proper fun part, his Saturday morning ritual – Blondie on the CD player, cup of tea on the dressing table, war-paint all lined up; like little soldiers about to go into battle.

He stares at his reflection in the mirror. Thinning blonde hair still damp, slicked back from a skinny face, pale from lack of Vitamin D. Long dull hours under factory fluorescent lighting, hidden from the sun. Hidden from the world.

David Turner, forklift driver.

He slings on loads of moisturiser – Skin Wisdom from Tesco, with its exotic blend of green tea extracts, chamomile and spring water. Then it's a luminous primer from The Body Shop, 'Glow Enhancer' this stuff's called, supposed to give you a dewy youthful glow. He needs to get some more cos it's running out. Then his Five O'Sharp Beard Cover – absolute godsend this stuff, hides a multitude of sins, especially if you're out all day and into the evening. Thankfully with him being so fair he doesn't have to lay it on that thick. It took him a few goes to get it right at first, but he's a dab hand now. He smiles to himself as he applies it to his chin and neck. If I ever get fed up with the PVCu door industry, he thinks, a glittering career in Hollywood surely awaits.

Next it's the foundation. He used to use Boots No7 Radiant Glow foundation in ivory, but then he read in the *Times Style* magazine about Dream Satin Liquid foundation by Maybelline. It was in their Top Twenty Beauty Products, so he's giving that a whirl at the moment. Gives an airbrushed finish apparently.

OK, now for the blusher; another Maybelline product, Dream Mousse Blush in plum. It's really natural and gives a good glow. Then on the cheekbones he uses this expensive but effective stuff called 'High Beam' by Benefit, which is a truly gorgeous make-up brand. They have a lovely counter in Hammonds and it's not just about the make-up, it's very much about the packaging, which is dead girly and witty. It's got a kinda vintage fifties vibe, with glam pictures of girls in sailor outfits and fifties dresses and names like 'Her Glossiness' lip gloss, 'Lust Duster' loose powder and 'Hollywood Glo' face gleamer stuff. Their philosophy is 'Make-up Is Cheaper Than Therapy', which he wholeheartedly agrees with. Anyway, the High Beam stuff basically just highlights your cheekbones and also gives more of that extra dewiness that all the girls crave.

Now it's the eyes. His eyes are his best feature, so he likes to take a bit of time with this bit. He applies some light brown eyeshadow then it's carefully on with the eyeliner. He's got this great eye pencil by Barbara Daly at Tesco. It's like a dark metallic blue called Kingfisher and it's very soft and easy to apply – some eye pencils nearly take your bloody eye out. They're sometimes too cold and the pigment of the colour doesn't seem to show. But this cheap Tesco pencil is ace. When he first started doing his own slap, he used to look like he'd put it on with a yard brush. Lindsey said he looked like Bette Davis after the funeral. But practice makes perfect, as they say. A trace of white eyeliner (brings out the brow bone), a bit of lighter foundation (brings out the cheekbones), another gulp of tea and then he gets busy with some pink eyeshadow from Mattese NYC, perfect for his pale blue eyes. According to the packaging, he now embodies the 'vibrancy and energy of New York City'. Which will obviously go down a storm in Princes Quay Shopping Centre, Kingston-upon-Hull.

Mascara; he's got a few on the go at the moment, cos he got some freebies with Boots No7. You're supposed to throw them away after three months but he never does. He's got a Boots No7 'Dream Lash', which has this weird bendy brush, and he's also got a Body Shop Super Volume mascara – both in black. Always black.

Next it's lipstick. He always uses Juicy Tube by Lancôme, evening or day. It's more of a sheer lipstick and it's dead natural. These are a bestseller for Lancôme and have become a bit of a must-have. All the make-up brands do them now but he's got the original that Lindsey gave him – it's lasted him ages, cos he doesn't use much. You don't need to. It's basically lip gloss in a little tube – his colour is raisin but this is more of a plum shade he would say.

Then it's a quick blast of perfume – currently Midnight Poison by Chrisian Dior. It's supposed to be more of a night-time scent, but he wears it during the day, cos he's such a rebel.

There – all done.

He gets his wig off its stand and adjusts it carefully on his head. Twists round on his stool, turning to face his new reflection from various angles. This is the moment when it's all worth it, all the shite and sweat and drudgery, all the boorish crap he has to put up with from them set of baboons, nine till five, Monday till Friday. This is where it all falls into place and he feels finally complete, whole, *normal*.

He looks amazing.

He feels amazing.

Fuck it, he *is* amazing.

He does his best Debbie Harry pout, and blows himself a kiss in the mirror.

Goodbye David.

Hello Denise.

Hessle Square: 10.45am

Chrissie's on her way out when Michelle gets back. She's putting her coat on in the hallway as Michelle opens the front door. Chrissie doesn't look too happy to see her.

– Have you spoken to your mother? she says.

– No, why?

– She's been trying to get hold of yer. Rang up here three times she did.

– What did she want?

– I've no idea. I told her, I said, I don't know where she is, I haven't seen her all day.

Chrissie winds a scarf round her neck, faffs about with her hair in the mirror. Shoots Michelle a look from the glass.

– I'd give her a ring if I was you, she says. – No one knew where you was.

– I told you I was off out.

– Yeah, well, you dint say you were stopping out all night. You could have been dead in a ditch for all I knew.

For fuck's sake! I'm twenty-one years old, thinks Michelle. I'm not a bloody bain.

She keeps her trap shut though, cos she is stopping in Chrissie's house after all. Besides, Michelle knows the score here. It's not her that Chrissie is pissed off with, it's her mam. They've never really got on at the best of times, but this flood business has really cranked the tension up. Basically, Michelle's mam thinks that her and Michelle's dad should move into Grandad Bill's house while he's in hospital and their house is getting done up. Michelle's dad's not said anything about this, not really, just sort of brushed the idea off, avoided the issue. But Michelle knows he thinks the same as Chrissie – that her mam's out of order. Like jumping in me father's bloody grave, Chrissie had said. And because Michelle's stopping at her house, she's caught in the middle. It's alright for their Nathan, he's at his mate's. And their Angie, she's got her own house with Carl and Ella and the other bain on the way. So it's Michelle who gets caught in the crossfire. Michelle doesn't know why she agreed to come and stop here. It's handy for the shops and buses, what with it being right on Hessle Square, but it's too close to her mam's for comfort.

– Are you off to me grandad's? Michelle asks her auntie.

– Not today I'm not, but our Nathan's going round

this afternoon. It wouldn't hurt you to pop in an'all at some point.

– I will do, says Michelle.

Chrissie gets off and Michelle starts running a bath. She makes a cuppa while she's waiting and puts her dead phone on to charge. It comes up with three missed calls from MAM and an answerphone message telling Michelle to ring her soon as she can. Michelle debates it in her head for three seconds then decides against it. Bollocks to her, she thinks, her and her sour-faced fuckin' moaning.

Then her phone beeps twice with a new text message.

It's from Darren:

U R AMAZIN

The Quadrant: 11.02am
Brian wakes up to raised voices.

Julie shouting and their Paul shouting and their Jennifer shouting.

He goes down to the front room and Paul's sat on the couch with the remote. He's flicking through the channels.

– What's up? Brian asks him. – What's going on?

Paul shrugs and flicks.

– Nowt.

Julie's in the kitchen in her dressing gown. She's stomping about like a maniac, emptying ashtrays into the bin, piling pots up and slamming 'em into the sink. Jennifer's sat at the table reading a magazine.

– Hiya Dad, she says.

Brian asks Julie what's up.

– Him, she says, pointing through to the living room.

– He's lost his bloody ring.

– What ring?

– That full sovereign your dad left him.

Oh for fuck's sake.

Brian looks at their Jennifer. – What you laughing at?

The grin's wiped off her face double quick.

– Nowt.

He goes back in the living room.

– Where's that ring gone?

Paul shrugs.

– Lost it.

– Lost it? Paul, your grandad left you that ring.

Paul frowns and points the remote at the telly.

Flick – a cartoon. Flick – a black and white film.
Flick – a footballer being interviewed.

– Where've you lost it? Brian asks, and then immediately realises what he's just said. – I mean, where did
you go last night?

– Round Fair.

– Did you go on any rides?

– A few.

Flick – some teen soap. Flick – the shopping channel.
Flick – back to the cartoon again.

Brian's gonna rive that bastard remote out of his
hand in a minute.

– Paul, that ring is worth a lot of money. It's over
fifty years old.

– I dint lose it on purpose, did I.

Julie shoots through from the kitchen, drying her
hands on a tea towel.

– He never lost it at Fair, she says, – cos he still had it on when he came home, cos our Jennifer saw him with it on! Don't tell bloody lies Paul! She flings the tea towel at him and goes stamping upstairs.

– WELL DON'T LISTEN TO HER, SHE DUNT KNOW SHIT! yells Paul.

– FUCK OFF WANKER, I SAW IT ON YER FINGER! Jennifer shouts from the kitchen.

– 'EY! BUTTON IT! Brian shouts. – THE PAIR OF YER!

They button it, the pair of 'em.

Pictures flicking on the telly. Julie banging about upstairs. Brian's heart banging about in his chest.

– I'm off out, says Jennifer and her chair scrapes back and then the back door goes.

Brian sits down on the couch next to Paul. Takes the remote off him and turns the telly off.

– Have you looked down the back of the couch?

Paul nods.

– On the floor an' right under an' all round?

Nods again.

Brian looks round the room. It's all been tidied up. All the pizza boxes gone, plates and glasses cleared away, ashtrays and saucers full of tab ends emptied. The sash window is open and the smell has gone.

– Who did you have back here?

– Just Gary an' Cookie an' that lot.

– Who's that lot?

– Just Gary, Cookie, Lee . . . that lot. They just come back for a smoke an' that. I fell asleep on the couch, an' when I woke up they'd all gone.

Lee?

Lee Allott?

If Lee Allott was here, thinks Brian, then it's odds-on his shadow was tagging along an' all. What's his name again, that ugly little smackhead bastard? Brian pelted him out of the shop a few weeks ago, a load of bacon up his jumper. Stood on the pavement outside screaming death threats before Brian chased him halfway up Prinny Ave.

Gibbo. That's it. Andrew Gibson.

– Paul, says Brian.

– What?

– Look me in the eye.

He's still staring at the telly. There's nowt there except his and Brian's reflections.

– Look me in the eye, Brian says.

Paul lifts his face up to his dad's but he's not looking at him. His eyes are wobbling up with water.

– Did you have your ring on when you came home?

– I think so, yeah.

– Was that Gibbo here?

– Yeah.

– When did they all leave?

– I dunno. Cookie an' them left about half one an' then there was just Lee an' Gibbo an' I must have fell asleep.

Brian considers this for a minute or so.

Then he says:

– Paul.

– What, says Paul.

– Did he take that ring off your finger? Did that Gibbo nick your grandad's ring?

Paul blinks, once, and looks back at the screen.

157

Water slides down onto his cheek. He wipes it away with his sleeve.

Silence.

Then a tap turned on upstairs. The sound of a bath being filled.

– Paul?

– What.

– Do you think he took it? That Gibbo?

He bites his lip and shakes his head.

– How do I know?

– Have you asked him if he's got it?

Paul laughs. But it's not a proper laugh.

– Why not? Brian says. – Are you frightened of him?

– Am I fuck.

Paul wipes his eyes with his sleeve again.

Neither of them says owt for a bit.

Then Brian stands up and slings the remote onto the couch.

Paul looks up at his dad. His eyes are red raw.

– What you gonna do?

– What do yer think I'm gunna fuckin' do? I'm gunna get yer yer ring back.

Paul turns the telly back on and Brian gets his jacket and shoes on and he leaves the house.

Boothferry Estate: 12.14pm

Easily led, that's Trevor. Always been the same. Ever since he was a bain. He's not proud of it, but it's true. He used to knock about with their Graham and all his mates, a big gang of 'em there was. If one of 'em had said put yer hand in the fire he probably would have done. He remembers one time they were all climbing up on the roof of the garages at the end of their street. Their Graham and Billy Arnold dared him to jump off onto this old Capri with a cracked windscreen that was parked in the tenfoot. So he did. Slipped and went through the windscreen. Cut all his leg to ribbons. Straight to Infirmary, twenty-eight stitches. Trevor was a big clumsy fat bugger even when he was ten. Especially when he was ten. He used to run behind 'em all bawling his eyes out whenever there was any bother and they had to give it toes. All them racing off like the clappers from a shattered window or a bonfire or a chowing neighbour. And big fat daft Trevor left to face the music. Him huffing and puffing like a bloody steam engine, the rough hand of a shopkeeper or a copper on the back of his fat little neck.

He sits around in the house for a bit and then decides to go for a pint. There's Norland at the top of First Lane or Schooner up Bethune. Might be too many familiar faces in there though.

So. Norland, then.

He'll leave the dogs in the house. They're doing his bloody head in, if truth be known. He thinks about tying 'em up outside but decides it would be a bit cruel. It's not over warm. Looks like rain, in fact. Besides, some robbing get would probably make off with 'em. Charlie especially. He's an ugly bugger, thinks Trevor, but they must be worth a bob or two, these Shar Peis.

The dogs both get up and trot to the door when they see him putting his jacket on. Charlie jams his nose right up against the front door. Jess sits there looking up at Trevor, tail thumping on the floor.

Trevor holds the door to the living room wide open.

– Go on, get back in, he says. Jess looks back into the room then up at Trevor and whimpers. Charlie leans his big daft head against the front door. Trevor tries to get his leg round him, push him backwards while he slowly opens the door, but Charlie just pushes back harder and then Jess bounds up and she tries to get out and they both get in each other's road and Trevor nearly takes Jess's snout off slamming the front door shut again.

Flaming bloody hell!

– Pair of twats! says Trevor.

He goes back in the living room and gets hided behind the door.

Bloody ridiculous, this.

After a few seconds they come trotting back through. Trevor whips back round the door behind them into the hallway and slams the door shut tight. Jess yelps. Charlie starts barking. Trevor opens the front door and regards the sky. Definitely looks like it's gonna piss it down. There's a big thick dark green jacket hung up in the hallway. Trevor swops it for his denim jacket. The dogs are still barking their heads off behind the door.

Sorry kids, thinks Trevor.

Dad's off out for a drink.

Hull city centre: 12.16pm

Any problems Denise gets during daylight hours are usually the result of staying in one place too long. If she keeps moving she can sometimes get through the day with no hassle at all. Alright, she gets the odd stare – bound to, really – but if she keeps walking quick enough she can usually stop the stares turning into comments. She can sometimes even convince herself that they're admiring glances.

But she does not dig this one little bit, stood outside Prinny Quay, done up like a dog's dinner for every little chav wanker to gawp at on their way to Maccy D's. She's stood up straight and proud with her arms folded, but that old familiar sickness is starting to swell up inside her, taking root in her belly like a poisonous flower. She feels exposed stood there on her own, exposed and vulnerable. It starts to spit rain and she retreats further into the entrance, under the big glass canopy.

Twelve o'clock on the dot they said, where the bloody hell is she, the silly little cow? Leaving her stood here freezing her arse off like some crackhead prossie on Waterhouse Lane. Probably getting Denise back for leaving her at Fair last night. Denise told her about the little lass and how she was lost and how she had to take her to the cops, how it shook her up and that, but all Lindsey was interested in was her own wounded sense of injustice. How could you leave me there, she'd whined, in that filthy bloody van. Typical Lindsey – me, me bloody me. So she's probably doing this on purpose to get her back. Probably sat in front of the telly in her dressing gown with a fag and a cup of tea, while Denise is stood here like a prick.

Bloody selfish bitch. She knows Denise is not ready to do Town during the day. Not on her own. Not without her.

This little bag of shit in a shell suit does a double take as he lopes past, his kegs halfway round his arse, knuckles virtually dragging on the floor. He nudges his mate, and they both give it the rubber neck, trying to take her in. His mate nearly walks into a bloody lamp-post, he's that enthralled. Denise looks away quick, but she hears the wolf whistle followed by some no doubt hilarious witticism that she doesn't quite catch.

Fuck off little boys. Don't look at what you can't afford.

Lindsey, where the hell are you?

There's a bus stop twenty paces away, a taxi rank beyond that. She could be home in fifteen short minutes. Back in her warm little house, safe. Out of the cold. Away from all these eyes.

She digs out her mobile and speed-dials Lindsey's number.

– *Your call is being forwarded to the . . .*

Bitch.

The number 55 swings round the corner and hisses to a stop. People get off and then people get on. Denise could be one of those people. She could get on the 55. Straight to the back, seat next to the window, head down, home. Cup of tea, bit of jam on toast, watch a DVD while the rain spatters on the window and the world outside turns without her.

She tries Lindsey again.

– *Your call is being forwarded to the . . .*

Oh you absolute fuckin' bitch.

Denise takes a couple of steps out so she can look down Carr Lane and then up Whitefriargate. She's willing Lindsey to come swanning through the crowd of shoppers, that familiar strut of hers, like she's royalty moving through her subjects. But then her stomach lurches and she thinks she's gonna puke, cos here comes another familiar face, and it's fuckin' Kenny, headcase Kenny from work. He's sauntering past Thorntons with some woman, hands in his pockets, wearing that same sneering gob that he has at work. This woman, Denise presumes it's his wife or his bird, she tugs at his sleeve and they stop to look at something in a shop window.

He's not seen Denise.

But now he's pulling his missus away and in ten seconds' time he'll walk right in front of her.

Denise spins round, heads straight through the doors and into Princes Quay. She moves quick, or as quick as she can in these shoes. Quick past the fixed smile of the woman selling life insurance, quick past the two lairy-looking young lads suited and booted at the double glazing stall and dead quick round the corner, only slowing down when she gets onto the main shopping deck.

Princes Quay: Denise hates this bloody place at the best of times, it's even worse on a Saturday. It's the usual semi-human horror show; a mindless shuffling parade of cut-price polyester sportswear and tacky cheap trinkets. Teenage lasses pushing bawling sticky-gobbed bains in second-hand prams. Dead-eyed gorillas in rugby and football shirts getting dragged up and down the escalators by their hard-faced wives and girlfriends. Sour-faced old gimmers sat on benches, stuffing their kites full of shite. Groups of young lads in baseball caps lolling about, leaning over the railings. Welcome to Hull, the Gateway to Europe. It's a shame al-Qaeda never ventured this far north, thinks Denise, we could do with a few strategically placed bombs up here. Just announce a sale on gold clowns at H Samuel, watch 'em all swarm in like a load of demented animals and then press the detonator. Ker-boom! A shower of burnt shell suits scattering softly onto the Humber. Wonderful. More fresh air for normal people.

She moves through the tide of shoppers, fixing her gaze above the heads of the cold-eyed and the curious alike. Yes, people, she thinks, I am fuckin' gorgeous. Take a bloody good look, it's the only bit of glamour you're likely to get today. Go on, feast your eyes, give your tiny little minds a treat, then go home and collapse on your DFS couches in front of *Pop Idol* or *X Factor* or whatever shite you fill your empty little heads with. Pass judgement on people you've never met while you shovel Iceland pizza and chips down your ugly little necks and then drink yourselves senseless till bedtime. I should be charging all you dreary bastards a tenner each just for the privilege of looking at me.

Denise is trying to control her breathing, but she can feel the panic rising in her chest. She keeps swallowing hard, but it's like there's summat stuck in her throat. She want a cig, desperately wants a cig, but you can't smoke in here now and anyway she hasn't got any cigs cos she doesn't smoke, she's jacked it in and she is not caving in now, no, not at the first tiny bit of pressure . . .

But this is not pressure, no pressure here, just her, Denise, out shopping, just like any other normal woman on a Saturday.

There's no decent bloody shops in this town. None for girls like her, anyway, girls who want summat a bit different. If you want standard high-street tat three months after everyone else in the UK has slung it in the charity shops, then you're laughing. But if you want a one-off piece, summat a bit individual, forget it. And if you're nearly six foot tall with size ten feet and hands like shovels then you're looking at . . .

. . . what the fuck is he looking at? That security guard? Who the fuck does he think he's . . . looking at someone beyond her, someone behind her, not her, not Denise. She glances round; some horrible little bag-heads hanging about outside Virgin. They clock the guard heading over and they melt away into the crowd. That's what she's got to do, just lose herself, be invisible, disappear . . . it's alright Denise, it's OK, no one's looking . . . keep looking . . . in . . .

. . . shops, shops, shops, get in a shop. She hovers about outside Dorothy Perkins and then New Look, but they're both too full, too many people. The assistants are hovering about near the doors, smiling at everyone as they wander in; hello how are you, need any help?

No.

Keep moving.

Then she catches sight of her reflection in Wallis's window. It stops her dead in her tracks and her stomach lurches up again. Oh shit, she thinks, I look wrong, the entire look, it's just wrong; the long blonde hair, it looks cheap, too blonde . . . me eyes, too black and heavy, I look like a fuckin' panda . . . and me face, she thinks, oh me face, it's bright bastard orange, shining like a beacon, too heavy on the foundation, oh fuck oh fuck oh no, oh . . .

. . . no. That's not you, Denise, that's just your reflection, all warped and wobbling under the lights, these horrible harsh artificial lights. It's like the Hall of Mirrors at Hull Fair, it's not really you . . .

. . . you . . .

. . . are . . .

. . . beautiful.

Move on.

She's outside River Island, looking in. It's not too crowded, just two or three people dotted around, big spaces to move about in. She can go in there, easy, no problem. There's two young lasses near the door, two assistants. They're stood yapping to each other, oblivious.

A deep breath and she's in, past the two young lasses, moving among the rails. They're playing Britney Spears dead loud through the music system and she hums along under her breath as she flicks through the clothes. She holds a couple of things up against her then puts them back. Numpty-looking tops and skirts that she wouldn't be seen dead in. She keeps her eyes on the rails as she moves around the shop.

Someone brushes past behind her, says excuse me, and Denise moves aside without looking round. Then she glances up and there's this young lass, bonny young lass with red hair, bit studenty looking. She says thank you and gives Denise a smile, no fear or aggression in her eyes, just a proper warm and genuine smile that melts the frozen ball of ice that's clenched in her belly.

A smile and a thank you and then she's turned away, heading towards Accessories. Denise wants to run after her and hug her. Instead, she watches her spinning a display case around. She's totally at ease with herself, natural grace of movement, head cocked to one side, smile still on her lips as she picks up beads and bracelets and dangles them from her fingers. Just a normal happy bonny young girl out shopping on a Saturday. And she's left Denise feeling like sunshine inside.

Denise has a look at a few more bits and bobs, but there's nothing here that she really fancies. She could do with something new for tonight though, not clothes, maybe just a bit of bling, summat cheap and cheerful – tacky even. Yeah, a daft bit of tacky tat to piss Lindsey off, the silly little cow. Thinks she can mess with Denise's head by leaving her stood on her Jack Jones in the middle of Town? Think again lady. Nowt but a posh little fag hag. A spoilt little tart from Willerby who needs to grow up and learn some manners. Thinks she knows it all, but she knows absolutely nothing. Needs a few short sharp lessons in life does that one. Well, from now on she can find someone else to play with, cos Denise has had enough of her and her stupid head games. She certainly don't need any . . .

– You alright there mate? Need any help?

A young lad at her elbow, a grinning young lad in a black glittery T-shirt and an arm full of bangles. He's got one of them stupid cockatiel hairdos, a walkie-talkie on his hip and a face full of acne. He's grinning at Denise like a village friggin' idiot.

She can feel the heat rising up her throat, her stomach bunching up in knots again.

– What . . . did you call me?

– I was just asking if you . . .

– No, what did you *call* me?

– I dint call you owt, he shrugs, – I just asked . . .

– Mate. You called me mate.

He shakes his head. – I was just . . .

– Yeah, well just don't, cos I'm not yer fuckin' mate. Alright?

His eyes go wide for a split second and then he grins that stupid fuckin' grin again. Denise is sure she's seen him before somewhere. The club mebbe. He's a fag, definitely, she thinks. She looks over his shoulder and there's another couple of snickering little idiots loitering near the paypoint. They see her looking and turn away dead quick, one of them's holding his mouth, like he's trying to stop himself laughing out loud.

– Yeah, whatever. If you need owt, gis a shout. And then the little faggy bastard winks at her and flounces back over to his mates.

Before Denise knows what she's doing she's right behind him and she's got the little cunt by the arm, spinning him back round to face her.

– WHO THE *FUCK* DO YOU THINK *YOU* ARE? EH? YOU UGLY POCKMARKED LITTLE *QUEER*!

A shower of spittle flies out her mouth and hits his face. He flinches and tries to pull away, but she's got tight hold of his arm.

– Let go of me! he says. – Get off me – *now*!

He's back-pedalling but Denise still has hold of him and she can't let go, partly because she's so fuckin' livid, but mainly because her legs have turned to water and if she leaves go of him she'll crumple onto the floor in a heap.

A young lass comes flying over and tries to get in between them.

– Excuse me! EXCUSE ME!

The three of them are wheeling around, pushing backwards and forwards knocking into rails and dragging clothes off hangers. Denise goes to clatter this lad but he ducks out of the way and she nearly catches the young lass a pearler across the chops. The lass grabs hold of Denise's hand and she loses her balance. A pair of trousers get taffled up in her feet and she goes arse over tit, dragging all three of them down with her. They send a rail over and go crashing onto the deck in a big tangle of bodies and clothes.

This kid pulls free, jumps up and stands there looking at his bare arm. There's a red mark on it from where Denise has had hold of him.

– He's marked me! Fuckin' freak's bruised all me arm!

This young lass gets to her feet. She's panting hard, her face all flushed and her top is all twisted round.

– That's enough! Liam! Go to the staffroom!

– Look at me fuckin' arm!

She points to the back of the shop.

– Staffroom! Now! I'll deal with this!

The entire shop is looking at them. Everyone, shoppers and staff, the red-haired sunshine girl, they're all stood gawping. Denise's wig's come off an'all. She scrambles about in the pile of clothes on the deck trying to find it as the queer little cockatiel-haired bastard slopes off, muttering and chuntering about claims and actual bodily harm.

– I'LL GIVE THE BASTARD ACTUAL BODILY HARM! shouts Denise, – I'LL TAKE HIS FUCKIN' UGLY ACNE-RIDDEN FACE OFF FOR HIM!

This young lass, the manageress, she's stood over

Denise, banging on about offensive language and threatening behaviour and calling the police and all the rest of it. Denise find her wig, jams it back on and turns round to face her.

– Do what you fuckin' like!

She pushes her out the road and stomps past her, out of the shop, onto the main deck. Out the corner of her eye she sees a fat bastard of a security bloke running down the escalator, yapping into his walkie-talkie. She stops, takes her shoes off and runs like fuck, weaving in between prams and bains and shoppers as she heads for the car park exit. Someone shouts something, and one young kid tries to grab her but she shoves him onto his arse and she's through the big glass double doors and onto the car park. There's a door for the stairway just after the paypoints and she crashes through it, nearly breaking her bastard neck as she leaps the concrete stairs two at a time, shoes and bag in one hand and the other hand on her head, keeping her wig in place as she bounces off the walls.

Then she's out, weaving round the barriers and racing out the car park, pelting down Roper Street, past the empty warehouses and the boarded-up buildings. A cop car zips across the end of the street so she does a sharp left down an alley and then she's in some big empty courtyard, strewn with empty lager cans, smashed vodka bottles and used johnnies. An old rusting trailer full of tyres and a load of rotting blue pallets stacked up against a wall.

Denise collapses against the pallets, clings onto 'em, presses her forehead into the damp wood, her breath coming hard and ragged. Her head feels like it's about to explode. She can feel the veins throbbing in her temples.

She throws up, two hot jets of acid, once, twice. She drops her shoes and handbag and holds her hair out the way of her mouth as the puke hits the ground between her stocking feet.

Oh Jesus fuckin' fuck . . .

She wipes her mouth and leans against the pallets, trying to get herself together. It's quiet in here. You can almost forget you're in the middle of Town, with all the cars and the people. No noise in here, except the pigeons gathered on the guttering above, and Denise below, panting and spluttering like an animal.

She feels her guts lurch again and she thinks she's gonna let another load go, so she pulls her wig off and backs away, bent over double as she starts retching. It feels like she's bringing razor blades up, it's like her chest and throat are on fuckin' fire.

Oh stop, she thinks, stop, please stop . . .

But it has stopped, and she's just dry heaving now. Just waves of empty agony lurching up from her stomach. Her mouth gaped open in a silent scream, but there's nothing left of her to come out.

Hull city centre: 12.30pm

Michelle doesn't think much to this new shopping centre. They've been hyping it up for months now, with all the artists' impressions in the paper and the promise of a twenty-first-century shopping experience and all that carry on; but now that it's opened Michelle thinks it just seems like a big fuss about fuck all. A big draughty corridor, that's all it is. Her dad says it's an eyesore, that it was thrown up in a hurry. Michelle doesn't know anything about that, all she was interested in was the shops, but they're nothing to go overboard about either. Mainly the same high-street chains that were all in the city centre before. There's a Zara and an H&M, but that's about it. The rest of the units are all just Next and Topshop and Sports Direct. All the same shite they had before, just bigger and newer. Michelle took their Ella to Build-A-Bear, which is alright if you're four. There's going to be a pictures and a Gala Bingo upstairs, so at least Michelle's mam'll get some use out of it. But as for the rest of it, Michelle can't say she's that impressed. Her and Jennie have a quick scoot round TK Maxx but there's nothing on the racks so they go to Maccy D's and have a burger.

Michelle tells Jennie about her dad and the bust pipe and all the stress about the house and her mam and her Auntie Chrissie getting on her case. Jennie tells Michelle about their Paul and how her mam is kicking off at him for losing his ring. It was some sovereign ring his grandad had given him before he died that was worth a load of money. So her mam was giving him loads this morning. Then her dad got out of bed in a right mood cos he's on nights, and then he started as well. Jennie says she's sick of all the rowing and she wants to move out and get a flat. Michelle tells her to count her in, big style. No way is she going back to her mam's after the place gets finished. Not a chance. She'd rather tow that bloody caravan away and go and live in the middle of a field.

Jennie asks her about Darren and she can tell by

Michelle's face that she's made up without her even saying a word.

– That good? she says.

– He's spot on, says Michelle. – Best lad I've met in ages.

Michelle fills Jennie in on all the details, about how he's dead laid-back and quiet and actually takes an interest in what she's got to say, unlike that other brain-dead tosser Scott the Stoner. More mature, she says, not just some daft young kid. Jennie asks if he's a good shag and Michelle tells her that's for Michelle to know and for her to never find out and Jennie laughs and says Michelle's a jammy cow.

Michelle tells Jennie about this mental bitch kicking off at Fair and Jennie says not to worry about it, Town's full of 'em and besides she's got loads of mates who'll back her up if this lass or her sister pop up out of the woodwork again, no problem.

They finish their Big Macs and have a wander round in Prinny Quay. There's a real nice top in Envy but it's nearly forty quid. A bit steep for me, says Michelle. Looks like it's gonna have to be New Look again.

As they're going up the escalator this security guard with a walkie-talkie comes flying down the other one in the opposite direction. Everyone turns round to have a gawp and this woman comes pelting out of one of the shops. There's a load of shouting and bawling and a lad gets put on his arse as she disappears through the big glass doors and out into the car park.

– Shoplifter, says Michelle.

Jennie leans out over the side of the escalator to try

and see what's going on as the stair moves them slowly upwards.

– D'yer reckon they'll catch her? she says.

– Dunno. Hefty cow wan't she? I wunt wanna get in her road.

First Lane: 12.43pm

Norland used to be Eight Bells. Trevor used to come in here sometimes with Bald Arnold and all that lot. Landlord was called Maurice, if he remembers right. Little bald feller with a 'tache. Trevor can't see him anywhere though, or anyone else he recognises. He goes through to the bar and sees one familiar face, Barry Pederson, the roofer. He's sat on his own with the paper and a pint. He glances up and for a second Trevor thinks he's recognised him, thinks he's going to say summat. But he just sort of half nods and goes back to his paper. Looks half pissed up, which would be about right. You could do half a dozen spells in the big house and the one thing you could guarantee every single time you came out would be Barry Pederson with his arse to an anchor in Norland bar, his van full of tools rusting in the car park outside.

Apart from Barry there's two kids stood at the fruit machine and another old feller with a pint of mild and that's it. Still early. Trevor gets a pint of lager and a bag of salt and vinegar crisps from the young barmaid and sits down by the window.

A bloke comes in and starts fiddling about behind the bar. Must be the new landlord. His hair's all wet and slicked back and he's got a bit of bog roll over a shaving cut on his chin. Only a young bloke, younger than Trevor. He hums a little tune as he's pottering about with the pumps.

— Picked any winners Pedro? he says to Barry.

— Nah, load of shite.

The landlord picks a remote control up from behind the bar and points it at the telly on the wall. Channel 4 racing. Trevor watches the horses pad round the track as the names come up: Irish Fantasy, Noble Boy, Fourinhand, Far Flung Shore. Trevor doesn't know what people are looking for when they pick out horses. To him, any one of 'em looks just as likely to win as the next. Or fall flat on their arses and get carted off to knacker's yard. Big bloody powerful things they are though. Barry's took his glasses off and he's looking up at the screen.

— Far Flung Shore, Trevor says to him. Barry looks over. Trevor nods at the telly. Barry looks in his paper and then back at the screen. He shakes his head.

— Nah.

Trevor puts his name up on the pool and sticks ten bob on the side of the table. One of the lads stares at him as he chalks his cue tip. He moves Trevor's money to one side when he puts the chalk back down. Trevor gets another pint in and watches the race. Noble Boy wins it, pisses it by a mile. Trevor doesn't hear Far Flung Shore's name mentioned once.

One of the lads pockets the black and Trevor gets up and takes a cue off the wall rack.

— Best of three, mate, says the lad.

— Alright.

Trevor shoves his money in and the balls come rumbling down the chute. He squats down and starts loading the triangle, arranging the balls. Then he stands up and chalks his cue.

– No, we're playing best of three mate. The lad points at himself and then his mate.

– Winner stays on innit? asks Trevor.

The lad shakes his head and takes a fifty pence piece off the table and flips it up. Trevor's fifty pence piece.

– Heads, his mate says. The lad looks at the back of his hand.

– Tails. I'll break.

He bends down to line his shot up. Trevor's still stood at the end of the table behind the triangle of balls. The lad looks up at him.

– What?

– Nowt.

Trevor sits back down. He watches 'em play for a bit then one of them pots the black and they set up and break again. Trevor gets another pint and a short in and watches 'em play another two games. Then he sups up and goes to the board, wipes his name off and walks out of the pub.

Newland Avenue: 1.23pm

Paul loved his grandad, and his grandad loved him. No, that's not right – he absolutely idolised him. My little treasure, he used to call him. Used to sit him up on his knee when they were watching telly and Paul would try and unbend his fingers, his stiff old fingers that were all gnarled up solid with rheumatism and stained yeller with baccy. Come on Muscles, try and get me rings off, he'd say to Paul and their Paul would be in

176

fits, helpless with laughter, pulling on the old man's fingers.

Brian could never really get on with the bloke. To be honest, growing up, he was petrified of him. He was alright when he first married Brian's mam, when Brian and his brothers were little. Used to bring them all goodies and toys back from sea. But as Brian got older the old man got worse and worse and by the time Brian was about eleven or twelve he used to despise the cunt. Typical fisherman, thought Brian. Always pissed up and wanting to start a row. Complete gobshite. Brian's mam, on the other hand, she was one of the loveliest women you could ever hope to meet. Never had a bad word to say about anyone that woman, and he was a complete arsehole to her was Mac. Led her an absolute dog's life he did.

Brian remembers the first time Julie came to the house down Grassington. Can't have been more than a month or so after they'd first started properly going out together. Course she'd heard all about Mac. Who hadn't? Big Bad Bobby McHarold, the bloke who battered a boat full of Danes on Dock, sparked 'em all out outside Sportsman, one after the other, and then bought 'em all a pint afterwards. Hardest bloke on Hessle Road and now the hardest bloke on Bransholme. They'd see him around, out and about when he was home from sea, usually staggering out of a pub or stood glowering in the doorway of a bookies, sucking on a tab. But Julie never clicked he was owt to do with Brian till he'd shouted and bawled at them one day when they were coming out of Centre. He come staggering out of some house with blood all down his shirt front and Brian grabbed Julie's arm tighter and hurried her on, pretending he hadn't seen or heard him.

– It's that Bobby McHarold, she said. What the hell does he want?

– That's me dad, Brian said.

And then the first time she was introduced properly they were in the back kitchen, just finished their Sunday dinner, and he comes crashing through the back door, falling all over, pissed out of his brains. Brian's mam managed to get him sat down at the table and then she got him his dinner out the oven. All dried up and ruined it was. He sat there staring at his plate. Then he looked up at Brian, then Julie.

– What the fuck you doing with him? he says to Julie. – Look at the state of the cunt. Tony fuckin' Curtis!

After that he'd call Brian Spartacus if he was there when Julie came round, which wasn't that often cos Brian usually tried to time her visits for when the old man was at sea. Fuckin' Spartacus. Mac thought it was hilarious. Used to leap up out of his chair and shout – I'm Spartacus! Just doing his best to start a row. And once he realised Brian wan't biting, he'd start abusing their mam, making some comment about her hair or her clothes, or her cooking or whatever, calling her from a pig to a dog. Just trying to get a reaction out of someone. They all used to just ignore the old bastard, but it used to make Brian's fuckin' blood boil.

One time Brian was in Nightjar on his own, just stood there playing the bandit. Mac and his old cronies were all holding court in the corner and he shouted across to Brian – Oi, Spartacus, get me a fuckin' drink! Well, by this point Brian had had enough of his constant slaver, and he'd had a good drink himself that afternoon. So Brian told him to get fucked.

All Mac's mates started laughing and winding him up and saying are you going to stand for that Mac, so then the old man's up and over, telling Brian to get the fuck outside. So Brian went outside with him and Mac starts taking his tie off, like it's Queensbury fuckin' rules or summat. Brian was half tempted to crack the old bastard there and then. But then Mac started taking his jacket off and folding it up all careful like, laying it over this little brick wall. He was that pissed he could hardly stand up, kept nearly tottering over as he's trying to fold this fuckin' scruffy old jacket up.

Brian knew there and then that he wasn't going to touch him.

The old man's stood there with his dukes up, swaying and snarling and Brian just put his fists down and stuck his chin out and said – Go on then, Mac.

He looked at Brian sort of confused for a second, then he sneered and swung one at him, but he was that pissed Brian could see it coming from the middle of next week and he just tilted his head back as it whistled past his bugle. Mac tried a couple more digs; same thing – just swiping at fresh air. And then the old man lost his rag, went to grab Brian's shirt so he could stick the nut on him, but Brian just pushed him away, not even hard like, a hand on his chest to shift him back, and the old man went falling arse over tit, backwards over this wall and cracked his head.

Brian helped him up and got him back into his

jacket, the silly old bastard. He had a big lump on the back of his loaf. They got back in the pub and Mac went and sat back down, still hurling abuse at Brian as he tried to fasten his tie back up. Brian fetched him a double rum and then nodded to his company, who were all sat there gobsmacked. And then he went back to the bar, supped up, and got off home.

Never had any bother with him after that.

Then Brian and Julie got married and soon after that his mam finally saw sense and pelted the old man out. He moved into the maisonettes on Bransholme and they never saw that much of him after that. But when Paul came along and then Jennifer, Julie said they should see their grandad. Said it wasn't fair on them. And to be fair to the old bastard, he had calmed down a bit. He was great with the bains when they were little. Brian thinks the old man could relate to bains better then he could to adults. And the bains loved him. Especially their Paul. He used to be Mac's favourite out of all the grandbains. Mebbe cos he was the first one; or more likely cos he was a lad. Their Paul used to be round there all the time. He even used to go round after they'd moved, trek all the way back over to Bransholme and go errands for his grandad, put his bets on, get him his baccy and what have yer. When he got proper badly Paul was there more than Brian, every weekend and nearly all the school holidays. And just before Mac went into the hospital with his emphysema, he got a pair of bolt croppers and cut his sovereign off his twisted old finger and told Julie to take it to Hugh Rice in Town and to get it re-soldered, re-sized and give it to their Paul.

They buried him two weeks later.

And their Paul's never had that ring off his finger since.

Brian's thinking about all this as he walks up and down Grafton Street, looking for this Gibbo lad's house. Used to piss Brian off a bit, the way their Paul thought his grandad was such a big fuckin' hero, he must admit. Paul just saw him as this funny old fucker in a busted armchair, telling him stories about deep sea fishing and dodging icebergs and thunderstorms and battering pubs full of Danish seamen. He didn't tell him about terrorising his family when he was out of his fuckin' head on rum, or batterin' his wife round the kitchen or pissin' all his money up the wall every time he came home.

But Brian never said owt. You can't shatter a bain's illusion, can you?

All Brian could get out of their Paul about this Gibbo was that he lived down Grafton Street near the Grafton Pub and he had a blanket in his window. That narrowed it down to virtually ever other shit tip down here. Scruffy street this, thinks Brian. Full of students and druggies and asylum seekers. Bins and black bags spilling out all over the pavement. Washing machines and old tellies in the front gardens. Even a busted old couch left in front of one house. Makes Brian laugh how people call East Hull, say it's run down and that, but this neck of the woods, Newland Ave, it makes Holderness Road look like North Ferriby.

There's two houses with blankets near the Grafton, one two doors down and another one another four doors down.

No answer at the first one.

Brian can hear music coming from the next house. Sounds like it's coming from up the stairs. He presses the bell a couple of times. There's no sign of life, but there's definitely music on, so he bangs like fuck for two or three minutes, his face pressed up against the glass.

Eventually a figure comes down the stairs. Brian takes a step back and this black-haired lass in a grubby white dressing gown opens the door.

– Do you have to bang so hard?

– Sorry. Is Andrew in?

– Andrew?

Music coming from up the stairs. Brian can smell strong weed. Smells like skunk.

– Andrew Gibson. Gibbo.

She shakes her head.

– Never heard of him, sorry, she says, and she shuts the door.

Brian has a wander up and down. There's a few more windows with blankets and club night posters. He bangs on the doors, but there's either no one there or he just gets knocked back. So Brian heads back home to have a wash and a lie down before he has to change into his uniform again.

Their Jennifer's in the kitchen with a tray of doner meat and chips. She tells him that her mam is across the road at a neighbour's and that Cookie has been round for their Paul and they've both gone out.

And then she tells Brian that the bloke in the kebab shop at the end of Hall Road has got their Paul's ring on.

Little Switzerland: 1.37pm

It's a decent walk from Norland down to Hessle Foreshore. When Trevor was a kid him and his mates used to walk from Gypsyville when they were twagging school. Used to seem like miles. They used to take bottles of cider and shake 'em up with a load of tablets, sup 'em in that old quarry near the bridge. Little Switzerland. Trevor can't think why they call it that. He's never been to Switzerland but he imagines it to be all clean air and fresh mountain streams. Goats and yodelling, all that lark. Not a septic lake full of newts and midges in a disused quarry. But they used to have a laugh down there and all around the foreshore.

He stops in Hessle Square and gets four cans from Kwik Save. When Trevor got old enough to start supping in pubs he'd sometimes come into Hessle Square, but there'd usually be bother with the Hessle kids and Boothferry. Makes Trevor laugh when people go on about how violent it is nowadays. It was miles worse in the eighties, he thinks. No CCTV for one thing. Hessle Square was like a bloody battlefield most Saturday nights. People getting kicked all over, glassed, the lot. Trevor was never into scrapping, not like Graham and all his mates. But more often than not Trevor would cop for it, what with him being a big daft bugger and that. Obvious target.

So he gives the Hessle Square pubs a swerve and keeps going till he gets to the top of Ferriby Road and the little footpath that takes you down into Little Switz. It's starting to rain, just spitting really, but he's boiling in this big thick jacket. Starting to sweat like a pig in fact. There's a bench at the bottom of the steps. He cracks open a tinnie and has a sit down.

They've done this place up since he was last here. It used to be all wild and overgrown but now there's proper footpaths and benches and picnic tables and signs telling you where to go and all that carry on. The signposts have all got little animals carved into 'em, badgers and squirrels and owls and that. They're a bit weird looking. Trevor wonders who did them. Probably someone on day release, repaying their debt to society.

Should have brought Charlie and Jess, thinks Trevor. They'd love it down here, all this space to run about in. He wonders if their owners ever bring them. Then he starts to feel bad about leaving them both locked up in the house. At least they've got each other though, thinks Trevor. It would have been nice to have a bit of company today, someone to talk to. He wonders if the owners would let him come back to the house and see them both again. Take them out for a walk or summat, even if it's just on park.

He practises calling out for them:

– COME ON JESS! COME ON! COME ON CHARLIE! THERE'S A GOOD LAD!

Then he remembers that it's supposed to be their Graham looking after them, not him. It would maybe cause too much bother if he turned up and announced himself as their new mate. Trevor imagines the owners opening their front door and their faces when he told them he'd been stopping in their house, drinking their cans, sleeping in their bed, playing their organ, wearing their clothes. Who the hell are you? they'd say. You weren't supposed to be here.

One of the signs says BRIDGE and points down a footpath through some trees. Trevor sups his tin and dumps it in a bin. It's starting to sling it down now. He pulls up the hood on the jacket and follows the wooden arrow down the path.

It's coming down hard now, but the trees keep most of it off. They used to kip out in here when they were kids, make shelters and light fires. Run around all night looking for ghosts, frightening each other to death. Trevor tries walking along with his eyes shut for a bit. All he can hear is the pattering of the rain above his head and the crack of branches under his feet. It's nice. Comforting. It's like being inside when really you're out.

Trevor can hear barking.

He stops dead and opens his eyes and there's this big black bugger of a dog galloping down the path towards him. It skids to a stop in front of him and they both stand there looking at each other.

– Alright boy?

The dog barks once and then wheels round and goes racing back up the path and round the bend. Trevor can hear a feller's voice and then they both appear, the black dog and him, an old feller with a cap on. He's got the dog by the collar and the lead wrapped round the other hand, one of them metal chain jobs.

– Alright?

The feller gives him a nod and walks the dog round him. The dog's straining and pulling, trying to get near Trevor, but the feller keeps a tight hold and they both disappear down the path and through the trees.

There's a pub up near the bridge. Trevor has a piss behind a bush. Then he opens another tin out of his carrier bag and pushes on.

Newland Avenue: 2.23pm

Sky telly is fuckin' shite. Ninety-odd channels of relentless boredom. Carl only got it for the football, but even that's getting completely tedious. Sixty minutes gone, Arsenal nil Bolton nil. It's like watching wood warp. On too much money, he thinks, these cunts. Hundred and twenty grand a week. You'd think they could at least pretend to take an interest in their work. That fuckin' Adebayor, he spends half the match walking around with his hands on his hips and the other half hurling himself to the deck, like an extra in a cheap western. Look at him now, rolling round like a fanny. Defender never even touched him.

– Look at this knob, he shouts through to Ange. – Grown fuckin' man.

No answer.

– ANGE!

She appears in the doorway, puts her finger to her lips. She's on the phone.

He can hear her yapping as she walks back into the kitchen.

– Yeah . . . yeah . . . yeah, alright then, Kayls . . . well, soon as possible really, I'm in all day . . . you what? . . . Oh, alright, fair enough . . . yeah, OK, tomorrow afternoon, then . . . brilliant . . . Thanks Kayleigh. Thanks love . . . you what? Michelle? No I've not seen her . . . Oh aye, yeah, I told me mam, oh too right, yeah . . . well, like I say, I knew our Michelle was seeing someone but I dint know who it was, exactly . . . oh yeah, I know . . . I know who he is now . . . well, yeah, there's no smoke without fire is there? . . . Don't know if me mam's seen our Michelle yet though, or even spoken to her . . . I don't think she wants to tell me dad, what with me grandad being so badly and that . . . oh aye, cancer, yeah . . . he's going back in on Monday . . . Oh I know . . . Alright love, ta-ra.

The ref goes in his pocket for the yellow and holds it up. But it's not for the defender. He's booked Adebayor for diving. The sullen Togo striker suddenly forgets his agonising ankle injury and leaps to his feet. The ref's surrounded by red and white shirts.

– Cockney tossers! Fuck off! Grow up!

Ange puts her head round the door.

– Stop effing and blinding. Did you find that book for the boiler?

– No. I'll look for it after this.

– Don't bother. I've got someone coming tomorrow to look at it.

– Who?

– Bloke who lives next door to Kayleigh. He's a plumber. He sorted her mam's out for her.

– I told yer I'd get Shane to sort it for us dint I?

– You've been saying that for the last two weeks. We need it sorting out now. Nearly bloody winter.

– Who does he work for?

She shrugs. – Dunno. Think he just does guvvies.

– How much does he want?

– Forty quid. Plus any parts.

– Forty quid!? What is he, a plumber on his mother's side?

187

She waddles through and stands above him with her hands on her hips.

– And what's that supposed to mean? she asks.

Is she fuckin' right or what? He turns the volume on the telly down.

– What it means is, does he know what he's doing? We don't want some cowboy fuckin' about with it do we? Make it even worse. End up paying a fortune.

– Ha! You make me piss you do! You've been sat on your arse for six weeks while we slowly freeze to death and soon as I do summat constructive, summat to get it sorted, you start moaning!

– Oh aye yeah, here we go. Now we're getting to the truth of the fuckin' matter. It's not the boiler that you're pissed off about, is it? It's the fact that I'm out of work.

– No, it's the fact that this house is like a fuckin' ice box and all you seem to care about is what time football's on or how much dope you've got left.

He looks down at the joint he's rolling.

– It's weekend. Entitled to a fuckin' smoke at weekend.

– Life's one long weekend to you Carl. And I'm telling you now, as soon as this bain comes you can pelt all that lot in the fuckin' bin, I aren't having that round a newborn baby.

– Yeah, right.

– Yeah right. You wanna sort your priorities out. Sat there moaning about paying someone to fix the boiler, you don't mind lining people's pockets for weed do yer?

– I told you, it's not the money. I just wanna know it's getting done properly.

–Yeah well, whatever. It's getting done. If we'd waited for you to sort it we'd be waiting till friggin' Christmas.

She frowns, puts one hand to her back and leans on the wall. Takes a few deep breaths.

– You alright?

– Yeah. I'm alright.

She arches her back, breathes in and then out.

– Where's Nathan got to? He's supposed to be taking Ella to Fair.

Carl just grunts. Uncle Soppy-Bollocks Nathan, he thinks, with his McFly hairdo and his drainpipe fuckin' jeans. Carl's been meaning to take Ella to Fair, but Nathan asked if he could take her. Saturday night and he's taking bains round Fair. Should be out on the piss, lad his age. Summat wrong with him.

Ange rubs her back and swears.

– Is there owt I can do? he asks her.

– Find that book, that's what you can do.

And she goes back through to the kitchen.

Fuck me, he thinks, no wonder I have to have a smoke.

He turns the sound back up on the football.

Free kick to Arsenal.

Boothferry Estate: 4.29pm

This is daft, Rose tells herself. She shouldn't be frightened of going back on the site just because of one sad old Percy Filth. Anyway, it was probably just a young kid messing about. The laptop sits looking at her on the kitchen table. What did her Malcolm used to say?

When a horse throws you off, don't mess about, get straight back on the bloody horse.

Leo's waiting for her at the side of the screen.

LEO123: alright rose? how was fair?

Yorkshire_Rose: It was fine thanks. Bit dear though! It gets dearer!

LEO123: jessica enjoy it?

Yorkshire_Rose: Oh aye, she always does. Second only to Christmas in her book.

LEO123: gd gd ... i just stayed in and watched telly, bit boring really LOL

Yorkshire_Rose: did you see that film with Richard Gere? Quite good.

LEO123: no, I watched X factor, I sky plussed it from last week. that welsh lad is a great singer

Yorkshire_Rose: I've not seen any of that

Hang on just one bloody minute . . .

Yorkshire_Rose: Leo, how do you know my granddaughter's name?

LEO123: you told me ... don't u remember?

Yorkshire_Rose: No, I wouldn't have told you that Leo. I don't give out personal information on the internet. How did you know her name?

LEO123: you told me!

Yorkshire_Rose: I did NOT tell you Leo! HOW DO YOU KNOW HER NAME?

LEO123 has left the private chat

Saturday 4.32pm

LEO123 is inviting Yorkshire_Rose to private chat

LEO123: sorry rose, got booted . . .

Yorkshire_Rose: How do you know my granddaughter's name? And DO NOT say that I told you because I DID NOT!

LEO123: ok, yes, I know, you didn't I am sorry

Yorkshire_Rose: Tell me how you know her name. WHO ARE YOU?

LEO123: somebody told me her name rose

Yorkshire_Rose: WHO?

LEO123: u wldnt believe me if I told u

Yorkshire_Rose: JUST TELL ME!

LEO123: malcolm

LEO123: rose? r u there?

LEO123: rose? hello? pls speak to me . . .

LEO123: rose?

LEO123: ROSE?!?!?!

Yorkshire_Rose: Yes, I am here.

LEO123: rose, pls don't go, i can explain everythnign . . .

Yorkshire_Rose: Who are you?

LEO123: u don't know me

Yorkshire_Rose: Well you must know me because you know my husbands name.

LEO123: no, i don't, not apart from on here . . .

Yorkshire_Rose: Did you know Malcolm?

LEO123: not while he was on this side, no. but i have spoken to him

Yorkshire_Rose: This side? What are you talking about?

LEO123: u kno the church i told u about? where I go with my mother?

191

Yorkshire_Rose: Go on . . .

LEO123: it's a spiritualist church

Yorkshire_Rose: What does that mean?

LEO123: it's a church where we practise clairvoyancy and healing through the spirit world

Yorkshire_Rose: Are you having me on?

LEO123: rose, I am a medium

Yorkshire_Rose: You mean a psychic?

LEO123: we prefer the word medium

Yorkshire_Rose: I prefer the word charlatan!

LEO123: so how did I know malcolm's name?

LEO123: rose?

Yorkshire_Rose: Because you either know me or you knew him or someone told you and if you wasn't such a bloody coward you'd tell me what your real name is instead of hiding behind a computer screen.

LEO123: ok, rose, I'm gonna tell u what my real name is and I'm also gonna tell u something else – something only you and malcolm know and then maybe u will believe me . . . ok?

LEO123: ok . . . you and malcolm went round the med on a cruise for your fortieth wedding anniversary and you both agreed that when you got back home you would renew your wedding vows at st nicholas church which is where you both got married . . . you were sat on the deck of the boat just off Majorca when you decided to do this and you were that happy you decided to get a bottle of champagne and you both got drunk and spent all night dancing and then malcolm got up with the boat band and did some frank sinatra songs ... but when you got back malcolm had a heart attack in the back garden on the sunday after and died on the way to hospital ... and four weeks after he died you found the pills he was supposed to have been taking hidden behind his shaving mirror in the bathroom he was meant to take them but they made him light headed so he never took them ...

LEO123:   rose?

Yorkshire_Rose: I'm here.

LEO123:   rose, my name is dennis jordan and I have been a medium since i was a child my mam is a medium as well and our church is the new dawn spiritualist church on matthew street, just behind the mecca bingo ...

LEO123:   rose, malcom wants to talk to you ... come to the church tonight at half past seven and you can find out for yourself

Yorkshire_Rose: I don't believe in the occult.

LEO123:   occult is just another word for hidden rose ... and things only stay hidden if you don't know where to look ... just come and have a look, that's all I ask

LEO123:   rose?

Yorkshire_Rose has left the private chat

Admiral View, Hessle High Road: 4.34pm

Their Nathan came round this dinner time to do that thing for his college project. Bill thought that when he said he was going to record him, he meant with a tape recorder, but he turned up with one of them film recorders. A video camera, y'know? He's doing a project on Hull's fishing heritage. Bill wishes he'd have said it was for the telly, he'd have got a bit spruced up like, put a clean shirt and tie on. But Nathan reckoned he wanted it to be all natural and sort of off the cuff, y'know? Informal, like. So Bill made them both a cup of tea and they sat down in the front room and Nathan set his gear up and he asked his grandad how he got started and how they carried on at sea and what it was like and all that caper.

Bill didn't really know what to tell him at first, so he just told him about his first trip. Fifteen-year-old he was, 1947, cook's assistant. They were on their way to the grounds off Bear's Island. He remembers he went out for a piss and it was blowing a gale. They were steaming at about 11 knots, sea coming onboard, y'know? And there he was, first trip away, full of seasickness and busting for a piss, trying to get across this open deck to the toilet, which was at the stern end, right next to the quadrant. Course, he was a greenhorn, had no idea how to walk across a ship, so he's slipping and sliding all over the shop. Took him about twenty minutes to get in the can and then, on the way back, she give a big lurch and a knock of water sent him arse over elbow. Well, he slid all the way back down the deck to the quadrant. Nearly disappeared into the gears, all grinding away, inches from his face, like. Fifteen-year-old Bill was. Didn't put him off though. After he got over his sickness he was up on deck every chance he got, taking it all in, like. Learning the ropes, as they say. He showed promise as well. Two trips later he was a deckie learner. Kept signing on for trips and worked his way up; deckhand, third hand, bosun, mate and then finally got his skipper's ticket in 1959. One of the youngest in Hull he was.

Nathan asked Bill to explain a working day, how the watches used to work and what the chain of command was and all that caper. The conditions they had to work under. So Bill told him best as he could, tried to make it a bit interesting, like. But there was no way of really dressing it up, y'know? It was just graft. Repetitive; that was the word that Bill used. Up to your waist in freezing cold water for eighteen hours at a time, hauling and shooting, packing all the fish away in ice, cleaning the gear, hauling and shooting again. Twenty-one-day trip. Hardly any time to eat, sleep or piss, y'know? Bill reckons on one trip he never took his trousers off for about ten days. It all sounded like a bit of a hard-luck story by today's standards, but at the time they never considered it like that. Bill supposes they were a bit restricted in their thinking, y'know?

They just got on with it.

Nathan asked his grandad if he had any regrets about going to sea. Bill said no, not really. But then Bill had a bit of a think and he told him about Dickie Smith.

It was round about this time of year. He knows it was, because Hull Fair was on, and Dickie was all keen to be getting back and taking his bains round on the last night. You tended to miss out on all that sort of caper at sea, birthdays and going out and special occasions and what have you. But the way this trip had panned out, they were gonna be home for the last night of the Fair, weather permitting. They'd not done bad on this particular trip, plenty of fish, got quite a bit of oil an'all – the cod liver, y'know? So it looked like it was going to be a good settling.

They were steaming home, about two days from dock, everything hunky-dory. All the lads were chuffed; they were going to be home for Hull Fair. Bill got in his bunk about midnight and had a read of his book for a bit, and then he bobbed off.

About four o'clock in the morning, the mate wakes him up. Says they can't find Dickie Smith.

The watch used to change over at three and Dickie was due to take over. What generally happened was Dickie would make a fresh drink of tea and take it up to the wheel, so he wasn't expected until about ten past three, quarter past, y'know? Well, it gets to about half past and the guy on watch says to his pal, where the bloody hell's Dickie with that tea, y'know? So the mate takes the wheel and they go and look for him. Looked all ends of the ship and they couldn't find a trace of him.

So of course that's when they came and woke Bill up. They had another look, but he wasn't anywhere.

Well, Bill knew there was only place he could be.

They turned the ship round and went to have a look. By this time there was a bit of a storm kicking up and a strong wind. They went back for a good few miles, spent a good few hours scouring the water for him. Sent a message to the shore station, an urgency message, y'know? Man over the side, all ships to keep a look out. But the chances were negligible, to be strictly honest about the deal.

He didn't turn up.

All Bill could think was that Dickie was carrying the tea and got hit by some water coming on board and he maybe fell and got knocked unconscious and swept over the side.

Course this was all noted in the log book and there was a big inquiry when they got ashore. Bill went to see Dickie's wife. Four little lasses she had. It was a shame. Some people reckoned she'd brought it on herself, said she'd gone and waved him off from dock. Waved her husband away to sea, as they say. But Bill reckoned that was a load of baloney. She knew better than that, course she did. Dickie had been going to sea for years.

It was just one of them things, y'know?

Bill thinks their Nathan was finding all this a bit boring like, so he spun him a few anecdotes. Sailed with some right characters over the years. And they did have some laughs. Like the time Georgie Mussel got hit by a mollie when he opened the bridge window and peered out into a snowstorm. He'd been looking on the radar and saw what he took to be another ship heading towards him. But it was snowing like a bastard so he was getting all this clutter on his reading, y'know? Georgie opened the window up and stuck his head out, trying to see ahead through all this snow and wind and shite. Course, it's dead of night so all the deck lights are blazing and they must have blinded this bloody big mollie, cos it comes spinning through the window and wraps itself round Georgie. He fair shat himself did George. Thought Old Nick had got him by the neck he did.

Mind you, says Bill, he was a comical bugger was George. Bill remembers one other time George signed up on the Arctic Corsair with his cousin Freddie. Freddie was a bad-tempered sod, not like their George. One teatime on this particular trip the cook had done a load of steaks, right nice they was, they had 'em with mashed tatie and a drop of gravy. Well of course, they had to go down to the galley in sittings, in pairs like, and George and Freddie were the last two to go down. So Georgie gets down there while Freddie's still getting a swill down and there's the last two steaks left on the table, one big 'un and a little titchy 'un. So, course, Georgie starts scoffing the big 'un. Freddie gets down and sees this and blows a bloody gasket. You rotten selfish bugger, he says! If I'd have got down first I'd have saved you the big 'un and I'd have had the little 'un. Well what you bloody moaning about then, says Georgie, you've got the little 'un!

Tickled their Nathan, that did.

Bill told him about the talent shows they used to have over the VHF when all the ships were rested up. They'd all gather round the set and fellers would take turns doing a bit of summat or other, bit of singing or what have you. Telling jokes y'know? One guy called Johnny Nelson, he used to do a bit of tap dancing. Over the airwaves, like. Course, he'd have took his boots off and was hammering 'em on the table while someone held the handset up, y'know? And then the other ship would come back and say, aye, we'll consider that, and one of their fellers would try to top it. Do a bit of juggling or summat. Daft really. But you had to do summat, says Bill, else you could go a bit barmy. Mind you, he says, I think some of 'em were half barmy to start off with.

Then they got onto the home life. Or what home life they had. Most of it, to be truthful, was spent in the pub. Used to have some good piss ups. All the old characters, like Dillinger and Alfie Mack and the Shepherdson Brothers. Some right good sessions they had.

The thing is though, as Bill tried to point out to him, they might want to know all about the fisher kids and their barmy antics now that it's all been and gone, but at the time they weren't well liked, trawlermen. A load of Flash Harrys they used to call them. Mebbe cos they liked to sling their bread about when they came back. Chuck money in the streets for the bains. And have a good drink of course. Nathan wanted to hear all about that side of things, so Bill told him a few tales. Like the time Dillinger called a taxi to Rayners to take him from the bar to the snug. He gets in the cab, it takes him ten yards round the corner. He pays the driver, gets out and goes straight in the other door of the pub to the snug. Then there was the time Wally Jackson swapped all the bains round in their prams outside Wash House and the women all went home with the wrong bains. Stuff everyone's heard a thousand times before, really, but it seemed to tickle their Nathan.

Bill thinks it's odd how they all go on about it now. Their Chrissie asked him to go and see this play with her, this thing at Spring Street about the trawlermen. A drama, y'know? Fiction, like. Some feller from London had written a play based on the ships going down, the three trawlers that got lost just after Christmas that time. Late sixties, it was. Bill remembers Madge was carrying their Joseph. Three ships lost in about the space of a week – the *Romanus*, the *Peridot* and the *Ross Cleveland*. Fifty-odd men dead. Fifty-odd widows and all them bains without their dads. Terrible business.

How the hell can they hope to turn summat like that into entertainment?

They had a couple of hours recording and then they wrapped it up. Bill made them a brew with a dram in it. He doesn't know if Nathan got the material he was after, exactly, but he seemed happy enough with how it'd all gone. He got himself off about half past three. Said he was taking Ella round Fair, Angela's bain. She'd already been once with her mam but Nathan had promised her as well, so she got to go twice.

Bill'd take her himself if he was feeling up to it. Been a few years since he went round Fair. They all say it's real dear now and all the rides are death traps. He told their Nathan to be careful, and to keep an eye on the bain and himself and Bill slipped him a few quid.

For the bain, like.

Hall Road: 5.15pm

The place is called Zandi's. It's next to the hairdressers on the arcade opposite the flats. Brian's been past it a million times, but he's never been in. He never eats kebabs these days, or any of that greasy fast food gear, on account of the old ticker. He can't say he misses it much, but he did use to like a doner after a few pints. Plenty of chilli and garlic sauce an'all.

He parks the moped up outside, takes his helmet off and goes in.

Brian clocks the feller as soon as he's through the door. There's two of 'em behind the counter, one of 'em serving and the other slicing meat off the kebab that's revolving on the spit.

And there it is, there's the ring on his right hand, the hand holding the knife. It's their Paul's, definitely. No two ways about it. His grandad's sovereign ring. Brian would know it a mile off. No ifs or buts.

The first bloke looks at him.

– Yes mate?

Brian points to the other feller.

– Need a word with your mate.

The other feller turns and looks at Brian, then looks away. Keeps slicing. The meat is falling off in long strips and he's catching it in a small metal tray.

– Alright mate, Brian says to him.

– Alright. What's up mate?

– Can we go somewhere for a quick word? asks Brian. – Won't take a minute.

– What is it?

– In the back. Like I say, won't take a minute.

The feller looks sidelong at his oppo, who just shrugs and starts shovelling chips into trays. There's two lads sat waiting on the bench in the window. One of 'em nudges the other one.

– Just say what you wanna say mate, the feller says. – Say it here.

Alright, clever cunt, thinks Brian, have it your way. Brian points to his hand.

– That ring you've got on.

– What about it?

– It belongs to my lad.

– No it don't. It belongs to me.

And the cheeky bastard puts the knife down and holds his hand up for Brian to see. Spreads his fingers wide and waggles 'em about.

– On my finger. See? Mine.

– Where d'yer get it then?

– None of your business innit mate.

And he picks up his knife, turns his back and starts slicing away again.

Brian's jaw tightens and he feels his fists clench hard round the helmet strap.

. . . one . . . two . . . three . . .

– Two doner meat and chips, says the other feller. He puts the two steaming trays on the counter. The lads get up for their grub and then turn for the door.

– Alright Bri, says one of 'em. Brian has no idea who he is. He gives him a nod, moves aside and lets 'em both pass.

They stand outside eating their chips and watching through the window.

Kebab man looks over his shoulder at Brian like he's a piece of shit.

– You want food?

– Look, Brian tells him, – I've had about five fuckin' hours' sleep an' I am not in the mood for this. That is not your ring. You bought it off a dirty little fuckin' bag-head an' he stole it off my son. It's his ring, and I want it back.

The feller just shakes his head.

– So, if you don't want food please leave.

The knife swings round and points at Brian, then the door.

– Leave, please.

. . . four . . . five . . . six . . .

A quick picture flashes up in Brian's head: Brian leaping over the counter, smashing the feller over the nut with his helmet, grabbing him by the hair and ramming his fuckin' face onto the red-hot griddle again and again and . . .

. . . *seven . . . eight . . . nine . . . ten.*

– Now, says the bloke.

Brian swallows hard.

Very fuckin' hard.

And then he turns on his heel and leaves.

Boothferry Estate: 5.45pm

Trevor's a bit arseholed by the time he gets back to the house. It takes him a few goes to get his key in the lock and when he gets into the hallway it takes him about four goes to get the wet jacket off.

There's summat up though.

He goes through into the front room and the house feels cold and there's no noise except the ticking of the clock on the mantelpiece.

Then he sees the back kitchen door's wide open.

– Oh Jesus. Oh Jesus bloody Christ.

But they're not gone; they're there, Charlie and Jess, stood in the back garden. Jess is snuffling about near the fence. Charlie's chewing a toy rubber bone he's got between his paws.

Trevor shouts at 'em both.

Jess looks up and trots over. She leaps up at him and tries to lick him, gets mud all over the front of his jumper. He doesn't chow at her though. He's relieved to see her. To see both of 'em.

– Come on then Charlie!

Charlie's not bothered.

Trevor looks down at Jess's happy barking face and

he lets her lick his cheek and mouth and he ruffles her lugs up.

– I'm pissed up, Jess, he tells her.

Princes Avenue: 7.28pm

Linnet, half seven, and Morgan's getting 'em in as Chops and Shane head off to the bogs with their little bag. It's a new gaffer in here. Looks exactly like the last one though – shaven-headed feller with the obligatory goatee and crap tats. He's put an England flag and a City flag up behind the bar. Installed some new fanny an'all, notes Carl. One of 'em looks vaguely familiar, a saucy little brunette with jacked-up tits and three inches of orange war paint. There's a blonde bit an'all, and a student-looking bird with a pierced lip. She serves the pints up and Carl gives Morgan a hand with 'em over to the table in the corner.

– She'd fuckin' get it, he says, sitting down.

Carl looks to the bar.

– What, her with the gob full of scrap metal? She'd rip the end of your cock off!

– No, silly cunt, the other one. Her with the tits.

– You mean her who Chris was shagging? says Chops. Him and Dan are back from the bogs. He slips Carl the bag under the table.

– Chris? Chris Beaumont? Morgan looks totally confused. – Are you sure?

– No, Chris, er, thingy. Deano's mate Chris, him who works for YEB.

Morgan nearly chokes on his pint.

– What, that big daft dopey cunt? Comes in here with that little kid in the baseball cap? Always on the bandit?

– Yeah, that's him. Fucked her all over.

– Fuckin' hell. I can't believe it.

Morgan looks devastated. Shane kicks Carl's foot under the table and nods at Morgan.

– Yeah, I heard about that, says Shane, his face as straight as a poker. – Apparently she's a right mucky cow an'all. Takes it all ways.

– Oh aye, yeah, says Carl. – I remember now. Deano told me all about it. That Chris and his mate got her in the works van after last orders one night. She sucked 'em both off, one after the other. Right fuckin' hooer.

Morgan is looking from Carl to Shane, his eyes like dinner plates. Carl takes a long swig of lager to hide the big grin that's creeping across his kipper.

– You're fuckin' winding me up, says Morgan. But he sounds more hopeful than certain.

Shane shrugs and sups his pint. – Fair enough.

But the seed of doubt has been sown. Morgan gazes towards the bar like a man hypnotised.

– I'm sure someone said she was seeing one of the Tylers, he says. I think she's got a bain to one of 'em.

– 'ey Carl, says Chops, – your lass must be about ready to drop by now? When's she due?

– Two weeks.

– Do you know what you're having?

– No, but if it's another lass it's going straight back.

Carl tips Shane and Chops a wink and he gets up and heads for the bogs, the bag clenched tight in his fist.

You'd have thought the new landlord would have done summat about these bogs, thinks Carl. They still fuckin' stink to high heaven. More than two sniffs in here and you're a greedy bastard. Only one of the traps has a door you can lock. The other one's hanging off its hinges.

He bolts the door behind him and does a couple of bumps off his cash card, one up each nostril. Fuck chopping lines out in here, every square inch of the gaff is drenched in either piss, puke or lager. There's a load of dotted tabs floating about in a pint pot sat upright in the pan. He stuffs the bag in his pocket, gets his cock out and fills the pint pot full of piss. The tab ends swim over the top of it and run down the sides like dirty little tadpoles.

When he gets back to the table, Morgan's still banging on about the barmaid.

– How the fuck did he manage that? And that little twat with the baseball cap? Can't believe it. Can't fuckin' fathom a bird, can yer?

He shakes his head and gazes into his pint.

– 'ere y'are, says Carl, and taps Morgan's leg under the table. Morgan's eyes light up. He takes the bag and slips off to the bogs.

The new landlord appears, with a fist full of glasses.

– These dead?

– Them two are, says Chops, and nudges a couple of empty pint pots across.

– 'ey mate, Carl says to the landlord, – can't you do summat about them bogs?

– Why, what's up with 'em?

– What's up with 'em? Have you been in 'em yet?

– Yeah, what's the problem?

– Fuckin' hell, they're not exactly, what's the word, salubrious are they?

– They're for pissing in mate. You're not supposed to hang about socialising in 'em.

– They're a fuckin' disgrace.

The landlord puts the glasses back down on the table and leans in.

– Listen, they're clean at the start of every shift. Spotless. If people treat 'em like a shithouse while we're busy serving there's not a lot I can do about it, is there?

– Why don't you have an attendant like they do at train station, chips in Shane, helpfully. The landlord stares at him.

– Yeah, I might do. Good idea, yeah. Might stop people using 'em as a bloody drugs den, eh?

– Yeah, you wanna do summat about that an'all, says Shane. – There was a syringe in the piss trough the other night.

– Yeah, I know. Don't worry. It's all in hand.

The landlord points at a notice on the wall. Big black capital letters on a piece of white A4. It's been photocopied and Blu-Tacked on virtually every pillar and post throughout the boozer:

ANYONE
CAUGHT USING OR DEALING
DRUGS IN THIS ESTABLISHMENT
WILL BE INSTANTLY BANNED.
NO WARNINGS WILL BE GIVEN.

Chops nods thoughtfully.

– Quite fuckin' right. I admire your stance mate. Someone has to stand up to this scum.

The landlord gives him a look, but Chops isn't King

of Tuesday Night Poker for fuck all. His face betrays nothing, not even a hint of a suggestion of a wind up.

He raises his glass.

– All the best.

Curt nod from the landlord, and he gathers the glasses up again.

– Hang on a minute, says Carl, – that sign says no warnings will be given.

– That's right, says the landlord, – they won't.

– Well that's a warning in itself, innit? 'Anyone caught using or dealing drugs will be banned'?

– That's right.

– Well you said no warnings will be given!

– They won't.

Fuckin' hell, thinks Carl, talk about thick. He's even thicker than the last landlord and he *was* thick. Do the brewery only employ dimwits? Carl was only winding him up, but the coke rush is kicking in now and he can't let it go. He jabs a finger at the sign.

– Well what the fuck's that then? It's a warning! What can't you understand about that?

The landlord points a fistful of glasses at Carl.

– I'll tell you what that is pal, that is zero fuckin' tolerance, that's what that is. And it applies to cheeky cunts as well. If you don't like it, sup up and fuck off. Alright?

Morgan picks this moment to arrive back from the bogs. He's sniffing like a bloodhound with a bad dose of flu. He sits down and looks round at the circle of tight-lipped grins and raised eyebrows. The landlord with his fistful of glasses, glowering above it all.

– What's up? What's going on?

Carl sups his pint and gets up.

– Come on. This place has gone right downhill. Let's fuck off.

Hull city centre: 7.50pm

It's not what Rose expected. It doesn't look much like a church, for a start. At least not from the outside. From where she's stood, it just looks like somebody's house.

At first she wasn't going to come. But then she looked the place up on the internet and she reckoned she would. It seemed public enough and safe enough, like they always stress on the site. And Rose wants to meet this Dennis Jordan character, see where he's got his info from. There's only two people in this world that knew about them pills and that's Rose and their Donna. No one else – or at least no one Rose has told. So for this Dennis Jordan to know that info, either their Donna must have told him or she's revealed it to someone they both know who's gone and told him. Whichever way it is, whoever's told him, Rose'll get the truth out of him, oh aye, don't you worry. And then she'll give him a piece of her mind. She'll tell him exactly what she thinks of him, mark her words. He won't need to be bloody psychic to work that one out.

She stands outside for what seems like an age, then she gathers herself together and gives the door a tap. No answer, so she gives it a proper good knock.

A chap eventually answers, a youngish chap, early thirties. Rose can hear singing coming from some-where behind him. He asks if she's there for the service and Rose tells him she's been invited by Dennis, Dennis Jordan. His face lights up in recognition.

– Ah, yes, of course, do come in.

He shows her through to a larger room at the back of this house or church or whatever you want to call it. There's about twenty-odd people scattered among a few rows of chairs, all sat facing a small raised floor and altar. There's a woman with long mousy-coloured hair and a tubby little chap sat up there, both of them late forties or early fifties. Everyone's singing a song, a hymn. The young feller shows Rose to a spare seat on the end of one of the middle rows, and he goes and sits at the front.

She scans all the sides of the faces she can see and the backs of the heads in front of her, but she doesn't recognise any of them. They're a mixed bunch, mainly women, pairs of women, some of them mother and daughter she would say, but one or two couples and then a nicely dressed younger lad who seems to be on his own, mid-twenties, a couple of chairs down from Rose. There's a few proper old timers here an'all, two of 'em in wheelchairs. Most of 'em don't seem to notice her, their eyes shut, lost in the song they're singing. Rose can't place what hymn it is, but it's one of them you swear you've heard before, even if you couldn't put a name to it. It sounds lovely, actually, thinks Rose, a bit like a Christmas carol, or summat you'd sing to get a bain off to sleep. She finds herself singing along, though she doesn't really know any of the words, just la la la. She does know the tune though; or seems to know it at any rate.

Rose wonders which one of 'em's Dennis Jordan? If that's his real name, that is.

The hymn murmurs to a finish and the chap behind

the altar gets up. He starts off by saying what a lovely day he's had with his grandchildren and what a gift from God they are, and he hopes they've all had a day as nice as his. Then he says summat about the weather, how it's proper Hull Fair weather and everyone has a chuckle. He then goes on to talk about the phrase 'stormy weather', about when times are difficult and people are frightened or confused and how important it is to have belief and hope, belief *in* hope even, and how that same belief can help people, heal them, by sending positive thoughts out so that people who are frightened or lonely can hear those thoughts and maybe feel less alone. He asks everyone to think about the mothers and children in the war-torn countries, and of course the families closer to home who were victims of the flood here in Hull, people here among them, he says, or people they know, friends, family, people close to them who have had their world turned upside-down. And then he asks God to lift the veil between this world and the next one, and allow their loved ones to prove to everyone that they live on after their passing. He nods at the long-haired woman and sits back down again.

This woman stands up and pours herself a glass of water out of a jug that sits on the altar. Drinks a few big gulps down and then tops it up full again.

– Thank you John, thank you very much. You'll have to excuse me everybody, I tend to drink a lot when passing on messages. So if I have to run off halfway through . . . you'll know why.

People laugh. She sends a big warm smile around the room.

– It is just water, I promise you! OK . . . well, I have a lady here with me, she walked in with me actually, and she's been nattering away non-stop and she wants me to come to you, sweetheart . . .

She points at a woman somewhere behind Rose.

– . . . yes, you in the red cardie love . . . yes, that's right.

Rose's instinct is to have a quick glance round, and see who this woman is, but for some reason she feels it isn't the right thing to do. Like it would be somehow improper, rude even. Invading on someone's private space. So Rose keeps her eyes on this medium or psychic or whatever she's meant to be and just listens.

– . . . this lady, she's an older lady . . . trouble with her joints? . . . (. . . erm . . . don't know . . .) . . . yes, she's saying her joints were hurting . . . I can feel it all in me fingers, felt it the minute I walked in . . . (. . . errr . . .) . . . this could be a long way back . . . on your father's side, she's saying . . . (oh, right . . . well . . . maybe . . .) . . . speak up love, loud and clear if you don't mind love, because the sound of your voice does help the spirit make a stronger connection sweetheart . . . (RIGHT . . .) . . . are you understanding this memory now love? She's very definite; it's her fingers, the finger joints . . . trouble with circulation . . . with her blood maybe? (. . . oh aye, her blood, yeah . . .) . . . does that makes sense love? . . . (. . . yeah, I think so, yeah . . .) . . . yes, this is the proof that she's showing me now, look . . . yes, yes ok, ok, sweetheart . . . she's showing me . . . is there someone you know who's in a bit of trouble? . . . or who thinks they might be in trouble . . . worried about something? . . . (. . . er, well, yeah . . .) . . . is it someone close to you love? . . . (. . . yes . . .)

... yes, well this lady is telling you that the person concerned will make the right decision ... so don't you get chewed up by it love, because there's nothing you can do, do you see? ... (... *yeah, I do get chewed up by things, yeah* ...) ... well don't love, she's saying don't ... this person has to find their own way ... OK? ... (... *yeah, yeah, thank you* ... *makes sense, yeah* ...) ... Well, I feel I haven't much more from this person, the energy is retreating ... yes, so I'll leave her love with you and move on ...

Another gulp of water, another big smile and her eyes are round the room again.

– Yes, the lady sat near the radiator ... no, not you love, I beg your pardon, the lady behind you with the headband on ... yes! Now, I'm being shown a load of bills spread out on a table ... can you make something of this, love? ... have you got an understanding of what this could mean? ... (... *yes, definitely, yes* ...) ...

Rose knows what her Malcolm would have made of this. He'd have said they were off their bloody heads, the lot of 'em.

The woman goes from person to person, asking them various things; boring stuff really, general chit-chat. Some of what she says strikes a chord with people, some of it falls flat. But it all seems very vague to Rose. A couple of times she seems to get on a right track and then it all gets a bit confused in the fine detail, like. But she spends a good few minutes with every person she picks out, and Rose notes that there's a genuine thank you from each and every one of them at the end. I'll leave you with their love, this woman says. Other things she comes up with seem to be bang

on the money though: a couple of names, specific inci-
dents. One couple right in front of Rose, the woman
starts talking to them about a young girl, a young girl
on the spirit side and how she's safe now and being
looked after, and the chap just bursts into tears. Hangs
his head and weeps. His wife's got tight hold of his
hand in both of hers and she's nodding away and smiling
through her own tears, yes, yes, thank you she says,
thank you. Another woman picked out is sent a message
from her sister-in-law who tells about her husband who's
apparently still a lazy bugger even on the spirit side.
They all have a good laugh about this and Rose finds
that she's laughing as well, even though she doesn't know
any of the people they're talking about, alive or dead.

She leaves their love with them.

After about half an hour of this she comes to the
lad sat a way down from Rose, the young lad on his
own. He's been sat staring at the floor throughout all
the other messages, head down, chewing away on his
thumbnail.

– The man there with the white shirt on . . .

He looks up.

– . . . yes you love . . . I'm speaking to a lady here
. . . a girl, a younger girl . . . a girl with . . . yes, OK
sweetheart, I'll tell him . . . a girl with a lot of hair, a
lot of long, curly hair . . . are you understanding this
memory love?

– No.

His head bobs back down and he's chewing away
on his fingers again.

– . . . she's someone known to yourself love, or
known to someone close to you . . .

This lad's just staring at the floor and shaking his head. All the side of his face flushing up red.

– . . . I'm seeing a different . . . it feels like a different country . . . I can feel the sun, can feel it on me face . . . a warm sun . . . she's saying Spain . . . no, Greece . . . sorry, yes love, OK, OK . . . are you understanding this memory of Greece, love? . . .

– No. Sorry but, no.

A woman sat behind him leans forward and puts a hand on his shoulder but he swats it away like it's a wasp.

– Darren, she says, this woman sat behind him, – come on Darren, love.

– Are you alright love? asks the long-haired lady on the stage, and there's kindness in her voice, genuine concern.

–Yeah, *I'm* alright, he says. But Rose thinks he looks a long way from alright. He's on the edge of his chair, rocking back and forth, arms folded up tightly across his chest. She can almost feel the anger burning off him. The atmosphere seems to chill, like he's sucking all the warmth out of the room.

The lady on the stage though, she just looks down and smiles at him.

– . . . well . . . OK . . . alright . . . we'll move on then . . . now then, I have a message for the lady . . . over there . . . yes, you love . . .

And her voice carries on floating round the room from one person to the next, offering up memories, sending messages, sharing little bits and bobs.

Leaving love all around the room.

This lad next to Rose though, he looks far from

happy, he's all chewed up about summat. Rose doesn't know whether he did understand that Greece message or whether he's maybe just been dragged along against his will, but he obviously doesn't want to be there. He looks like he's ready to spring up and bolt out the door. The woman behind him keeps trying to put a hand on him, but he won't have it. Eventually she gives up and lets him alone.

Every time a message finishes the lady on the stage scans the audience till her eyes fall on a particular face. And every time her eyes move over Rose, Rose is thinking come on then Malcolm, if you're there. I'm listening, love.

But the lady doesn't call on Rose, and then she says she's getting tired and must stop now but she's glad to have passed on so much love to those in the room and she apologises to those who didn't get a message. The tubby chap gets up and asks everyone to join him in singing the adopted hymn of the church, the one they always finish on: Eternal Father.

Rose does know this hymn, it's the one they sing for the fishermen, 'For Those in Peril on the Sea.' This is the one she had at Malcolm's funeral. Rose mouths the words along with everyone else.

— *Oh Trinity of love and power/Our brethren shield in danger's hour; From rock and tempest, fire and foe/Protect them whereso'e'er they go/Thus evermore shall rise to Thee/Glad hymns and praise from land to sea.*

The song comes to a close and she has to swallow hard to stop herself filling up. Such a beautiful hymn and they all sung it with so much . . . well, the only word is love, thinks Rose. They sung it with love. Like they really meant every single last word. Like they'd thought about what those words meant and how the strength of those words can lead to action, to help people. To heal 'em, even. They breathed life into those words, thinks Rose.

She fishes about in her handbag and gets a tissue.

– That's it, thank you so much, the chap on the stage says. – We leave you with love, every single one of you. See you on Thursday.

Everyone rises to their feet and starts to exit. The young chap sat at the front, the one who let her in, he waits for Rose at the door.

– Can I get you a cup of tea?

They go through to the front room and he gets Rose a brew and tells her his name is Paul. He asks her if it was her first time at the church and she tells him yes and he asks her if it was what she'd expected and she tells him no.

– People are often surprised. They expect flapping curtains and candlelight, or tables being raised off the floor.

– Well, Rose says, – I came here with an open mind.

He goes on to tell her about the church's history and how they got started, but Rose is only half listening. She's glancing about looking for this Dennis Jordan. Rose counted five other chaps apart from the fellow on stage, but she can only see a couple of them now. Unless the others are still in the main room. That young lad, he was off like a robber's dog as soon as all the chairs scraped back.

Paul shows her some books written by a local lady – well, not books, pamphlets really. But they're all properly bound and printed up like books. They look very professional. He says they might help Rose find some of the answers to her questions and how they helped him when he first came to the church. She asks him if he knows Dennis Jordan and he says yes he's known Dennis a long time and then he smiles and nods at someone over her shoulder.

– Hello, you must be Rose?

She turns round. A small balding chap with glasses, slightly built. Her age, or thereabouts. He's holding out a hand, which she dutifully shakes. She didn't spot him back in the other room. He must have been at the very back. He's not what Rose expected, even though she doesn't really know what she was expecting. Paul says he'll leave them to it and he disappears over to the other side of the room.

Dennis Jordan smiles. It's a nice smile, almost shy. A genuine smile.

– I am so glad you decided to come Rose. He nods at her half-empty cup. – Would you like a top up?

– I'm alright ta. Where's your mother?

– She's talking to her friends. She'll gab all night if I let her.

Rose looks across to where he indicates. A woman in a wheelchair among a small group sat round a table. She looks to be the oldest there. Must be in her eighties, late eighties. She doesn't seem to be doing any talking. In fact she looks like she's dropped off asleep.

– She used to channel, but she's getting on a bit now. It takes it out of you, you see.

– Oh aye, you said. She's a medium as well isn't she?

– She is.

– Does she still . . . hear voices?

It sounds a bit daft saying it like that, like Rose is saying she's crackers or summat. But that's the only way she can think to describe it, to sum up what she's just seen.

– Oh yes, the gift never leaves you. But like I say, she gets tired quickly now. I tend to have the most contact these days.

– How do you know my daughter? Rose asks him.

– I don't, I've never met Donna.

– Oh, but you know her name though.

– Yes. Malcolm told me.

You rehearse situations like this in your head, thinks Rose, you prepare yourself for them, but often times they don't turn out how you envisage 'em. Rose thought she'd feel anger, stood here now face to face with this man. But that's not the case. She just feels totally disarmed. This man, coming out with all this, this man who she's been happily chatting away to for the last two or three weeks but she's never met before in her life. He's not being defensive or aggressive or trying to convince her of anything. He just says these things so matter of fact, like they're discussing an old friend who they've both known for ages and not her dear husband dead of two long and lonely years, the man who Rose lived, loved and laughed with and saw go through them curtains her own self.

– So how come he never came and gave me a message tonight? Only talk through you does he?

Dennis Jordan gives her his warm and gentle smile. – Well I get the impression he's quite a shy man, isn't he? Not one for speaking in public?

Rose has a flashback to Malcolm's sixtieth, that big do they had for him in The Bosun, everyone sat down having their buffet, their Donna getting up and reading that poem she'd written about her dad and everyone cheering and clapping and then shouting speech speech at Malcolm, him waving them all away, saying he'd had too many drams. But her knowing there was more chance of the Titanic rising from the seabed than him rising from that chair and talking to all them people.

– Is he here now?

– Yes, nods Dennis Jordan, – he's here now.

Rose can feel her jaw tightening up and she swallows hard.

– No, he's not, she tells him. – He's not here.

Dennis Jordan puts his hand on her arm.

– Rose, do you remember how you felt when Malcolm first started going to sea? How you was worried sick at the thought of summat happening to him?

– Mr Jordan, I . . .

– . . . and then, after he'd done a few trips, you got used to not seeing him and if he did come into your thoughts it wouldn't be because you were frightened or thinking anything bad had happened . . . it would be because you had been reminded of him, maybe picked one of his jumpers off the floor, or . . .

– Look Mr Jordan.

– Dennis, he says.

– Dennis. Can't you see how this could be upsetting for me, someone else claiming they can talk to my husband?

– Don't you ever talk to Malcolm?

– Well . . . yes. But that's just . . . a comfort thing. He doesn't answer me back does he.

– Maybe he does but you haven't heard him.

– I see, says Rose.

But she's still not sure if she does.

There's a bit of an uncomfortable pause. Well, uncomfortable for Rose. This Dennis, he just stands there and smiles at her.

– Why do you call yourself Leo? she asks him.

– Ah, star sign. Well, Leo with Scorpio rising, but I thought that was a bit too long.

He starts to say summat else, but she interrupts him.

– Listen, there's summat I have to tell you. You might think I'm totally barmy but I need to get it off me chest. I went to Hull Fair yesterday. Well, you know that, I told you on . . . well, I told you didn't I?

He nods.

– I went to see a Gypsy. You know, one of them in the caravans on Walton Street. Me daughter egged me on, it was just a bit of fun like. But she said I'd meet a man with a gift. That's what she said.

Dennis Jordan gives a little chuckle, shakes his head.

– Well, what happens here is nothing to do with crystal balls or Gypsies, Rose. This is a church.

– Aye, I know it is, I can see that. I know that now. But it's . . . well, it's just strange, don't you think? A man with a gift. That's what she said. That's what you just said an' all.

– Well, it can sometimes be a curse too, he says and then he sees the anxiety on her face.

– Rose, it's a coincidence, nothing more. Gypsies at Hull Fair . . . well, come on. It's just a way of getting money out of people. Mumbo jumbo. It's got nothing to do with us, this church, or why you're here.

She's still not quite sure why she is there. She doesn't say this, but Dennis must have seen it written all over her.

– Look Rose, it doesn't really matter where the message comes from; it's how you act on it that counts. As long as you act out of love. And you have done, haven't you? You're here now. You're here because you want to speak to your husband, he says. – To Malcolm.

– Malcolm, she says.

They find themselves a quiet table in the corner and Dennis tells Rose about Malcolm, how he first started hearing his voice when he was talking to her on the site. How Malcolm told him he was her husband and how he'd left her so suddenly. Dennis said that Malcolm still loved her and would always love her and a love like theirs was so powerful and strong that it lasted for ever, that time didn't exist how they knew it here on earth – the earth plane, he calls it – and that Malcolm wanted her to know that he was happy where he was because he had the best time on earth with the finest wife any man could ever have hoped to have. Dennis tells her that him and Malcolm have a laugh and a joke about the old days at sea, some of the times Rose and him had over the years, and how he's so proud of the kids and of Jessica, how he can see her growing up into a lovely young lass. He says he's sorry for being such a daft bugger and not taking his tablets like the doctors told him to, but there was no pain where he was now and that his mam and dad was there with him and his older brother and some of the old pals he lost at sea. Dennis says that when he talks to Rose on the internet Malcolm is often there with him and it's like the next best thing to talking to her himself. Dennis tells Rose that Malcolm's spirit is watching over her every single minute of every single day and night and that she should never be worried or upset because she has a golden aura of love around her, wrapping her up safe and warm wherever she goes.

Dennis tells her all this and he's holding both of her hands in both of his cos she's in proper floods now, but not cos she's angry or upset any more, no. It's because she's happy.

She is so happy.

The place starts to empty, people drifting off, and Rose and Dennis get their coats on and wrap his mother up and push her chair through the streets down to the taxi rank where he wheels his mother into the big black cab. Rose waves them both off and watches them move through the traffic lights and disappear down Ferensway.

The bus home is full of young people dressed up, all yelling and bawling, all excited at the thought of the night in front of them. Rose sits at the front and watches the lights and cars flash by. It's cold and wet outside, the rain running down the steamed-up window, but she is wrapped up warm in golden love and nothing on this earth can touch her.

Princes Avenue: 8.28pm

Fuckin' Moz, he's only gone and won two hundred quid on that daft fuckin' bingo game! Someone gave him the Viennetta ice cream this dinner time and then about half six he finds the missing piece of the puzzle, the Fairy Liquid, picks it up off the deck along with a couple of decent tab ends. Result! Carol weighs him in for the two hundred sovs and he's happy as fuckin' Larry. Brian has never seen him so made up. He's amazed he's still here, thought he'd be straight in Linnet but Moz says no, he's going for the big prize, the holiday in Thailand. Says he's on a roll and it'd be daft to stop now. Anyway, he says, it's not the winning, it's the taking part. Everyone who comes out of Jackson's gets asked for a bingo card and if they want a *Big Issue*, sir, madam. His good mood seems to be rubbing off on people as well, cos he seems to be selling a few more than normal.

Brian asks Moz if he knows this Andrew Gibson and Moz asks him why and Brian's telling about what went on and what he's going to do later on, and as they're yapping this Citroën Xsara turns off Prinny Ave and pulls up next to the community centre at the top of Belvoir Street. The window comes down and a voice shouts Brian's name over this deep thumping bass. He looks across and it's full of baseball caps and smoke. The lights flash on and off.

– Hang on a minute Moz.

Cookie's in the driver's seat with that Gary Miller riding shotgun. Brian goes across and sticks his head in the window. There's four more of 'em squashed together in the back, their Paul among 'em

– Alright Bri, says Cookie. He takes a drag on the dog end of this joint and offers it across.

– No ta, says Brian. Cookie shrugs and takes another drag, flicks it out the top of the driver's window.

– What time you on here till Bri?

– Two in the morning. Why?

– We'll come an' get yer.

– Why?

– We're here for yer Bri.

– How d'yer mean?

– Go an' do that fuckin' Paki. Get your Paul's ring back.

Cookie twists round in his seat and nods at their Paul.

– Fuckin' right innit Paul? he says, and all the caps go up and down like a row of little daft nodding dogs.

Brian clocks the other faces in the back. There's Cookie's little brother in there, but he doesn't know the other two lads.

Brian tells them to leave it, but Cookie launches into this rant about mates and respect and fuckin' Pakis taking the piss. He's leaning across Gary, one hand on the wheel and jabbing his finger at Brian, telling him they can't let this fuckin' Paki cunt walk about wearing Paul's ring that his grandad gave him, this is his Grandad Mac we're talking about, and how Paul's his best mate, right, and how he respects Brian, how everyone respects Brian, right, and they can't just sit back and let this cunt take the piss. He looks half demented, his eyes bulging and his teeth grinding together. Bits of fleg flying out of his gob as he's snarling and pointing.

Charlied up. Brian can tell. They all are.

Brian reaches across and turns the stereo down.

– Right, Cookie, listen. For a start, no one's fuckin' doing anyone. Right?

– Who says?

– I fuckin' say.

– Yeah but fuck's sake, Bri.

– But fuckin' nowt. Don't be a fuckin' prick, Cookie. You go anywhere near that shop and you'll either get arrested or you'll get your fuckin' throat slashed. You stay away, do yer understand? Brian points into the back seat at the row of baseball caps. – All of yer, he says.

– Yeah but Bri, says Gary, – you can't let that Paki cunt get away with . . .

– Right, listen, Brian tells him, – for a start, he's not even a Paki, right? He's a fuckin' Turk.

One of the lads in the back laughs and starts singing under his breath – *I would rather be a Paki than a Turk* . . .

Brian leans right in and points at their Paul.

– Do you hear me Paul? Stay the fuck away. I'll deal with this. Me. Understand?

– Yeah, but Bri, he says.

Bri he calls him. Not dad. Fuckin' Bri.

. . . one . . . two . . . three . . . four . . .

– But fuck all Paul. You go near there, any of yer go near that shop and I'll be handing out fuckin' slaps. Proper ones. Understand?

He looks across at Cookie.

– Understand?

. . . five . . . six . . .

Cookie reaches under his seat and pulls out the end of a baseball bat. The handle.

– Don't worry about no knife Bri. He won't get chance to pull no fuckin' knife. He'll get this round his fuckin' head, fuckin' good style.

. . . seven . . . eight . . .

– Don't be a prick, says Brian.

. . . *nine* . . .

– What's up, says Cookie, – fuckin' scared of 'em or what?

Brian loses it completely, reaches right into the car, and gets a grip of the little bastard by the scruff of his neck. Drags him right across Gary Miller, who starts yelping.

– DON'T MAKE ME COME ON FUCKIN' TOP WITH YER COOKIE! shouts Brian. – DON'T FUCKIN' DO IT SON!

Their Paul's out the back door and he's got hold of Brian's arm.

– DAD! DAD! PACK IT IN!

Brian lets go of Cookie and shrugs their Paul off. He spins round and starts walking away.

But then he turns round and goes straight back.

He gets hold of their Paul by his shoulders.

– Don't you go anywhere near that shop! Do you understand? Do you hear me Paul?

– Yeah, but what about me grandad's ring?

– I'll get you your grandad's fuckin' ring!

He points to himself.

– Me, he says. – I'll get it.

Brian lets go of his son and walks back across the street to the shop, where Moz is doing his best to not look interested.

– Gis a cig, Moz.

– I've only got one!

– I only fuckin' want one, yer cunt.

Moz lights him up and they stand and share the cig as the Xsara does a quick gear-crunching three-point turn and wheel-spins out into the traffic and away down Prinny Ave.

Hull city centre: 9.01pm

Darren's already in Punch when Michelle gets there. He gives her a kiss and a big hug, almost crushes the life out of her. He's a bit unsteady on his feet and Michelle can smell whisky on his breath.

– How long you been here? she asks him.

– Not long, he says.

They have a couple in Punch and then go down Whitefriargate and into Old Town. They have one in Mint, one in Three Johns Scott, a couple in Barracuda, but it's mobbed in there and it's taking too long to get served, so they go across the road and into Revolution.

There's this big group of lads over in the corner. Michelle thinks she recognises one or two of them. One of them is the lad who was sat in Linnet beer garden last night. Then she sees their Angie's bloke Carl stood among them, clutching a bottle of Becks and swaying about like he's on a ship's deck in a storm. Michelle waves to him, but he just stares right through her. He looks in a right state, completely off his head. Then the lad from Linnet, Shane, Michelle thinks his name is, he sees her waving and he comes over.

– Alright, says Michelle.

– What you doing with that cunt? he says.

He points over to the bar, to Darren, who's got his back to them both, getting served.

– You what?

– Him. That Darren fuckin' Foster. You was with

228

him in Linnet last night wan't yer.

– Yeah, so? Who are you, me fuckin' dad?

– Don't you know who he is?

– Yeah course I know who he is. Why? What you on about?

– He's that cunt who murdered that lass in Greece.

Michelle bursts out laughing.

– Yeah right.

– Threw her off the balcony at the hotel.

Michelle's smiling, but she doesn't know why she's smiling. She feels herself start to freeze up inside. Shane looks totally psychotic. He's gripping the neck of his bottle like he's about to batter someone and he's leaning right into her, eyes bulging out like golf balls. His jaws are chewing away ten to the dozen and there's beads of sweat stood out on his forehead.

– Fuckin' telling yer, he says, – it was in all the papers an' that.

– The papers? What papers?

– The fuckin' paper. Murdered his bird. He got off with it an'all.

Michelle shakes her head.

– I think you've got it wrong mate.

– Ask your Angie then. That mate of hers was out there with 'em when it all happened.

– Our Angie's mate? Who?

– What do they call her, Carlie is it? Her who goes out with Mark Gladstone?

– Kayleigh?

– Kayleigh, that's the one. Gladdy battered him while they were on holiday. Telling yer, you wanna fuck him off Michelle. He's a nasty little cunt.

229

Darren comes back with the drinks. He hands Michelle a bottle of WKD and looks at her and then Shane and then back to Michelle again.

– Everything alright? he says.

– Yeah fine, she says, and then to Shane she says – Yeah anyway, cheers Shane, see yer later.

Michelle grabs Darren's arm and pulls him away, towards the door.

– What's up? he says. – Who was that?

Shane says something and Darren turns round, but Michelle keeps pulling him away.

– Come on, she says.

Michelle leads him across the road and over to Bluebell. She sits him down in the back room and tells him what Shane said and then she asks him what the fuck is going on.

– The truth, Darren, she says.

He sits there biting his thumb for a bit and then he starts. He tells her about this bird called Zoe and how a load of them all went to Zante for their holidays last June, about twelve of them there was, a load of couples and family, cousins and that, all going mad and partying every night. Michelle asks him if he knows Kayleigh and Gladdy and he says he didn't really know them before they went away but someone he knows knew them or someone this Zoe knew. Anyway, yeah, they were there as well, he says, and Michelle's heart sinks like a stone but she says go on and Darren chews his thumb and says him and this bird Zoe had an argument in some club and went back to the hotel. They were both off their heads, been drinking all day, had loads of Class As as well, and then they went back to

230

the apartment and were sat out on the balcony having a joint and he went inside for a piss and when he came out she was hung over the balcony railing, hanging on by her fingertips and he tried to grab her, pull her back up, but she let go and fell all the way down. Six or seven floors, he says. Bounced off the roof of a bar below and got run over by a car in the street. And that was it, he says. They took her off in an ambulance and she died in hospital the next morning. Internal injuries, he says. Massive internal injuries.

He says some more stuff but Michelle's not listening. It's just a noise now. After a bit he stops and just sits there, his head in his hands.

Michelle feels sick.

She feels sick to her stomach.

She tries to think of something to say.

She says, – Did you love her?

He shrugs and says something but he's got his head down and she can't hear it.

– You what? she says.

Darren looks up at her. All the colour has drained from his face. He looks utterly terrified.

– It was an accident, he says.

Michelle feels like she's going to spew. She just wants to go, get up and go, get right away from him. But as she rises up from her seat he's grabbed tight hold of her wrist.

– Michelle, wait, he says.

– Darren, let go.

– No, listen, please listen to me Michelle. I dint do owt.

He's hurting her wrist.

– Let go of me, she says.

– I hear her, Michelle, he says. – I sometimes hear her voice . . . can't sleep . . .

– Voice? Whose voice?

– . . . fuckin' nightmares . . .

She tries to pull her arm away.

– You're hurting me Darren, she says.

– Don't go . . . please Michelle. Don't go.

– Let go of me.

– Michelle, I went to a church.

– You what?

– A church . . . earlier on . . . tonight . . . me auntie wanted me to go . . . she knows this woman . . . she told her all about me . . . says she can talk to spirits . . .

– Darren, what the fuck are you on about?

– . . . dead people. She talks to dead people. She said it would help me . . .

– Darren, she says, – you're hurting me. Let go of me. Now!

He shakes his head, tears spilling down his face.

– I need someone to help me, he says.

– Now, says Michelle.

He lets go of her, scrubs his eyes and face on the sleeve of his jacket.

When he looks up she's already gone.

Hull city centre: 9.35pm

There's a line of black cabs parked up outside Revolution. Michelle goes to the front one in the queue. Her hands are trembling and it takes her three goes to get the door open. She slides into the back seat and the driver tilts the rear-view mirror.

– Where we going love?

– Hessle, she tells him. – Itlings Lane.

– Itlings, Itlings . . .

– Just before Square?

– Oh aye yeah, he says.

They move out into the traffic heading slowly down Lowgate, going past all the pubs and the pissed-up drugged-up party people in their skimpy dresses and their shirt-sleeves spilling off the pavements and out onto the road, past King Billy on his golden horse and out through the lights and right onto Castle Street, past the marina and all the boats, past the Ice Arena and the Odeon, out onto Clive Sully Way and past Arco all lit up red blue purple green and yellow, past McDonald's and B&Q, the Humber wide and cold and black and silent beside the road, the Bridge looming up in front, the red and white lights blinking high above them as the car comes off the slip road and through the new lights, past Sainsbury's, the car park vast and empty as they swing a left down towards the square, towards the place she used to live.

Muffled ringing from inside her bag on the floor between her feet. She reaches down and kills it.

She doesn't want to hear it.

She doesn't want to talk about it.

She wants to go home.

She wants her mam.

Boothferry Estate: 9.46pm

Trevor wakes up on the couch and he doesn't know why and then he realises the phone's ringing. It takes him a while to find it, down by the side of the organ.

One of them cordless jobs. He crouches down and picks it up and says hello but it keeps ringing. Then Trevor realises you have to press this little green button. He presses it and it stops ringing.

His head hurts.

– Hello?

– Trevor?

A woman's voice. Janice's voice.

– Janice?

– Is that you Trevor?

– Yeah. It's me, yeah.

Bloody bastard hell. His head's like a struck bloody gong.

– Oh, right. It dint sound like you.

There's a pause and then:

– You got there then. Everything alright? Dogs alright?

Dogs.

Trevor looks round for the dogs.

Jess is curled up in a chair asleep. Charlie's on the couch. Sleeping? Hard to tell through his gunked-up little eyes.

– Yeah, they're fine. Everyone's fine.

– What's that weird noise?

– What weird noise?

– I can hear like a weird noise. Is there summat wrong with the phone?

– Don't think so. I can hear you alright.

But she's right, there is a noise. At first Trevor thinks it's just the noise inside his head, but then he can hear it outside of his head as well. Outside of him. It's like a humming noise, a deep low drone. Like a swarm of bees.

234

Janice is talking to him but all Trevor can hear is this bastard humming.

Then he clicks what it is. He's on his hands and knees next to the organ and the bloody thing's still turned on. He drops the phone and gets up and flicks the big red switch next to the keyboard. There's half a bottle of Lamb's on top of the organ.

The noise dies down and then disappears.

Janice is still yapping away on the floor. Trevor picks her up.

– It was the organ.

– 'ey? It was the what? Are you alright Trevor? Have you had a drink?

– I'm alright. Listen, don't you worry about that wanker. Don't you worry about him.

– Trevor, what are you talking about?

– Him, that wanker. Our Graham.

She tells Trevor she's not worried about Graham and that he should forget all about it and then Trevor tells her that he'll look after her and she says she knows he will, but she doesn't understand and Trevor tells her no, he'll properly look after her, her and the bains and she says yes I know you will love, so then he tells her he loves her and then there's this massive silence on the other end of the phone.

– Janice, he says.

– I think you should go to bed Trevor. I'll give you a bell tomorrow.

Then it goes dead.

He shouts bastard and slings the phone at the couch. Trevor grabs the bottle and he staggers up to bed, a room full of barking behind him.

Itlings Lane: 9.49pm

The lights are all on at her mam's, and the front door's wide open. Michelle can hear music coming from upstairs. There's a light on in the caravan as well, but there's no one inside.

Michelle stands at the front door of the house.

– Mam, she calls. – Mam? Are yer there?

She steps into the hallway and she can see her mam in the kitchen. She's in her dressing gown and slippers, a glass of wine in one hand and a cig in the other. She's got her back to her. Michelle sees her dad's legs stretched out on the floor.

– Mam? Mam, what's happened?

Michelle goes into the kitchen. Her dad's got his head in the unit under the sink. There's a muffled banging and swearing, then he wriggles out backwards and stands up. He's panting hard and his face is streaked with sweat and dirt.

– Fuckin' bastard thing, he says.

He looks at Michelle.

– Hiya Shell, he says.

Michelle's mam turns round and clocks her. Michelle can tell she's half pissed. She looks at Michelle for a second and starts to say something but then turns back to address her dad.

– Is it sorted now? she says.

– Aye, should be, now, he says. – Fuckin' thing.

– So can I have me bath now?

– You can when I put the water on.

– Well go on, gerrit on then.

– I will do, hang on.

Michelle's dad picks a can of Stella up off the draining

board, tips his head back and belts it down in two long hard gulps. There's a load of empty cans plus half a bottle of white wine and two other empty bottles. Her dad belches, crumples the can up and chucks it into the sink.

– D'yer wanna drink Shell? he says.

– I do yeah, ta.

He cracks another two cans open, hands her one over.

– Right, he says. And he goes down the hallway and out the front door. Michelle's mam drops her tab end into one of the empty cans, reaches into her dressing gown pocket for her packet and taps another cig out.

– Mam, Michelle says.

– I wanted to fuckin' go out, says her mam.

She fires her fag up, exhales, looks at Michelle again, like she's just realised she's stood there.

– What you doing here anyhow? she says.

Before Michelle can answer, her dad comes back into the kitchen. He turns both taps full on. There's a judder and a gurgling from somewhere down below and then water starts spluttering out of one then both of the taps. Three seconds later it's a raging torrent, bouncing up off the bottom of the sink and spraying all the draining board.

– Fuckin' hallelujah, says Michelle's mam. – Get that boiler on.

Then there's two big bangs from right under the sink. They all look at each other.

– That dint sound good, says Michelle.

Her dad kneels down, opens the cupboard door and peers in.

– Oh for fuck's sake, he says.

He reaches his hand in and then suddenly pulls it out again, like he's been bitten by a snake. A jet of water comes pissing out from under the sink, hits him square in the chest and he's shouting and swearing, scrambling backwards and falling flat on his arse.

Michelle's mam goes mental:

– OH I DON'T BELIEVE IT! I DON'T FUCKIN' BELIEVE IT! DO SUMMAT! JOE! DO SUMMAT!

Michelle's dad gets to his feet, drenched, and pelts outside.

The water's just pissing out. A small lake forms on the kitchen floor, moving slowly out from under the unit. Michelle and her mam take a few steps backwards as it comes towards their feet.

– JOE! screams Michelle's mam.

– FUCKIN' HANG ON! shouts Michelle's dad from outside.

The jet of water slows down, falls away to a dribble and then stops.

– BASTARD SHITTING CUNTING HELL!

Michelle's mam kicks at the puddle of water and throws her wine glass at the wall. It shatters, glass all over the floor, a dark stain slapped up the freshly dried plaster.

– Mam, says Michelle. – Mam, please, don't.

Michelle's mam bursts into tears and sinks to her knees, slowly curls up on the floor, hugging herself to her chest. She's sobbing and wailing like a bain.

– I CAN'T STAND ANY MORE OF THIS! IT'S RELENTLESS, SHELL! IT'S JUST FUCKIN ...RELENTLESS ...

Michelle's straight down to her, cradling her mam in her arms, rocking her and shushing her, stroking her hair and trying to make it all better while the water creeps slowly around them, seeping under Michelle's knees and soaking her mam's dressing gown.

– I know it is Mam, says Michelle. – I know it is. But it won't be for ever. I promise yer.

– It seems like it Shell, says her mam. – It seems like for ever.

Princes Avenue: 11.50pm

Respect. It's a word Brian hears a lot these days; mostly from the youth, kids like their Paul and their Jennifer and all their daft mates and the kids he pelts out of here. And they hear it off the telly and on DVDs and records and out of the mouths of every half-baked plazzy gangster who sits in the back room of the pub bragging about their petty little moves and dealings.

Respect, thinks Brian.

They don't know the fuckin' meaning of the word.

He's still fuming about their Paul and Cookie and their dopey little vigilante mob when the first lot of piss-heads come swaggering over from Linnet. They come barging down the aisle, knocking stuff off the shelves and generally acting the cunt.

– Bastards, says little Dougie. – Took me ages, them cornflakes.

Brian follows 'em down the aisle and up the next one. They head for the fridges where they keep the beer, which are all shuttered up. One of 'em, this little wanker in a Stone Island jumper, he starts banging on the metal shutters.

– Fuck's going on then, he says. – Where's the fuckin'
ale?

– Past eleven mate, Brian tells him. – All finished.

He turns round and looks Brian up and down.

– Who the fuck do you think you are, you?

. . . one . . . two . . . three . . .

Brian grabs the bastard by the jumper and slams him
up against the shutters. The lad's head bounces off the
metal. Brian's nose right up close to the lad's sneering
face. Hot breath through clenched teeth.

– Me? he whispers. – I'm fuckin' Spartacus.

Fuck it.

Fuck it.

Brian lets go of the lad and goes through to the
back and gets his coat and his waterproofs and his
helmet. Carol is in her little office looking through
some files. She looks up from behind the perspex
window as Brian's getting into his gear.

– What's up?

– Everything, he tells her. – Everything's fuckin' up.

– Where you going?

– Won't be long.

– Brian, you can't just take off when you feel like
it . . . Brian!

And she's up and out of her little office.

– BRIAN! BRIAN! YOU'RE NOT ON! I'M
GONNA HAVE TO CALL LOCKINGS, YOU
KNOW.

– CALL THE CUNTS THEN, he yells over his
shoulder, as he starts wheeling his moped out the back
door.

There's a bottle of rum in the caravan. Michelle's mam has got dressed and her and Michelle's dad and Michelle sit cramped up and close together, getting pissed and listening to the radio.

– Our Angie told me about that lad, that Darren, her mam says. – I tried ringing you up, but there was no answer.

– I know, it's alright Mam, it's all sorted.

– I don't want you anywhere near him, says her dad. – Do you hear me, Shell?

–You don't have to worry on that score, says Michelle.

–Yeah, well if he comes anywhere near you I'll break his bastard neck, he says.

Michelle laughs, but it's not a proper laugh.

– I mean it, he says. – Break his bastard neck I will.

– He won't be coming anywhere near me, says Michelle. – Honest. Don't worry about it Dad.

– He dunt know where you live does he? asks Michelle's mam.

Michelle starts to say summat, but then shakes her head.

– No, she says.

– Are you sure?

– I'm sure, she says, and Michelle picks up the bottle of rum and gives them all a top up. – I told him you were living in a caravan, she says, – but that's about it. No shortage of them round here, is there?

– He's been inside you know, says her mam. – Did you know that? Bet you dint know that did yer? Been in jail for violence.

– I dint know that, says Michelle.

– Aye, our Angie told me, says her mam.

None of them say anything for a bit.

– We do worry about you Shell, says Michelle's mam. – We worry about all of yer, all our bains. I know we ant had a lot of time for you and our Nathan lately, but it's been nowt but stress, what with one thing and another.

– It's alright, Mam, she says.

Michelle didn't tell him where she was living. Not exactly. She just said her auntie's off Hessle Square. She's sure she didn't tell him what street. Almost certainly sure she didn't tell him that.

Michelle's dad says, – Wait till I get my hands on them fuckin' builders.

Michelle sups her rum and looks out of the window. The skip full of their old kitchen lit up underneath the street lamp. Michelle can see the rain coming down hard in the halo of yellow light.

She still feels a bit sick, but she'll be alright. She'll sleep here, in the caravan, with the rain on the roof, just like when she was little and they all went to Reighton Gap on their holidays. She'll get up tomorrow and she'll be fine.

There's a dull ache deep inside, gnawing away at her. She puts one hand on her belly and presses hard. There's nothing in there, she tells herself. It's all in me head. It's just the shock of it all.

That and the drink.

That's all it is.

Hull city centre: 11.52pm

. . . round Town, a few more pubs in Town, bag of charlie long gone, big dab of MDMA then another one and then

another one just for luck and they're moving through the streets of Town now, big crowd of them, who's this lot, Carl doesn't know hardly any of this lot, a couple of spliffs lit and passed around as the rain starts to come down in a fine driving mist, the pavement under his feet and the orange and yellow lights above his head as they're going past their reflections in shop-front glass and the pubs thumping with people and noise and . . .

. . . then they're outside another place, purple light above the door, MDMA rushes kicking in big-style now, massive belts of sickness coming up from his shoes, up the back of his legs, shuddering through him, gasping for air, leant up against the purple lit brick wall outside this place, black bomber jacket on the door, arm held out, small hard blue eyes boring into him, fuck that, going in, need to get in, a hand on his shoulder, then Shane in front of him, Shane and the black bomber jacket, all smiles, summat about Hull City, Boothferry Park and Lincoln away and then back slaps all round, they're in, we're going in, digging the money out his front pocket, past a lass, through a black curtain and in . . .

. . . to hot, hot and dark, red and gold light on dark walls, blokes in dark suits and pink faces and brown faces and red and gold faces, loose laughing mouths, loosened ties, music, thumping R&B and oh look there's . . .

. . . a bird up on the stage and she's the wrong way up, she's upside-down, legs wrapped round a pole, sliding slowly down, upside-down, all her hair hung down, hands on her tits, holding her tits and her flat golden belly and the beat, the beat goes thud thud thud deep in his guts, deep breaths, breath deep, don't spew don't spew don't . . .

. . . doncha wish your girlfriend was hot . . .

. . . in here, too hot, someone up at the bar, Chops up at

the bar shouting and waving his money about, what do you want he yells, Carl, lager, he's shouting from underwater, his big sweaty face in Carl's face, Carl, laaaaager, nod, yeah, yeah, this will pass, this will pass this . . .

. . . lass on the pole, the right way up now, arching backwards, one hand on the pole, one hand pulling on her nipples, circle of faces below her gawping up at her, he can't look, he can't look anywhere, eyes can't rest, everywhere he looks there's . . .

. . . lasses draped all round the edges of the room, in short skirts, in underwear, hanging onto blokes, stood in pairs, sat in groups, legs crossed, arms folded, handbags by their hips, spike heels dangling, tits, legs, bare arses, blonde hair and dark hair and red hair and made-up mouths and made-up eyes and staring, staring, don't stare, don't stare, don't . . .

. . . doncha wish your girlfriend was hot like . . .

. . . summat ice cold pressed into his hand, bottle of Becks, label wet and peeling, another wave of nausea, another deep breath another, it's too hot, too hot, he needs to take this . . .

. . . off for a piss, bumping and barging through bodies, tripping over carpet, feeling along the walls, sign, show him the sign, where's the . . .

. . . light, harsh cold white light, cold hard white tiles, lean over the trough, forehead pressed against a poster, DON'T DRINK AND DRIVE, a never-ending piss . . . dick dead and heavy in his hands, pissing, pissing, piss . . .

. . . splashing, splashing his face with water, cold water, staring at his eyeballs in the mirror, dark saucers, this MDMA belting through him like a train, he's rushing, he's . . .

. . . Fucked, mate, he says, you what, a bloke next to him in the mirror, washing his hands, shaking his hands, shaking

244

his head and then laughing, walking away in the mirror, the shriek of the hand dryer starting up behind him, waiting, waiting with his head on the wall till the shrieking stops and the dull thump outside swells up again as he opens the door and he'll . . .

. . . be alright, be alright, get back out there, get his arse to an anchor, his back to a wall, his . . .

. . . feet under the table, slide into a seat, a different lass up on the pole, tall skinny blonde lass, pink feather boa wrapped round her shoulders, can't see the rest, can't stand up, legs like lead, can't move, don't want to move, don't stand up, stay still, stay . . .

. . . still rushing, not as bad now, slowing down now, no . . .

. . . more big seasick waves smashing him around, just a gentle . . .

. . . lapping, a . . .

. . . warm steady . . .

. . . flow, it's . . .

. . . nice and cool, and

. . . then . . .

. . . heat . . .

. . . against his leg, and . . .

. . . a sudden bitter-sweet scent and . . .

. . . there's a . . .

. . . lass sat down next to him, leg pressed up tight against his, a lass dressed up as a nurse and she's sat right up close next to him, her hand on his arm, her big brown eyes smiling into his, Jesus fuckin' Christ, look at that, transfixed, hypnotised, beautiful, she is beautiful, she is proper proper gorgeous, he is staring down into the face of an angel, dark shoulder-length hair, heart-shaped face, the perfect line

of her jaw, that little gorgeous snub nose, oh look at them big full lips, lips painted pale pink, and them eyes, eyes all painted dark, like pools of melted chocolate, oh look at you look at you look at . . .

. . . you OK baby she says, he's nodding, her hand on his forehead, sweating she says, she pushes the hair out of his eyes, straightens his collar, better, she says, nods again, can't stop looking, don't stare, it's rude to stare, she leans into him and she's spilling out of that tight shiny white PVC, her tits pushed together and her smell oh Christ she smells like heaven, her lips, her mouth, her . . .

. . . name is Anna or Anya and his is Carl, you been here before, no, yes, don't know, smile, you like a private dance, oh fuck, oh yeah, oh no, in a minute, wait, hang on, just having a drink, she smiles, you don't have a drink, look down, no drink in his . . .

. . . hand, she's got hold of his hand and she's standing up and walking him across the floor, she pulls a curtain back, leads him through, they're in a tiny space, a tiny dark space, dim light, the beat, thump thump thump, that's his heart, thump thump thump and she turns round to face him and he's stood right over her and she's smiling and holding something out, she's holding open a little gold bag and there's money inside and she's asking him for money and he digs some folded-up paper out of his pocket, the queen's head, can't unfold it, how much, can't make it out, fingers fat and clumsy, hold it all up to show her, she peels one off and puts in her bag, throws it on the floor, a hand on each shoulder, pushes him down and down he goes, sat down, knees pushed apart and she's standing between them and moving, swaying, her hands on his chest, moving down to his hips, smiling, looking right into his eyes, right into him, and now her hands

246

wandering all over herself, slowly unzipping that white PVC, one foot up on the seat, the back of her leg, the curve of her tight little arse six inches above his hand and oh christ, her hands again, one hand slowly rubbing her brown flat belly all the way up to her bra and then wriggling out of that white tunic, she's turning round and slowly bending over, a hand reaching up between her legs and pulling aside . . .

. . . the curtain and then CRACK! he's up on his feet and he's spun around and his arm is jammed up against his back and his face is on fire and his head is ringing and BANG! BANG! BANG! he's being clattered round the back of the head again and again as he's pushed through the curtain and there's hot snarling breath on his neck, and then the cold rain on his face as a door is booted open and he's flung into the outside and he bounces off a wall and onto his hands and knees, his head pulled back and the eyes staring down into his are small and hard and blue and they're the last two things he sees before everything goes black . . .

Princes Avenue / Hall Road: 11.53pm

Brian gets out onto the pavement and fastens his helmet on. Moz is stood there gawping at him.

– Fuck are you looking at, Brian says to him.

– You alright, Bri?

– Never better Moz, says Brian, and he kicks the moped off, twists the throttle and inches out onto the road, looking for a break in the traffic.

Moz picks his bag of *Big Issue*s up, slings them over his shoulder and comes trotting over.

– Are you gunna go an' do it now Bri?

– Yeah. Won't be long.

A taxi slows down to let a load of lasses out and Brian moves out onto the road as the gap in the traffic appears. As he twists and goes, he feels this weight sink down behind him and two arms wrap around his waist. He nearly cockles the bastard bike over. Brian twists his head round and there's Moz clinging on behind him.

– Moz, what the fuck are you doing?

– I'm coming with yer Bri.

– Don't be fuckin' stupid, get off.

– You aren't going on yer own. Besides, I owe you one don't I?

– Fuck's sake. Hang on then.

So Brian zips down Princes Avenue with this mad ex-smackhead bingo-card-collecting tramp on the back of his moped. An ex-smackhead bingo-card-collecting tramp with no fuckin' helmet. He whips down the first of the Avenues, reckoning to keep off the main roads. Moz is hanging on like a limpet as they shoot down the backstreets and tenfoots till they get to the end of Hall Road. They bomb down to the flats and pull up opposite the arcade.

Brian parks the moped up just as the police car is pulling away.

At first Brian thinks they're too late cos the front window has been put in. There's glass all over the pavement and inside the shop. A young Turkish lad sweeping all the debris up. The main man behind the counter on his mobile, one hand resting on the counter, right next to this big machete. He's still got the ring on.

Fuckin' Cookie, thinks Brian. What a fuckin' muppet. Probably took one look at that blade and shat himself.

The young lad looks up as Brian and Moz step inside, glass crunching under their feet.

– We are closed, he says.

The man behind the counter looks up and sees Brian.

– I call you back, he says, and shuts his phone off.

– What do you want? he says to Brian.

His fingers close round the handle of the machete.

– We are closed. What do you want?

– You know full well what I want mate, says Brian.

– I am sick of this, the Turkish bloke says. – I am sick of it! And he picks the machete up and swings the counter flap open.

Brian has a quick glance behind. The lad with the brush has shat it, he's edging towards the door. No danger there.

Brian takes one step forward.

. . . one . . . two . . . three . . .

– What you gonna do with that then?

The Turk points the machete.

– Leave! Leave now!

– Or else what? You gonna cut me are yer? Come on then, silly cunt!

. . . four . . . five . . . six . . .

Beads of sweat on the Turk's forehead. Brian's knuckles wrapped around the strap of his helmet. The blade waving around in the space between them.

– You ant got the fucking balls mate, says Brian.

. . . seven . . . eight . . . nine . . .

– You bag of shit, says the Turk, and he moves to close the gap between them.

– Alright, mate, goes Moz, – fuckin' hell, alright!

He pulls a roll of money out his pocket and steps between the two men. A cylinder of ten-pound notes bound with an elastic band. Holds it up for the Turk to see. The man stops dead in his tracks and looks from Moz to Brian to the money.

– How much did you pay for the ring? says Moz.

– Moz, says Brian, – there's no need . . .

– Fuck it, Bri, it's alright, honest.

Moz slips the band off the roll and fans out the notes.

– Come on, he says, – how much?

The Turk shrugs.

– Eighty pounds.

Moz peels off eight tenners, slaps 'em on the counter.

– There y'are. Eighty quid, yeah? Now give him his fuckin' ring back.

The Turk picks the notes up and counts them, sticks them in his back pocket.

– And for my window?

– Fuck's sake, says Moz.

He peels another five off and puts 'em down.

– And that's yer lot. Alright?

The Turk shrugs.

– OK.

And he puts the machete down on the counter. Pulls the ring off and lobs it across to Moz, who passes it to Brian.

Brian slips his stepdad's sovereign ring onto his little finger and holds it up so it catches the light.

It's heavy. Proper heavy. Brian never realised before how heavy it was. He makes a fist and holds it up to Moz.

– What d'yer reckon? he asks him.

Moz grins.

– Bargain, he says.

Sunday 21 October

Hull city centre: 12.01am

They spill out from Propaganda and strut across to the club like a pride of glittering peacocks, their heels click-clacking on the shiny wet road. It has to be said, she looks absolutely stunning. All the girls who go to Fuel make a special effort on a Saturday night, but tonight Denise is without doubt the jewel in the crown – full-length gold lamé dress, white fox-fur stole, six-inch spikes and a cheeky little diamanté tiara. She's had a pill and there's another one in her purse for after. She feels about fifty foot tall and it's only going to get better. Nothing matters now, not the shitty day she's just had or the shitty week she'll be having starting Monday. All that matters is the here and now.

Saturday night – it's what she lives for.

Hull city centre: 2.04am

Mick's on his way back to his flat when the job comes in on the head: North Bransholme, going to Hessle. Worth a tenner at least. Mebbe more if they're pissed up. Which they probably will be, this time of the morning, oh aye. Mick accepts the job and spins the car round on Freetown Way, points it back over the river. The clock on the dash says 2.04. Not been a bad night. Most of the clubs have chucked out now, most of the ones in the city centre anyroad. Last job, then he'll turn it in.

He guns the motor back up the dual carriageway, turns Lincs FM up. He prefers it to the other stations, all that headbanging stuff they play. Same three bastard songs they play an'all, over and over again. Does Mick's head in. He either has Lincs on or Magic or just plays his CDs – Johnny Cash, Waylon Jennings, Merle Haggard, oh aye. The classics. Can't beat a bit of Some Cunt From Preston. Cracked that one to three pissed-up young lads he took back to Orchard earlier. Come out of that Welly Club they did, so they'd have been full of all that thumping bang-bang-bang shite. Full of bloody tablets they were. Mick can always tell. Eyes like headlamps, all of 'em chewing and yapping ten to the dozen. – What's this fuckin' shite, Drive? one cheeky little twat says. – Some Cunt From Preston, Mick told him. Whoosh, straight over his fuckin' head.

Doing nights in this job, ninety per cent of people are fine. No problem whatsoever. They just wanna get home. It's the other ten per cent who are the pain in the arse – slinging abuse, puking up, pissing thersens, shitting thersens. Fucking off without paying. And the lads are even worse. You get to know, though, oh aye. You get to know the balloon heads and where they go drinking and you give 'em a wide berth. Problem with most of 'em, they work all week in a fuckin' job they hate and then it gets to the weekend and they wanna prove a point to someone. Wanna assert themselves in some way don't they? Oh aye.

Like this silly bastard here, reeling about in the gutter, kebab in one hand, waving his other arm into the road.

Mick whips round him and gives him a blast of the horn. Gerrout the way, silly cunt! He recedes in the rear-view, angry little dancing feller in a white shirt. No jacket. Must be fuckin' freezing. Good. Mick hopes the daft bastard lives in Beverley.

He gets onto Bransholme, past Northpoint shopping centre, onto Bransholme North and slows right down as he turns down Saddleworth. It's totally deserted, just a few house lights dotted about here and there. He winds his window down and flashes his lamp slowly over the doors: 32, 34, 36 . . . two of 'em without numbers.

Here we go, 44.

All the lights are off.

Mick kills the lamp and winds the window back up. Two quick bibs on the horn. No way he's getting out the car, not round here. Some of the drivers he knows won't even come up North Bransholme after dark. One lad on the firm, young Shane, he got his head belted in and his bag took on here, not that long ago either. Dropped a job off, three of 'em, one of 'em a lass, and they'd put all their bags in the boot. Asked Shane to open it up so they could get the lass's purse out and square up, and then they pulled a fuckin' lead cosh from this holdall and battered him all over his car. This was at half six in the evening an'all, fuckin' teatime. Some fuckin' wrong 'uns round here. Shame – used to be lovely when they first built it, back in the early seventies, oh aye. Nice place to live. All them green fields. Now the fuckin' window cleaner uses a sander.

Number 44 opens up at the third lean on the horn.

Young lad, probably late twenties. He's got a short-sleeved white shirt on and slacks, shoes, best bib and tucker. Looks like he's just got in from going out. He goes to the back door, tries it, taps on the window and Mick realises he's got the central locking on.

Mick clocks him in the wing mirror. Definitely on his Jack Jones. He flicks the central and the lad gets in. Mick rearranges the rear-view mirror so he can see him.

– Where to my mate?

– Hessle Square.

– Okey doke.

Mick does a three pointer and spins it back out towards the main road. He can do Hessle from here in about fifteen minutes at this time of night, less if he gets a pelt on. He turns the radio down a touch, glances in the mirror. The lad's leant back, chewing on his thumbnail, staring out the window.

– Been round Town mate?

No answer. Mebbe he's a bit mutton. Probably just pissed up. Mick flicks the radio off and puts the CD player on. Hank Williams. Marvellous. Can't beat a bit of Ham Shank, oh aye.

– What?

Oh hello, thinks Mick, he speaks.

– Have yer been round Town?

– Yeah.

– Bit dead wannit? I was on me way home till I got your job. Mind you, week before pay day. Always a bit quiet, like.

– Yeah, he goes, but Mick can tell he's not feeling too sociable. Suits him. He's had people in his fuckin' tab all night. Nowt worse than some lairy cunt pissed up in the back when you're stone cold sober. Last job, he took these four lads back home from Fair, top of Walton Street onto Willerby Road and would they fuck shut up. Singing, shouting, fuckin' arguing. Kept him waiting for about fifteen fuckin' minutes outside the 24-hour Tesco an'all while they loaded up on cigs and goodies. And then, when they'd pulled up outside the house, the cheeky cunts tried to have a fuckin' debate about the fare. Mick just opened the doors and told 'em to sling their fuckin' hooks. He knows where they live though. Well, one of 'em at any rate. A dish best served cold and all that.

They get to the roundabout at the top of Stoneferry and me laddo in the back leans forward and he says:

– Can you go through Town?

– Eh? I thought you wanted to go to Hessle?

– Yeah, but just go through Town.

– Be quicker to go straight out and down Clive Sully.

– I wanna go through Town.

Mick shrugs.

– You're the boss, boss, he tells him.

This is all Mick fuckin' needs at this time of night, a tour of Hull with a fuckin' mute. What's he wanna go round Town for? Look at all the pretty lights? Must be looking for someone. Mick bets it's a bird. Bound to be. Probably had some barney while they've been out and he's fucked off home early in a mood, been sat there working himself up into a frenzy and now he's looking to drag her back home. Must have a screw loose, Mick thinks. He'd just leave her fuckin' to it, let her wander round in the freezing cold, oh aye.

These young lads, they make him piss they really do. Get so wound up about their women. Waste of time. Whores and fuckin' harlots the lot of 'em, oh aye. Mick sees it every weekend – you pick 'em up from their house with one bloke and end up taking 'em back with a different one, oh aye, don't you worry, Mick's seen it with his own two eyes. Some of the things he's clocked in that rear-view mirror an'all, Jesus. No fuckin' shame some of these young lasses. Hands up skirts, cocks out, tits out, the fuckin' lot. Mick's glad he's got lads. No way would he let a fuckin' daughter of his out in this town on a Saturday night. Any night, even.

Mick gets his tabs out his top shirt pocket and sparks one up, lets the window down a touch.

– Do yer mind, he asks. – I know it's illegal strictly speaking, what with this being me work place and everything . . . d'yer want one?

He offers the pack over his shoulder.

– No.

– Very wise mate.

They go over North Bridge and into Town. A gang of lads spill out of Staki's and start staggering up the road, shoulders hunched against the cold.

– Look at them silly bastards, Mick says. – Makes yer laugh dunnit. I mean, they work their balls off all week, lining some other cunt's pockets, then they go out and piss it all up the wall on cards and roulette. Pissed out their heads. Wake up next morning and they don't even remember where their money's gone. Barmy innit?

He clocks the lad in the mirror. Not even listening.

Just staring out the window, chewing on his thumbnail. Mick hopes he's not spitting them fuckin' nails
all over his back seat.

They turn into Baker Street and there's this figure
coming down the street towards them on the other
side. At first Mick think it's a woman cos it's got a gold
dress on, but it's stomping along like a gorilla and it's
got arms like a prop forward. And then Mick nearly
shits himself cos it looks like it's carrying a human
head. It moves into the streetlight and Mick sees it's
one of them trannies from that queer club down here.
He's pulled his wig off and he's marching down the
street shouting and bawling.

– ALRIGHT THEN LINDSEY, FUCK OFF! SEE
IF I CARE! YOU DON'T KNOW WHAT YOU
WANT, YOU! YOU'RE JUST SOME SPOILT
LITTLE FAG HAG FROM, WILLERBY!!
YOU'VE NEVER KNOWN WHAT YOU WANT!
HYPOCRITE! FUCKIN' HYPOCRITE!!

Christ knows who he's shouting at. Himself, probably. As they go past him he slings his wig down on
the deck and starts stamping on it. Then he slips and
keels over, lands in a blubbering heap on the pavement. He pelts this blonde wig into the road and starts
screaming.

– JUST! FUCK! RIGHT! OFF! CUUUUUNT!!

Mick dumps his tab end out the window and winds
it up. Should stop smoking really. Everyone seems to
be stopping now. Well, it's inconvenient, more than owt.
Can't smoke anywhere now can yer? Making people
go outside in the pissing wind and rain. Gets on his
tits, that. What's it all for? Concern for people's health?

Yeah, right. Why stop at making people go outside then? If it's that bad for yer, why not just ban the filthy fuckin' things altogether, eh? Well, we know why, don't we, thinks Mick, oh aye. Cos smokers pay through the nose all their lives for this filthy habit. Then, when it's time for them to retire and get a bit back, they drop down dead. Fuckin' heart failure or lung cancer or some other horrific disease, oh aye. Costs the government fuck all in pensions. Very convenient. Never mind statues of Churchill, he thinks, they should just erect a monument to Mr Benson & Mr Hedges, or Lambert and his fuckin' Butler. Services fuckin' rendered.

Mick slips down the side of Prospect Centre and hangs fire at the junction out onto Ferensway. There's no one about though, no cars, fuck all.

– Seen enough, my mate? Shall we go to Hessle now?

– Yeah.

Thank Christ for that. Mick does a left and then they're out on Clive Sully and heading out west to Hessle. Past St Andrews Dock, or, rather, what used to be St Andrews Dock. Used to have ships from all over the place in there, thinks Mick as he whips past. Five abreast sometimes. Fuckin' hamburger bar now. Hamburgers and fuckin' settees. They belt it past the big lit-up B&Q sign and take the slip road off, past the Sainsbury's and down towards Hessle Square.

He turns Hank down.

– Was it just in the square you wanted my mate?

– What?

– Do you wanna be just anywhere here in the square?

– Er . . . yeah, this street here.

The lad leans over the back of the passenger seat and points down a little side street on the left as they come into the square.

– Right you are, says Mick.

A narrow cul-de-sac. Halfway down the lad says:

– Just here.

Mick parks up and turns the light on, clocks the meter.

– Twelve quid please my mate.

The lad digs a wallet out of his hip pocket and leans over, flips it open. He gets a tenner and a fiver out, hands 'em over.

– Much obliged, hang on my mate . . .

Mick reaches under his seat and gets his bag out. Tips out some sheckles.

– 'ere y'are. Two, two-fifty . . . three quid . . .

But the lad's already out the door, slamming it shut behind him.

Thank you and good night.

Mick moves off down the street. It looks like a nice quiet little street, few window boxes and neat front lawns. Tight little cul-de-sac at the bottom. He turns the motor round slowly in a three-pointer and heads back to the top.

There's matey boy, stood in the middle of the road staring up at this house. Gawping up at a bedroom window.

Mick slows right down a good couple of foot away from him and the lad turns to look, shielding his eyes against the headlights. Then he walks round to the passenger side. Bends down and taps on the window. Mick lets it down a touch.

– What's up? he says.

– Whereabouts is the Humber Bridge?

– You want to go to the bridge?

– Is it near here?

– It's up on Boothferry Road.

– Is that far from here?

– It's a fair walk.

The lad straightens up and looks around. Bobs down again.

– Which way is it?

Hank Williams on low and the running of the car engine.

Mick thinks, I know the fuckin' score here, oh aye.

– Look, Mick says to him, – I can take you up there, if that's where you want to be.

– I do. I want to be up there.

– No problem, says Mick.

He turns the central locking off and the lad gets in the back and off they go.

Mick remembers when they opened that bridge. Eighty-one or eighty-two he thinks it was. All the bains got a day off school to go and see the queen. Bright sunny day it was. Mick was working at drypool dock at the time. Took the day off and took the lads up early to Hessle Foreshore. After they saw Liz they took the dog in that old quarry near the big new bridge. Fuckin' thing swam out into the middle of this big stinking lake to get a stick that one of the lads threw in and got its fuckin' paw stuck on summat, old shopping trolley or summat like that. Right death trap that place was back then. They've cleaned it all up now. Anyway, silly bastard Mick here had to wade in up to his waist and free this stupid fuckin' mutt from drowning in shitty muddy germ-infested water. He took his jeans off and dried them on a bush as the lads filled jam jars with newts and taddies. Played up fuck they did when Mick made 'em empty the fuckers out again before they headed back to the car.

They drive along in silence through Hessle Square. No one about at this time of night. Just Mick, the lad and Hank. The red lights stop them as they turn left at the church.

– Do you want to go actually over the bridge?

Silence in the back.

Mick turns the tape down a touch.

– Hey, son. Do you want to go *to* the bridge or *over* it?

– Just to it, please.

– OK boss.

He turns Hank back up and they go out of Hessle and onto Boothferry Road. Speed cameras up here, so Mick gets into the left-hand lane and slows right down. It starts feeling a bit nippy so he switches the heating on. Full on. It shrieks into the car and within about two minutes it's roasting.

– That too warm for yer? Mick asks over his shoulder.

– It's alright.

They get up near the roundabout at the top and the bridge looms into view, red and white lights blinking at the top with a big full moon hung behind. A lorry is rumbling up behind them so Mick moves over to let it pass and then swings back into the left-hand lane.

– Stop here, the lad says. There's a couple of cars up their arse now. Headlights in the rear-view.

Sign at the first exit – TOLL.

– Can't stop here mate, Mick tells him. – If I turn off here I can't turn round and come back. There's cameras up there. And I don't suppose you wanna go to Barton do yer?

– No.

No, thinks Mick. No, I know you fuckin' don't.

Sign at the second exit – HUMBER BRIDGE CAR PARK.

– Look, I'll drop you off down there shall I? In the car park?

– Anywhere round here'll do.

They roll down into this massive car park ringed off with trees and a small fence. There's a souvenir shop boarded up with a corrugated iron shutter and a small footpath winding up through the trees to the bridge. Two cars parked up at the far side. Apart from that, there's just them.

– How much do I owe yer? says the lad.

Mick twists round in his seat to face him.

– What's your name, son?

– Darren. Why?

– 'ey, well listen to this Darren, you'll like this. I had a mate once. He went to Canada. The Niagara Falls. Ever been there? Fuckin' mad. He says they dress you up in a huge rain mac, you know, like deckie learners used to wear at sea? No? Well, you're too young to remember them. Anyway, they're stood there in these bright yellow capes an' hats on a little ledge with the spray coming at 'em, pissing wet through they are. And there's this bloke there telling 'em all about how high up it is, a guide like, yer know, saying how much water goes over the edge per second and all that lark. And my mate looks down into the water below, turns round to this guide feller and says to him 'Do people jump off here often?' And the guide says 'No, just the once' . . .

The lad doesn't say owt.

Just sits there looking at him.

– How much is it? he says again.

Mick shrugs. – That'll be . . . er . . . just call it another two quid.

The lad gets his wallet out and pulls out a note. A tenner.

– 'ere y'are.

– Have you got owt smaller? Mick says. – I don't think I've got enough change for that.

And the lad says: – Keep the change.

And then he opens the door and starts getting out.

– Hang on Darren, Mick tells him, – it's a lot of change that. You do know you've given me a tenner don't yer?

– Just keep it, says the lad, and slams the door shut.

Mick's out of the car like a fuckin' shot.

– Keep it? Really? Nice one. How much more you got, then?

The lad stops and turns round. Confusion written across his face.

– You what?

– How much you got in yer wallet?

– Eh?

– Well you might as well give me the lot son. Come on, gis it. All of it. The fuckin' lot.

It's freezing out here. Mick can see his breath hanging

in the air between them. The lad's face relaxes into a sneer.

– What are you on about? You silly old twat.

– Well you won't need it will yer? Not where you're going? Might as well just give me the fuckin' wallet.

He takes a step towards him and holds his hand out.

– Come on, Darren. Gis it. Now.

He's still got the wallet in his hand. Mick sees the other hand ball into a fist by his side.

The lad says: – Are you taking the fuckin' piss or what?

Mick laughs.

– Taking the piss? No son, I'm just being realistic. Come on, have you got yer cashcard in there?

The lad looks at Mick like he wants to fuckin' kill him. Pure hatred in his eyes.

– Come on, Mick says, – what's your fuckin' problem? Gis yer wallet!

He goes to grab at his hand, and the lad takes a step backwards.

– Any other cards in there? Ey, and don't forget to tell us yer PIN number.

– Fuck off you cheeky old cunt! the lad snarls.

His lip is trembling now.

– Who? Me? Come on, I'm fuckin' serious. Tell us your PIN number, then I can go and clean your account out. Why not? Won't need it where you're going, will yer?

– FUCK RIGHT OFF CUNT! screams the lad and he slings a fist at Mick's chest, more a push than a punch, but Mick grabs his wrist and starts walking him backwards.

– Don't be like that, son. There's no need for all that now, is there?

Mick slaps his forehead with his other open palm.

– Oh! Hang on! Silly me! I get it now! You've spent it all ant yer! Blown it all on one final piss up? Well, you inconsiderate bastard!

– FUCK OFF! screams the lad.

– Planned this have yer? says Mick. – Just my fuckin' luck. And here's me thinking this was just an off the cuff thing.

– FUCKIN' SHUT IT!

There's a wild animal look in his eye; Mick can't decide if it's fear or anger or what the fuck it is. Every time the lad pushes against him Mick grips his wrist tighter and pushes him back, reaching out for his wallet with the other hand.

– Well you're not exactly dressed for it, are yer? Bloody cold in that water, you know. If it was me, I'd make sure I was wrapped up warm. You ant even got a jacket on! You've obviously not given it much thought.

He's twisting him round as he backs the lad up. Back up towards the car.

The lad's panting and snarling like a dog.

– YOU DON'T KNOW! YOU KNOW ABSOLUTELY FUCK ALL!

The tears start spilling down his cheeks. His face is like a piece of burst fruit under the car park flood-lights. Their shadows spilling long across the tarmac, two dark giants locked together at the wrist in some strange grappled waltz.

– Correct, says Mick. – I don't know. And what's more I don't care. Don't give a fuck. But what I do know is, I aren't just gonna sit here and watch a load of money disappear into the fuckin' Humber. Now are you gonna give us that wallet or not?

– You absolute cunt, says the lad.

He's sobbing like a bain now. Really sobbing.

– I'm just being realistic son. This world is designed for living people int it? Not dead bastards.

The lad tries to push against him again but he's weak as a kitten now. Mick pushes him back and pushes him down, he's crumpling slowly and his legs wobble and go as he sinks to the deck.

And then he's on his knees, sobbing, shoulders heaving as Mick holds his hand in the big empty car park under the freezing cold moon.

After a bit Mick says: – Come on son, let's get in the car.

He's not moving. Mick puts his hand under his arm and gets him up slowly. His face is red raw with snot and tears. He looks away, looks down to the ground so Mick can't see him crying.

– Come on Darren, Mick says to him. – It's alright. Come on.

He gets him in the back of the car and slams the door shut. He can still hear him weeping and snuffling as he walks round and gets into the driver's side.

Mick starts the car up and they move off. As they swing round the car park their headlights move across a stationary Ford Escort and catch a big flabby white arse bobbing up and down in the back window.

– Wayhey! See that? says Mick. – Are they at it? They fuckin' are! Doggers! WAYHEY! DIRTY BASTARDS! GOOO AAARRN!

Mick gives his horn an almighty fuckin' blast, football-chant style and that gets a bit of a laugh from the back, a laugh like he's trying to catch his breath in between the last of his sobs. Mick digs a packet of tissues out of the glove compartment and slings 'em over his shoulder.

– 'ere y'are.

The lad gives his bugle a good blow and after a bit his breathing has calmed down and he's quiet again.

They go back up Boothferry Road.

Mick says: – Do you want to talk about it?

And the lad says: – No.

– Alright, says Mick.

He turns Hank Williams up full and guns the motor.

Hull city centre: 2.18am

Denise is at the bar talking to Camp Colin. She's telling him about today in Prinny Quay and that lairy little twat in River Island. Colin's helpless with laughter as Denise tells him how she scrambled about on the deck trying to find her wig. She tells him how this little get started bleating about Denise marking him and how he was gonna put a claim in and Colin laughs longer and harder. Then she tells him how she pelted down the stairs two at a time with her shoes in her hand and Colin nearly goes into meltdown.

– Stop it, stop it you, Denise, he says, wiping his eyes. – Don't tell me any more, I'm gonna piss meself!

Denise likes making Camp Colin laugh like this. It makes the day she's had seem less raw, less hurtful. He's called Camp Colin not cos he's camp, although he is, but cos of when he split up with his bloke, Raymond. It was a nasty break-up, with no end of bad blood on both sides and a lot of their mutual friends found themselves being forced to take sides. You were either in Camp Colin or Camp Raymond. Denise was in Camp Colin.

Colin was the first person she met on the gay/transgender scene when she started coming out to places like this. And even though she's boringly hetro, Colin showed her nowt but kindness and solidarity during those early weeks. It was a nerve-wracking time for her, but Colin and his mates made it a lot more bearable – fun even. She's not really one for screaming and flouncing about – she finds a lot of that sort of behaviour a bit tedious if she's being honest – but them lot were always a good laugh to go out with and in the early days Denise clung to Colin like a limpet to a rock.

– And what did Lindsey do? asks Colin. – I bet she went mental dint she?

– She wan't there.

– Who was you with? Was yer on yer own, yeah?

– Yeah.

– Aw, good for you Denise! Good for you!

And then Colin looks at her and he bursts into hysterics again, clutching onto the edge of the bar for support.

It was actually Colin who introduced Denise to Lindsey. He got Lindsey a job behind the bar in the club which, like all of her other jobs, lasted about three weeks before she fell out with somebody and left in a huff. Denise liked her straight off, liked her feisty attitude. She found it funny and exciting at first. She was feeling a bit fragile and she buzzed off Lindsey's confidence, her fearlessness if you like. And Lindsey was all over her like a rash. It was only after Denise'd been seeing her for about two months that her haughty demeanour lost its appeal and Denise realised she was actually a spoilt little fucker who wasn't clever or sharp or witty. She was just completely up her own arse and pointlessly belligerent. Still, it was a regular shag and Denise craved that human contact. Even though sex with Lindsey was usually more like unarmed combat.

She starts moaning on to Camp Colin about Lindsey and how she stood her up. How it put her on edge, put her on the defensive. Colin nods.

– Oh aye. She was right pissed off when you disappeared last night. How come you just took off anyway?

Denise tells him about the little lass and how David took her to the police.

– That's disgusting! Can't believe some people can yer? Some bains. Dragged up aren't they? Bloody breeders!

He drains his bottle off and slams it onto the bar.

– Anyway, bollocks to that.

He takes Denise's hand and pulls her off her stool.
– Come on love, come and have a bit of a boogie with me.

They get on the dance floor and they're having a right scream, twirling each other round and busting loads of daft moves. Colin's enthusiasm is dead infectious and Denise gets right into it, forgets all about the shittiness of the day she's had. After a bit the second pill starts kicking in and she kids herself she's not in Hull city centre, she's in Studio 54, New York City, tripping the light fantastic with Debbie Harry and Lou Reed and Andy Warhol. Loses herself in the film inside her head.

After a bit the dance floor starts filling up and she starts getting a bit hot, so she leaves Colin to it. He's dancing with some fit young lad, so Denise tips him the wink and goes to the bogs to readjust her face. Then she sees her mate Candy and her bloke Alex. They're with a big crowd and a few of them go and have a sit down and a natter in the back room. They're having a right good crack and Candy's as funny as fuck. She's telling them about this idea she's had for an invention: a magic pillow that stops your face getting all creased up in the morning. She's on about waking up next to Alex and how his features are all over his face first thing. Mr Potato Head she calls him. Alex takes it all with his usual sweet and mournful expression and they're all in hysterics, but it's good natured, nowt nasty.

Then Denise spots Lindsey out the corner of her eye. She's with some dashing young metrosexual type in a too-tight T-shirt. Denise makes a point of not looking across and instead concentrates on her company. But next thing she knows Lindsey's come and parked her fat arse on the arm of Denise's chair. She can feel her thigh pressed up next to her shoulder. Then she feels her elbow digging into her.

– Not talking are we?

– I'm talking to Candy.

– Well the least you can do is buy me a drink to say sorry.

Denise's first impulse is to stand up, push her off the chair, send her tumbling right onto her fat arse. But she takes a deep breath and just shakes her head.

Ignore her, Denise. Concentrate on the people in front of you, the normal decent people. Alex is ragging Candy now, some story about her sleeping in and getting up in a hurry. Denise laughs along with them, even though she hasn't properly caught what they're saying.

Elbow digging into her shoulder again. Denise looks up, trying to keep her composure. Lindsey's haughty face staring down at her, this simpering fool she's with floating about in the background.

– Do you fuckin' mind?

– Stop being a wanker and get me a drink.

Denise knows Lindsey won't leave it, so she makes her excuses and she gets up, goes and looks for Colin. But Lindsey is right behind her, banging on about leaving her on her own at Hull Fair and who did Denise think she was etc. etc. Denise thinks she's coked up, but it's hard to tell with that mad bitch, paranoid aggression being her default setting.

Colin's stood nattering in the main room. Denise taps him on the shoulder.

– Wanna drink Col?

– No, I'm good ta. He holds up his bottle. Then he spots Lindsey and gives her a big hug, starts gabbing away ten to the dozen while Denise makes her escape to the bar.

They're still talking when she gets back. She tries to slips past 'em but Lindsey is straight in her face.

– WHERE'S MY FUCKIN' DRINK!

Denise slings her double vodka and coke full in Lindsey's face.

– THERE'S YER FUCKIN' DRINK, BITCH! THAT DO YER?!

Lindsey's frozen to the spot for a split second, a look of utter astonishment on her face. She looks so comically shocked that Denise nearly bursts out laughing. But then Lindsey's nails are in her face and she starts kicking and punching. They're swinging each other round in the middle of the club, knocking into people. Someone clouts Denise round the back of the head and her tiara goes flying. She's trying to keep her balance on her spike heels, clutching at anything and everything around her, but Denise is about to go over on her arse. Again.

Fuckin' hell, she thinks, not twice in one day.

Colin's got hold of Lindsey round the waist from behind, trying to drag her off Denise, but she's absolutely demented, swinging and spitting like a thing possessed, screaming the place down, calling Denise all the cunts under the sun. The crowd parts behind them and Denise falls backwards, sending a table full of drinks flying.

Then the bouncers are over and she's being spun round and marched out the door. This big ape's got one of her arms jammed up behind her back. Denise can hear screaming and glass smashing behind her and next thing she knows she's on the street.

Lindsey and this young lad are right behind her. She goes for Denise again, but this kid has hold of her and he's telling her to leave it. He's pulling her down the street and Denise is marching after them shouting and bawling but she keeps falling over, she can't keep up with them and Lindsey and her bloke get gradually further and further away.

After a bit they disappear round the corner at the top of the street and Denise is left on her own. There's no one else about. Just the click of her heels on the pavement and the sound of her own demented wailing bouncing off the buildings.

She shouts at the passing cars as she totters her way through Town.

Hull city centre: 3.24am

After a bit the lad says: – Can I ask you summat mate?

– What, says Mick.

– Who the fuck is this?

– Hank Williams. Why, what's up, don't yer like it?

– Can we have the radio on?

– You cheeky cunt, says Mick.

Then he says: – Aye, alright then.

Mick flicks it onto Magic. It's The Platters, 'The Great Pretender'. He turns it up.

– Fuckin' 'ell, this is an old 'un. I remember this from when I was doing the rounds, '59 I reckon, no, tell a lie, it was '58, yeah definitely, '58. The Platters . . . they used to have this in Kevin Ballroom, you'll be too young to remember Kevin Ballroom, it's not there now, it's . . . Er . . . what's there now? You know, that big building in Market Place, opposite the Holy Trinity, what's it called, that? Been years since I went in there . . .

There's no answer from the back. But Mick knows he's heard him. He turns the volume up and gets his foot down. If he gets a shift on he can drop the lad off and be in his own bed before it gets too light.

Oh aye.

He can't get to sleep if it's light.

Newland Avenue: 8.11am

Ella goes running back upstairs wailing when she sees her dad's face. He's laid on the couch in the living room and he can hear the thump of her little feet across the ceiling as she goes flying into the bedroom, to Ange.

Angie's voice, thick with sleep.

– What's the matter? Ella, what's happened?

– Daddy's turned into a monster!

Boothferry Estate: 8.28am

Trevor wakes up on the bed with all his clothes on. His eyes are stuck together and his mouth is dry.

Head still banging.

He goes in the bathroom with eyes half shut and has a drink from the tap. Then he swills his face.

Then he gets all his gear off and he gets back into the bed.

Hotham Road South: 10.10am

The phone wakes her up.

She's laid out on the couch, still in all her clothes. She feels like she's been kicked from arsehole to break-fast time. A dead weight. No way can she move. She can't even lift her head. A shaft of daylight is spilling through the curtains and swirling with dust mites. There's a sour smell coming from somewhere. At first she thinks it's her, but it seems to be coming from somewhere else in the room.

The relentless bastard ring of the phone.

She feels sick as a dog.

The answer machine kicks in. If that's Lindsey, thinks Denise, she can go fuck herself. No way is she talking to that demented bitch.

– David? David, are you there?

It's their Janice. What's she doing calling her David? It's still the weekend. She's Denise. Saturday and Sunday, her name's Denise. Janice knows that. What's up with her? What's she playing at?

Well fuck her as well.

Denise doesn't answer to David on a weekend.

Then Janice tells her the hospice have called and her mam, David's mam, their mam, has taken a turn for the worst. That she had a very bad night and she might not make it through the day. That she's on her way there now and, well, she thought David should at least know.

There's a long high-pitched beep and then she's gone.

Denise lies there for a bit staring at the ceiling.

Then she gets to her feet and heads slowly for the bathroom.

Boothferry Estate: 10.23am

Bella's all worn out with her romp around the park but Rose, she's as giddy as a schoolgirl. She pushes the Hoover round upstairs and down while Bella has a snooze in her basket. Rose has got Frank Sinatra on the music system and she's singing along at the top of her voice.

Rose is cooking a Sunday dinner today. It'll be the first Sunday dinner she's cooked in the last two years. As soon as she's finished sorting this house out she's off to Asda to get the roast and a few more bits and bobs. Get a bottle of wine as well. Might even get two!

Rose and Dennis and Malcolm were up till gone midnight talking on the computer. She can't describe how wonderful it was to talk to her husband again. It was like he'd never gone away. Like Dennis said, it's just like opening a door and stepping from one room into another. You just have to know where the door is.

Rose gives the house a good hoover and washes the few pots up in the sink. It looks like it's going to be a nice day outside. Even her tatty old back garden looks like it's had a new lease of life. Them dahlias look like they're making a comeback, and she thought she'd seen the last of them.

A last run round with the duster and she gets her purse and puts her coat on and then she remembers summat. That dirty article who popped up on the site yesterday, that Jack bloody Sparrow character. She'll email the admin and report that bugger. It's a disgrace, ruining it for decent genuine people. Well he can't intimidate me, thinks Rose. She'll get right on to the people who run the show and get him traced and then banned. She doesn't care if it is just a daft young kid messing about, filth like that needs to be nipped in the bud.

The laptop is still on from last night. Malcolm and Rose bathed in Mediterranean sunshine, smiling from the screen.

She moves the mouse and they disappear.

Rose clicks on the blue e at the bottom of the screen. It seems to take an age to fire up but eventually the Google page appears along with her list of favourite sites on the left-hand side. She clicks on Local Link Up but nothing happens.

Oh come on!

Click, click, click.

Nothing.

She remembers Donna saying not to click it too much cos every time you click it you're asking it to do something. Computers haven't got a mind of their own, she'd said, they only do what you tell them to do.

So she goes downstairs, takes her coat off and makes a brew, gives it chance to warm up or whatever it needs to do.

When she gets back upstairs the little egg timer is still spinning round and round. She clicks on the Outlook button to see if there's owt going on there but nowt happens. The egg timer doesn't even move when she shifts the mouse about. She presses a few keys. Nothing again. Just that spinning egg timer stuck in the corner of the screen. Rose consults her little notebook and presses the Alt Control and Delete buttons. Still nothing happens.

Bloody thing! This is exactly what it did last time when it all went to buggery! That shop was supposed to have fixed all this, all this crashing and what have you. Well they didn't do a very good job did they, Rose says to herself. It was only a bloody month ago they had it, and now it's all packing up again!

She hunts about in her purse for the little card they gave her last time.

A&J PC Solutions

Anlaby Road Hull

Open Weekdays 9 til 5.30

Saturdays 10 til 4

Sundays 10 til 4

Emergency Call Out Service Available

A young chap's voice answers after six or seven rings.

– Hello, A&J?

– Yes, hello, you had my laptop in for repair about a month ago and it's gone wrong again.

– Oh Kaaaaay. What name is it please?

– Mrs Neadley. Are you the chap I spoke to before?

Rose recognises his voice, the way he talks. It is, it's the same young chap she spoke to before. Oh well, that's a relief. At least he knows what he's doing.

– I'll just check, Mrs Neadley . . .

The sound of a keyboard tapping.

– . . . sorry, when did you say you brought it in?

– About four weeks ago.

– Right. Oh Kaaaaay, well, first of all what's the PC doing?

– Doing? It's not doing anything, that's the problem!

– Is it turned on?

– Yes, but it's not doing owt, the little thing is just going round and round. The egg timer.

– The screen's frozen?

– Yes that's it. Frozen.

– Oh Kaaaaay, he says and there's more tapping. – Just trying to find you Mrs Neadley . . . ah yeah, Neptune Garth?

– That's me, yes.

– Right. Yes, I do remember you. Well I'm sorry you're having problems Mrs Neadley, but if you bring it in I'm sure we can sort it out for yourself.

– Are you the chap who fixed it last time?

– No, I don't fix them myself Mrs Neadley. We have a workshop that does all our repairs. Like I say, if you can get the computer over to us I'll get it looked at.

– Well what about your emergency call-out service?

– Ah yes, usually, but Dennis is off today so the best we could do is get him out to you tomorrow. Unless, like I say, you want to pop it in today and I can get him to look at it for you first thing in morning?

Rose doesn't say anything.

– Mrs Neadley?

– Dennis?

– I'm sorry?

– Did you say Dennis?

– Yes. My uncle. He does all the repairs.

Rose looks at the card in her hand.

– What's his second name? she asks.

But even before he answers, she knows what he's going to say.

Dove House Hospice, Chamberlain Road: 11.59am

The woman at the hospice does a good job of hiding her shock when she opens the door. Her eyes widen for a second but then her professional composure kicks in and she asks who Denise has come to see.

– Lily Turner.

– And you are her . . . ?

– She's my mother.

The woman nods, stands aside.

– Your sister's sat with her.

It's not like Denise expected, this place. She thought it would be a bit shabby and depressing, all nicotine-stained magnolia and tatty net curtains. A load of slavering old skeletons shuffling about on walking frames, or sat in their own piss, staring blankly at the telly. But it's nowt like that; it's all lemon-yellow paintwork and tasteful Laura Ashley-style wallpaper. There's the smell of Sunday dinner cooking and Denise can hear a radio playing somewhere. She follows the woman down a couple of corridors and then they stop at a door. The woman taps twice, and opens it.

Denise's mam's propped up in bed with her eyes shut, a drip attached to her hand and another one in her nose. Their Janice is at the bedside. She looks round when Denise comes in. She looks shattered, even more so than usual.

– If you need anything I'll be just in the day room, the woman says. Janice gives her a weak smile, nods, and the woman shuts the door quietly behind her. Denise pulls up a chair and sits next to her sister.

They sit looking at their mam. She looks like she weighs about seven stone, and her face looks like it's collapsed, like all the life has been sucked out. A broken little yellow-faced puppet with a sunken mouth and wires coming out of her. Denise tries to listen for her breathing but she's not close enough. She thinks she can see her chest moving, but she can't be certain.

– Is she dead?

– No. Won't be long though, they reckon. They've sent for Dr Kundu. I thought you might be him, actually.

Janice looks at her watch.

– I spoke to our Cath, she's on her way, but I don't know where our John is. I left a message on his mobile.

She looks at Denise.

– Did you have to come all dressed up?

Something starts up inside her, but she swallows it back down.

– This is who I am, Janice.

– Yes I know Da . . . Denise. But . . . still.

– Still what?

Their Janice just shakes her head. She looks so tired. She's six years older than Denise, but she's never looked her age. Always a bit of a looker was their Janice. She's starting to look her age now, though.

– How long have you been here?

– Since nine o'clock last night. They brought the district nurse to her and then rang me up.

– Where's the nurse now?

– That was her who showed you in.

Denise is surprised at this. – She was a nurse? Really? She dint look like one.

– Oh aye? And what does a nurse look like?

Denise doesn't know what to say to that, so she says nowt.

– Thanks for coming anyhow. Janice smiles and squeezes her hand.

– Yeah, well, I'm not stopping long.

Janice gives her a look.

– I aren't being a phoney bastard Janice. I aren't here for her, I'm here for you. Cos you asked me to come.

Janice sighs and rubs her eyes.

– Well at least stop and have a cup of tea.

– What, out of a machine?

– No, you can make a proper one. In the kitchen. Do you want one?

– Yeah, I could murder one actually.

Janice leaves Denise there with her mam, his mam, their mam. She looks at her for a bit, but she's freaking her out so she has a skeg around the room. It's a lovely little room this. Denise can't think why the old woman was so adamant she wasn't coming in here. It's better than that pokey little flat on Greatfield anyroad, thinks Denise. At least she hasn't got a load of screaming kids slamming a football against the garages or car alarms going off on the hour every hour. At least there's a bit of peace and quiet. Denise thinks she wouldn't mind coming in here when she's old and fucked and on her last legs. She wouldn't mind . . .

– Oh mamamama . . .

Jesus fuckin' Christ.

It's her mam. Her mouth is opening and closing, like she's trying to chew summat. There's dried white spittle on her lips and chin and she's chewing and making noises like mam mam mam.

Denise leans in to her.

– Mam? Mam, can you hear me?

The old woman licks her lips.

– The kids . . . the kids are in me eyes. George, the kids are in me eyes.

George? Denise's dad? He's been dead for years. Fuckin' hell, thinks Denise, has her dad come for her? Is that what happens? Is this how it happens? A fuckin' ghost comes to get yer? Or does she think Denise is her dad?

The old woman's lips are all dry and cracked, they keep sticking together as her mouth opens and shuts.

– Do you want a drink, Mam?

Denise says it loud. She raises her voice. Why the fuck is she raising her voice? She doesn't think the old woman can even hear her.

There's a bottle of water on the side. She unscrews it and offers it to her mother's lips, but her eyes are tight shut still. Denise doesn't know what to do. She can't just tip it over her mouth.

Then she sees a box of tissues, pulls one out and wets the corner, puts the bottle back down and dabs the tissue gently on her mother's lips.

The old woman's hand reaches up and grabs Denise's wrist. Denise tries to pull away but her mother's fingers are clamped tight.

– What's that? she says. Who's that?

– Mam, it's me, says Denise.

– David, she murmurs. – Our David. I was thinking about you . . .

Denise shakes her head and tries to pull her hand away, but the old woman's got tight hold of her, her fingers clamped fast round Denise's wrist.

– Denise, she tells her. – Me name's Denise, Mam.

The old woman says summat else but it's so faint

Denise can't make it out. Just sounds like senseless noise, like a baby babbling. Summat about staying, having a stay or going away or summat. Denise can't make it out.

Where the fuck is their Janice?

– What? What is it Mam?

Denise bends down and puts the side of her head to her mouth. Her mam's breath like a butterfly brushing against her cheek.

Another day, that's what it sounds like.

– What? Another day? Another day what Mam?

– Be Denise another day, she whispers. – Be my David now.

Denise peels her mam's fingers off her wrist and holds her hand, holds it properly with both of hers. She can feel her eyes getting hot and filling up. She's cursing herself for losing it, said to herself she wouldn't lose it, but she can't help it, she can't fuckin' help it . . .

– It's alright Mam. It's alright. I'm here.

She sits there and strokes her hand and talks to her for a bit, just daft stuff, nonsense really, telling her it's going to be alright, don't worry, everyone else'll be here in a minute, our Janice and Cath and our John, all of them, we're all together, we'll all be together. The old woman just keeps gasping and murmuring. And then she swallows hard twice and stops trying to talk. Just shallow breath going in and out, thin and wheezing breaths.

Denise can't think of owt else to say so she just sits there, watching her mam's face. Her little crumpled yellow face tilted back and resting on that clean white pillow, eyes still closed, her mouth open, breath rasping in and out, life, still, somewhere, there, somehow.

And then a breath goes out of her and it doesn't go back in.

Denise can hear a radio playing somewhere outside, somewhere, faint down the corridor.

This is what happens, she thinks. We walk around breathing, and then one day we stop. Everything else goes on, but we stop.

She pulls her hand away slowly till just their little fingers are touching. Her mam's little finger hooked round hers. Denise's cracked red-painted fingernail in the parched and cooling palm of her mam's hand.

They stay like that till their Janice comes back in with their Cath and Dr Kundu and a big tray of tea.

Newland Avenue: 2.43pm

Ange isn't speaking to Carl, but that suits him down to the fuckin' ground. Bit of peace and quiet at last. He gets a deckchair out and sits in the back garden with a spliff. The comedown is a vicious one. His head's still swimming and everything from the neck down feels like one huge throbbing bruise.

He gets a text off Chops:

HANDS UP IF YOU HAD A GOOD NIGHT!

Funny cunt. Where was he when Carl needed him? Where were any of the bastards?

At least Ella's calmed down a bit. She comes out the back door and into the garden.

– What happened to your face Dad?

– Fell over and banged me head.

– Had you been drinking mucky beer?

She comes up closer, fascinated by Carl's battered face.

– 'fraid so babe.

She smiles at him.

– Silly Daddy!

– I am aren't I.

– Mummy says smoking is silly as well.

Carl holds the spliff at arm's length so the smoke doesn't go near her.

– Where is yer mam?

– Bed.

– Is she asleep?

She shakes her head.

– She's in a mood.

– Yeah, well you shouldn't be out here without a coat on. It's cold. Get back inside, there's a good girl. Go on, curly tots.

– I'm not curly tots.

– Go on, get inside.

– Are you coming inside?

– Yeah, in a minute. Go on.

She trots back in. His spliff is burning down on one side, leaving big Elvis Las Vegas collars. Rolled it too baggy. Carl dots it with his fingers, snatching at the glowing red embers, then relights the end so it burns properly.

His hands are trembling.

Joyful nights bring sorrowful mornings. That was one of his mam's. She'd give him that one while she was tutting and twatting about the house on a Sunday, pushing the Hoover across the living room floor, shrieking in his head and shredding his nerves while he was dying on the couch. The smell of Mr Sheen attacking his guts and her going on about treating the house like a hotel and how she shouldn't have to put up with all this every weekend and how her and his father deserved a bit more respect and don't think you're gonna be laid out on there all day and blah blah fuckin' blah.

Carl thinks he should go and see his mam. Take the bain. He'll need to get her onside for when number two comes along. Babysitting and that.

This spliff is making him feel sick.

He dots it out, sticks it in his shirt pocket and goes back in the kitchen. Fills the kettle from the tap. Stares at his reflection wobbling up at him, stretched long-ways in the curved metal. Swollen eyes. Big thick lip. His nose feels like it's the size of a fist. He doesn't think it's broken though.

Carl sets the kettle down, clamps one nostril shut with a finger and fires a big clump of snot and clotted blood into the sink.

There's a banging on the front door.

Ange's voice from upstairs:

– CARL! DOOR!

He rinses the blood and snot down the plughole, flicks the kettle on and goes down the hallway. Ella trots out of the front room and stands behind her dad, holding onto his leg.

The shape of a feller through the frosted glass. Big broad-shouldered bastard.

Carl opens the door and there's this huge fucker

with a shaved head and a goatee. He does a double-take as he clocks the state of Carl's face. Then he looks down at this bit of paper he's got in his hand.

– Er . . . Ange?

– Yeah?

– Ange lives here?

– Who wants to know?

– I am sorry?

Foreign accent. Fuckin' hell, thinks Carl, another Swiss Roll.

– Who – are – you?

– Ah, I am Jan. For the boiler?

He makes a big show of looking at this bit of paper and then at the number on the door.

– Oh aye, yeah, come in mate.

Carl stands aside for him to enter. The feller looks relieved.

– I get some tools.

He grins down at Ella and gives her this daft little wave.

– Hello, he says.

Ella darts back into the front room.

He heads back to the kerb to this battered old Marina. There's a blonde woman in the passenger seat, smoking and tapping a fag out of the window. Two kids strapped into seats in the back. He flips the boot open, lifts out a bag of tools and strides back to the house, all smiles.

– Jan, he says.

He holds his hand out.

– Yeah, says Carl, – you said.

Carl gives his hand a shake then points at the Marina.

– Are you gonna leave them sat there?

– My wife and children.

– Yeah, well don't leave them sat out there mate. Tell 'em to come in.

– OK to come in? My little boy is ... well, he makes a noise.

– Show me a little lad who doesn't. Go on, go and get 'em, it's alright.

He goes and gets 'em out the car and they all shuffle on in, him, his bag of tricks, these two little kids and his missus, who Carl's sure he's seen somewhere before.

And then he clicks. It's her. Leather jacket. Blonde hair. Black roots. Gold chain round her neck.

– Ah, now then, says Carl. – Nursery, right?

She gives him a look that's close to horrified.

Then Carl remembers.

– Oh yeah, sorry about me face. Looks worse than it is, though. You wanna see the other feller.

They all look at him a bit blank. One of the little lads looks like he's gonna start roaring.

Ange comes slowly down the stairs, holding onto the banister.

– Is it Jan? I'm Ange.

– Hello! This is my wife Zofia and our boys, Filip and Kasper.

– I'll make a brew, says Carl.

Ange takes the bird and the bains into the front room and Carl fucks off back into the kitchen. Jan follows him through with his little bag of tools. He dumps them on the deck and has a quick skeg round.

– You're the plumber then eh?

Jan laughs.

– Yes!

Fuck's he laughing at, thinks Carl. It's not a trick question. He's either a plumber or he isn't, simple as that.

– You from Poland then mate?

– Yes, Lodz.

This puzzles Carl. Lots? he thinks. What's he on about, lots? Lots of what?

– Lodz is a place in Poland.

– Oh right. So who do you work for here?

– Cake factory.

– You're a plumber in a cake factory?

– No, I am a plumber in Lodz but here I am in cake factory.

Fuckin' marvellous, thinks Carl. I've got Mr Kipling fixing me boiler.

Jan points at him.

– And you?

– What about me?

– You are . . . ?

– Panel erector. Cold stores. Food factories and that.

– Ah yes, OK, he goes, but Carl can tell he hasn't got a fuckin' clue.

The kettle starts juddering as it comes to the boil. You have to stand over it and flick it off with your hand cos the switch is fucked. Carl gets the mugs in a row and drops the tea bags in.

– The boiler is where? asks Jan.

– Upstairs mate, in the back bedroom. The bain's room.

Jan nods.

– And the water?

– Sometimes it's on, sometimes it's off.

Jan looks puzzled.

– I am sorry?

– Water? You mean the hot water, yeah?

– I may need to turn off your water? Where is the . . .

A twisting motion with his hand like he's turning on a tap.

– Oh, right! Er, it's round the front, I think.

– OK. You show me the boiler?

– Just go upstairs mate, it's in the back bedroom, can't miss it. On the back wall.

Carl holds up a mug.

– How do you have it?

– Oh yes, please, thank you.

– No, I mean do you want milk, sugar?

– Just tea please.

– What, black?

– Yes please.

– What about your lass? Will she want one an'all?

– Yes, thank you. So, your boiler. What is it doing?

– Fuck all mate, that's the problem.

Jan smiles. But Carl can tell he's not sure.

– Nah, it just keeps going off and on, y'know?

– Off and on?

– Yeah, y'know . . . on . . . phew!

Carl fans himself and wipes his brow like he's sweating under a huge imaginary sun.

– . . . and off. Brrrr!

Wraps his arms round himself and shivers.

293

Jan nods thoughtfully and points upwards.

– Upstairs?

– Yeah. Back bedroom.

– OK, says Jan, and he takes his shoes off and disappears upstairs.

Clueless cunt, thinks Carl. How do they think they're gonna carry on over here if they can't speak the lingo? And that's not being racist, he thinks, that's just common fuckin' sense, innit.

As Carl is making the brews he's thinking he should have gone with him. Fuck knows where he'll be poking around. Straight in Ange's knicker drawer, probably. Mind you, Carl considers, at least he's not one of them Kosovans. Hanging round in park, big groups of 'em, leering at lasses. Dirty bastards.

Carl takes Jan's wife her brew through. She's on the couch yapping to Ange. The bains are sat on the floor with pens and colouring books.

– Here y'are. Mind out, it's hot.

She takes it off him with two hands.

– Thank you. Your daughter is beautiful. Her hair is so awesome.

– She's a curly tot, aren't yer Ella.

Ella goes all coy, scribbling away in her book.

Zofia points at Ange's belly.

– You will be Daddy two times.

– Yeah, well, says Carl.

– One is nice and easy. Two is sometimes crazy.

She nods down at her two.

– I'll look forward to it, says Carl.

– Have you took Jan a brew? says Ange.

– Just doing it now.

Up in the back bedroom Mr Kipling's got the airing cupboard open and the bottom section off the boiler. He stands there looking at it, rubbing his chin.

– Thank you.

He takes the brew and sets it down carefully on Ella's bedside table.

– Do you have the . . .

He unfolds his hands, palms upwards, like he's opening a book.

– Don't know where it is. Sorry mate. Why, can't you do it without the book?

– Oh no, no, it will be OK.

– Right. I'll leave you to it. If you need me, I'll be in the backyard.

Boothferry Estate: 3.04pm

One of 'em's pissed all over the carpet. Trevor lets 'em out the back way, shuts the door on 'em and gets some cleaning gear from under the sink. He takes the washing-up bowl out of the sink and fills it full of warm water and detergent. Then he gets on his hands and knees and scrubs the piss out of the carpet.

They're back tomorrow. He should do some washing up an'all.

Newland Avenue: 3.16pm

From his deckchair Carl can see him in the upstairs window, bobbing in and out of the airing cupboard. If he fixes that boiler I'll show me arse in Hammonds window, thinks Carl. And he can fuck off if he thinks he's walking out of here with forty quid of Carl's if there's still no hot water when he's finished. Stick to icing cakes pal. I'll get Shane's mate round to have a look at it, he thinks.

He fishes the half-finished bifter out of his top pocket and fires it up.

– Hello?

Zofia steps out into the yard, arms folded, pulling her jacket tight to herself against the cold. Carl nods at her.

– Alright.

– Have you got some lighter?

She holds up an unlit cig between her fingers.

– Yeah, here y'are.

He flicks his Clipper and offers the flame up to her. She bends down and holds her hair out the way of her face as he lights her up. She straightens up and exhales. Stands there smoking in silence.

Carl tries to think of summat to say to her.

– So . . . do you like it here, then?

She shrugs. – It's OK.

– Did you take the bains round the Fair?

– We went, but not to go on many rides.

– Don't blame yer, it's a dear fuckin' do. Two quid a pop some of 'em.

She doesn't say anything to that.

Then she reaches down and touches his cheek and his heart nearly leaps out of his bastard chest.

– I am sorry about your face.

What the fuck is she . . .

Oh.

Fuck.

Carl doesn't say owt.

– Don't worry, she says. – I won't say something.

They both smoke for a bit, him sat down, head bowed, her stood over him.

– Every time of dance takes some more . . . takes some more away from you, she says.

She flicks her cigarette into the flowerbed.

– Soon I will stop, she says. – I will stop before there is nothing left.

He can't look at her.

Then he says:

– Does your husband know what you do?

– Yes, she says.

– And he's not bothered?

– Does your wife know what *you* do?

Carl thinks for a second, starts to say summat and then he doesn't.

He looks up at Ella's bedroom window. Zofia's husband, Jan, looks down at him. He's holding something up to show Carl. It looks like a small piece of machinery, some part out of the boiler.

Carl gives him the thumbs up.

Jan smiles, nods, gives him the thumbs up back.

Boothferry Estate: 4.14pm

After they've had their walk Trevor does himself some eggs and beans on toast for his tea and gets them their biscuits and some fresh water. Trevor eats his on his lap in front of the box while they demolish theirs in the kitchen. Then he has a tinnie and another one and then a few more while he watches *Songs of Praise* and *Heartbeat*. Trevor likes *Heartbeat*. He got into it while he was in prison, but could never watch it in his last two months cos the lad he got padded up with always wanted to watch the other side. Said *Heartbeat* was for old women, the cheeky little twat.

Suddenly Charlie sits up bolt upright and looks towards the window. He drops down from the couch and pads across the room and stops dead in front of Trevor, blocking the telly. He's lifting his big head and making a rumbling in his throat.

– What is it lad?

Charlie doesn't move. Just stands there

– Come on Charlie, shift yer arse!

He won't shift. Doesn't look round. Just stands there, staring out the window, growling.

– SIT DOWN!

Bloody bugger takes no notice.

– BASTARD!

Trevor leaps up and grabs Charlie's collar and drags the bleeder into the kitchen. His jaws swing round for Trevor's arm but Trevor's wise to his game and he has him bundled away and the door slammed tight shut in one move.

He keeps the door pulled shut to while the dog slams himself against the other side, barking and going barmy.

– AND YOU CAN STAY THERE WHILE YOU CALM DOWN! BASTARD! YOU DO AS *I* SAY!

Jess leaps up from the couch and starts barking as well, but Trevor's proper lost his rag now. He screams at her to shut her fuckin' gob and he whips his belt off and waves the buckle at her nose and after a bit she goes quiet. She curls back down on the couch and keeps looking between Trevor and the kitchen door.

– NO! HE'S BEEN A BAD LAD! A VERY BAD LAD!

Trevor sits back down. He's trembling like a bastard. He turns the telly up to drown out Charlie's muffled howls.

They're trying to pin summat on Greengrass, but he's not having it. Trevor likes that Greengrass. That actor takes a good part, he used to be Selwyn Froggitt. Trevor used to like that an'all. When he was a kid, like. Sunday nights with Trevor and Graham in their 'jamas with the telly on and a cup of cocoa before bed.

Graham and Trevor.

Janice and Graham.

Trevor and Janice.

The older copper is following Greengrass across the farmyard. What's he been in before, that copper? He's been in summat before. But anyway, he's telling Greengrass to stop being daft and to get in the police car. But Greengrass isn't listening.

Barking and thumping on the kitchen door.

Bollocks to this lark.

Trevor jumps up and gets his coat out of the hallway, walks out the house and into the street, slamming the door shut behind him.

Dumb fuckin' animals.

Hull Fair: 4.37pm

It's coming in dark earlier every day now. If the sky wasn't so overcast, you'd be able to see the stars by now. Sometimes you can see them by three, four o'clock in the afternoon. Sometimes the moon is out all day.

There's a fair wind whipping up, this carriage is

rocking slowly backwards and forwards by itself, but it's not from the wind, it's from the momentum of the ride. Whoever is pressing the buttons has stopped her right at the very top. If it was light, she reckons she'd be able to see nearly the entire city from up here. She can see enough, even though it's getting darker by the second. She can see the red and white lights of the Humber Bridge over there in the distance, and all of West Hull spread out beneath her, the orange, white and yellow lights of the houses popping on one by one. The red tail lights of cars winding along the roads. They look like they're moving dead slow from up here. The infirmary is easy to spot, it's that big, the wards all lit up like a row of giant yellow eyes. There's some sort of spotlight beamed onto the side of it an'all, some local radio station logo. It keeps changing colour, blue to white, blue to white.

She can hear giggling and shouting. A couple of lasses in the carriage below her. They're trying to look up at her, trying to see the weird trannie bloke dangling above 'em. Every time her carriage rocks forwards she can see 'em twisting round and craning their necks to have a good gawp. One of 'em's out of her seat. She'll fall and break her neck if she's not careful.

Someone gets hurt every year at this Fair.

Denise looks down at the crawling mess of noise and colour below her and she wonders if there's any little lasses wandering around lost down there. Any mothers running around looking for them, worried sick. They should look after their kids. Take good care of them. Especially in a place like this. Keep tight hold of their hands in a place like this.

Anyway, she thinks, it all goes tomorrow. This Big Wheel will be pulled apart and packed away, along with the Waltzers and the Meteorite and the Jumping Jacks and all the rest of the rides. The gyppos'll load their big trucks up and cart all their tat to the next city, set it all up again. Is it Nottingham it goes to next? Or does it come from Nottingham? She can't remember. Doesn't matter anyroad. It goes, and that's the important thing. All that'll be left here tomorrow is a load of mess for someone else to clear up.

She takes another swig out of her vodka bottle and the carriage starts dropping forward and slowly down. Four, five seconds then it lurches to a stop again. They're letting the passengers off one by one. She'll be at the bottom soon. She looks round at all the lights and tries to remember where everything is. But they're starting to blur and wobble now. This wind, it's making her eyes water like she's crying. But she's not crying now.

She's not going into work tomorrow. Or the next day. Or the day after that. Fuck Marshall and his trucks. Fuck that stupid forklift and the pallets and the doors and Butch and Little fuckin' Stu and all them other stupid cunts she's had to deal with every Monday to Friday. Fuck the fuckin' lot of 'em. One life, you get. Just the one. She doesn't know what she's going to do with hers, but she knows she's not going back there.

She'll have a good lie in and then she'll have a clear out, she thinks. A proper one. That's what she'll do. She'll take all David's clothes to Oxfam and then she'll go in Town and treat herself to some nice new gear. A new wig, maybe a red 'un. A skirt. One of them maxi skirts. A jacket an'all, some decent boots maybe.

Summat practical. Summat to see her through the winter. It gets so cold in this city. That wind, it whips off the North Sea and it cuts you in half.

Best wrap up warm, Denise.

Wrap up warm and safe.

It's freezing cold now, and it's only October.

Boothferry Estate: 7.54pm

Schooner. A mate of his had his twenty-first in the back room here. That was about fifteen years ago now. Tonight it's just Trevor, two or three couples and some old fellers sat in the corner watching the rugby on the telly. Some noisy young lads stood at the bar. He thinks one of them is Bald Arnold's kid brother. He looks across at Trevor and then looks back again and Trevor thinks he must recognise him. Then Trevor realises it's cos he's been staring at him, so he looks away, up at the rugby. Leeds Rhinos V Bradford Bulls. These are the two big teams now. Used to be Hull and Rovers.

He has a few pints and two bags of crisps and the lads get off somewhere else and then the couples drift off and it's just Trevor and the old fellers and then the rugby finishes and before he knows it it's just him and the barmaid and the barmaid's asking for his glass and it's time to go home.

North Bransholme: 11.30pm

The downstairs curtains are drawn at number 44, but there's a light on. She can hear canned laughter from the telly as she walks past. She walks to the top of the street, stops and turns round, walks back down again.

The street is empty apart from her.

Number 44.

A light on downstairs.

Canned laughter, and a round of applause.

The plastic carrier bag and its contents, bumping against her leg.

Boothferry Estate: 11.31pm

He gets a bottle of Lamb's from the beer-off and takes a few belts as he walks back. Just one or two slugs to ward this flipping cold off. He's fairly pissed up, it has to be said. The streetlights are all blurred and the pavement's falling away from his feet, like he's on the cakewalk at Hull Fair. At one point Trevor thinks he's gonna go arse over tit and he leans up against a garden gate.

Whoa there yer bugger!

The curtain at an upstairs window flicks back and a face appears. A young lass. Trevor grins up at her. She's joined quickly by a shaven-headed bloke and he bangs on the window and waves Trevor on his way. He looks angry. Trevor waves back at 'em both, and pushes on down the road.

He's right pissed up here.

Hundred yards from the house Trevor goes into a hedge. He stays there for a bit looking up at the clouds moving across the moon. Then he thinks he's gonna spew so he pulls himself up. He's wet through all down his front. He's spilled rum all over himself. He goes to screw the cap back on the bottle but he hasn't got owt in his right hand. He puts the bottle down on the deck and goes through his pockets for the cap but it's not there. So he picks the bottle back up, has another good belt and after a bit he gets to the front door. Stands there feeling in his pockets.

No keys.

Bastard.

Trevor stands there for a bit trying to think what to do. He thinks about going back to the hedge and getting on his hands and knees but it's pitch black and he's wrecked.

Back way, then.

He goes round the back tenfoot and comes to the garden fence. It's about seven foot tall, barbed wire along the top. He tries the gate.

Bolted.

Trevor puts the bottle down, wedges his foot against the bottom of the gate, lifts the snick with his thumb and leans hard. It creaks under his weight and then there's a massive crack and he falls into the back garden.

A light comes on in next door's upstairs. He lies there for a bit but nobody comes out. The light goes out again. He gets his bottle and goes and stands up against the kitchen door, looking through the dimpled glass.

Dark.

Just a slice of light coming under the door to the living room.

Trevor takes his jacket off and wraps it round and round his fist. Two thumps, three thumps, and on the fourth the glass goes through. He knocks the bigger bits down onto the kitchen floor, unwraps the jacket and picks out the rest from the crumbling putty till he makes a hole big enough to get his hand through.

Yes! The key's in the lock.

Trevor turns the key, pushes the door and he's in.

It must have been stood waiting for him in the dark. It doesn't make a sound, doesn't even growl, just jumps straight up and at him. It goes for his throat, and Trevor's heart nearly leaps out his chest but he gets his arm up just in time and the jaws fasten on him hard and Trevor screams, he screams like a bain.

Trevor's on his knees and it's like his arm is trapped in a fuckin' vice. The pain is unreal. The dog starts snarling and shaking his head from side to side, slinging him about like a rag doll. The bottle of Lamb's is on the floor where he dropped it and Trevor scrabbles about for it with his other hand. His fingers close round the neck. He picks it up and hammers it down on the top of the dog's head. It lets go for a split second then clamps down again and Trevor can feel its hot breath and its slaver and its fuckin' teeth grinding down through his arm and Trevor batters it again and again and again till the bottle slips out his hand.

It slackens off and Trevor gets his arm out, pulls himself up to his feet. He can see it in the dark. It's swaying about, banging into the cupboard doors.

Its legs are going.

– Charlie! Charlie! It's me!

Jess barking on the other side of the door.

There's a steak knife on the draining board. Trevor picks it up and he bends down and jams it in where he thinks the dog's neck is, but he misses and gets it in the shoulder. The dog howls, spins round and snaps his jaws again, but Trevor jumps back and kicks it twice in the head, hard. The floor's wet through and Trevor slips and falls, lands full on top of the dog.

All four legs are thrashing about and it's breathing, breathing hard. Trevor finds the knife handle and pulls it out. He feels for the collar with his other hand and starts sticking the dog in the neck. It's making this horrible gurgling noise, like dirty water going down a plughole. The dog's trying to get up, but after about the fifth or sixth time Trevor leans down hard on the knife and he feels the fight drain away from the body underneath him.

After a bit the dog goes still.

Trevor gets up and leans against the wall trying to get his breath back. He's soaking wet. There's a stink of rum and piss. He don't know if it's his or the dog's.

Jess is barking away in the living room.

Trevor finds the light switch and flicks it on and the sudden brightness makes him clamp his eyes shut. Then he opens 'em and looks down.

Oh Jesus.

He turns the light off again.

For a minute he thinks he's gonna spew but he manages to keep it down. Then he slides down onto the floor with his back against the living room door. Jess has stopped barking. Trevor can hear her whining and pawing at the bottom of the door.

– Wait there Jess. Wait there, girl. I won't be a minute.

He's crying now. He's starting to sob. He tries to keep quiet in case someone hears him but it's no good and he's sobbing out loud like a bain.

– It's alright Jess. It's not your fault. It's me. It's all down to me . . . big daft fuckin' Trevor. But don't worry lass, I aren't gunna leave you now. I've fucked it all up again Jess, fucked it up good an' proper, just like I always do. But don't worry . . . I won't leave you here . . . not on yer own. Not without yer brother . . . Alright Jess? I'll mek it quick . . . over in a flash . . .' Alright girl? . . . Alright Jess?

Trevor's still crying when he goes outside and gets the spade from the tool shed. He has a cig in the back garden and when he's calmed down a bit he goes back in, shuts the back door behind him and lets Jess into the kitchen.

North Bransholme: 12.30am

The light from the telly goes off at number 44 and one minute later another light comes on upstairs. She slides back into the shadows as a figure appears at the window and draws the curtains. After a while, the bedroom light goes out and the house is in darkness.

She decides to count to a hundred. She whispers the numbers to herself, remembering to put the thousands in between.

– . . . *one thousand and one . . . one thousand and two . . . one thousand and three . . .*

Boothferry Estate: 12.31am

It takes him a good hour to get all the kitchen clean. He drags the dogs out into the garden and lays them next to each other. Then he scrubs the kitchen from top to bottom. He gets some black bin bags from under the sink and dumps all the cloths and kitchen roll and bits of broken glass. He washes the knife clean with detergent and puts it back in the drawer. Then he finds some masking tape and covers the hole in the back-door window with the back of a cornflake packet out the bin. Then he has another scout round in the tool shed and finds some bigger refuse sacks under a wheelbarrow. He gets the dogs into the sacks and covers 'em both up. Then he sets the organ going on GOSPEL, dead quiet, and he goes up and runs a bath.

North Bransholme: 12.31am
– one thousand and thirty-two . . . one thousand and thirty-three . . . one thousand and thirty-four . . .

Zoe always said they weren't real seconds unless you put the thousands in.

Boothferry Estate: 12.32am
He does some thinking in the bath. He thinks about ringing Janice up and saying sorry about last night. Try and sort everything out. He thinks about their Graham and what he's going to say to him. Trevor thinks that Graham needs to stop acting like a bain and start facing up to his responsibilities. It should have been him doing this, not me, he thinks. It's not on, he thinks. It's always me who's left to face the music.

It's starting to come up in a big bruise on his arm where Charlie's jaws clamped down. Went right through the flesh an'all. Big ragged bite mark. His arm feels all stiff. Might have to go to hospital and get an injection for that.

Once he's cleaned himself and got changed, Trevor gets all his gear in his bag and goes and locks the back door up. He puts the key back in the teapot. There's still a bit of money in there, so he has that an'all. Then he lets himself out the front door, clicks it shut on the Yale and slips back round the tenfoot and into the garden.

North Bransholme: 12.34am
– one thousand and ninety-seven . . . one thousand and ninety-eight . . . one thousand and ninety-nine . . . one thousand and hundred.

Coming, ready or not.

Boothferry Estate: 12.35am
The two sacks are still there. He pulls back the tops and looks at them both. Jess's eyes are closed but her tongue is hanging out. He tries to get it back in her jaws but it keeps falling out. He ruffles her lugs and then shoves her head down into the sack.

Charlie's eyes are open. All caked up still an'all. That big thick baggy neck.

– You big daft bugger, he tells him.

He wipes his eyes clean with his jacket sleeve and then ties both the sacks up. Then he lifts 'em into the wheelbarrow and pushes it out the back garden, down the tenfoot and out onto the street.

There are bright pools of light every few yards from the street lamps. But there's no curtains open and there's nobody about.

– Come on then, you two, he says. – Little Switz.

It'll be alright, thinks Trevor. He doesn't live round here any more. And nobody knows him anyway.

Nobody even saw him.

North Bransholme: 12.36am

She scans the neighbouring houses from her place in the shadows. A few lights on here and there, but no real signs of life. No prying eyes peering out of windows.

Kerry steps out of the tenfoot, walks across the empty silent road and up the path, right up to the front door.

She crouches down and takes the Fairy Liquid bottle from the Jackson's carrier bag, flips open the top and squirts the contents through the letterbox. She tips the bottle right up to get all of the liquid into the house. When every last possible drop has been drained she drops the bottle onto the floor and crushes it underfoot. Then she pushes the flattened bottle and the screwed-up plastic carrier bag through the letterbox.

She stands up, wipes her hands on her jeans and pulls the box of matches out from her jacket pocket. She slides the drawer open, strikes a match and flares the entire box alight. She posts the flames into the hallway and holds the letterbox open until her fingers get too hot and she has to let go.

Kerry turns and walks away from the house. She doesn't look round and she doesn't quicken her pace, not until she hears the far-off blades of the helicopter and sees its blinking red lights appear from behind the block of flats in the distance. She knows that soon there will be more lights, red and blue and white, sirens too, screaming and flashing, ripping the night apart and filling up the street. But she'll have disappeared long before they get there.

ACKNOWLEDGEMENTS

Massive thanks to Jon Elek and everyone at AP Watt; Drummond Moir, Jason Arthur and everyone at William Heinemann; James Brown, Michael Holden, Dean Cavanagh, Jonathan Owen, Simon Bristow, Steve Owen, Steve Thomas, Jonny Getz, Gill & Henry, Anu & Olly Kumar-Lazarus, the people of Kingston-upon-Hull and all the boys and girls of OMJ.

And a very special thank you to Sam North for getting me on the ride.

This book is dedicated to Ruth, Josie & Sonny and to my Mam and Dad.

In loving memory of Jack Nelson, Shalom Getz and Terry Rowan – who told all the best stories . . .